THE SEARCH
FOR
MY GREAT-UNCLE'S
HEAD

JONATHAN LATIMER

THE SEARCH FOR MY GREAT-UNCLE'S HEAD

INTERNATIONAL POLYGONICS, LTD.
NEW YORK CITY

THE SEARCH FOR MY GREAT UNCLE'S HEAD

Printed and manufactured in the United States
of America.

Quality Printing and Binding by:
ARCATA GRAPHICS/KINGSPORT
Press & Roller Streets
Kingsport, TN 37662 U.S.A.

Chapter I

WITH A HOLLOW RATTLE of its muffler the Greyhound bus disappeared down the cement road and left
me in the darkness. Water dripped through a cluster
of trees behind me, making a noise of rain, and I placed
my pigskin zipper bag on the pavement and held out
my bare hand. The air was chill, but no moisture was
falling, and although puddles on the white cement indicated a recent downpour, in the sky the clouds were pale
enough to transmit light from an opalescent moon.

I picked up my bag and glanced at my wrist watch.
It was eleven minutes past midnight. There was a strong
odor of woods around me, an odor of wet earth and
moldy leaves, of moist shrubs and plants. The dampness
penetrated my tweed coat, and with an involuntary
shudder I pulled the collar around my neck, delaying
my departure from the solid footing of the pavement. I
dreaded the hour's journey on foot ahead of me, around
Crystal Lake to my great-uncle's isolated estate, and I
hesitated before taking the gravel road which led to the
footpath by the water's edge.

Perhaps when I was younger I would have looked forward to such an adventurous trip, but I am thirty-two
years old, and as everyone knows, thirty-two is well past
the prime of a man's physical life; although my aunt
Nineveh snorts when I make this remark and warns me

that if I do not display some prodigality of temperament and cease spending my evenings with the Earl of Rochester and the Duke of Buckingham I will live to be a hundred, adding always, God forbid!

Since I fear I may be confusing you, I should explain that I am an associate professor of English history at Coles University and that I live in Colesville, California. My parents are dead, and my father's sister, Aunt Nineveh Coffin, with whom I live, is my closest relative. For the past seven years I have been doing research in connection with the Restoration period of English history, and in that time I have gained a reluctant and awed admiration for the rakes who flourished under the witty Charles; hence my aunt Nineveh's reference to the Earl of Rochester and the Duke of Buckingham.

Since completing my graduate work at the University of Chicago, I have, with the exception of a year spent in London going through Restoration legal documents, led a very secluded life. The present trip, which put me in the position of walking at midnight through a Michigan forest, was my first in four years. It was the result of a letter which came Saturday from my great-uncle, Tobias Coffin, who is my grandfather's youngest brother. It was a rather peremptory message, reading:

DEAR PETER:
It has been many years since there has been a gathering of the Coffin family, and I have a desire to see the members of the clan once more before I die. You will please be at my home not later than Tuesday night.
Sincerely,
TOBIAS COFFIN.

I had read this letter at breakfast and had already determined to make the journey to my great-uncle's estate near Traverse City, Michigan, when Aunt Nineveh came down to the table. She carried a similar letter in her hand, and we had a characteristically pointed conversation about the matter.

"Are you going?" Aunt Nineveh asked.

"I think I should," I replied. "Uncle Tobias used to entertain me on his estate when I was a boy, and I think this is the least I can do to show my gratitude."

Aunt Nineveh attacked her grapefruit furiously and said, "Well, I'm not going."

I expressed surprise.

"I know what that old skinflint wants," said my aunt. "He's got all the money in the family, and he wants to see us crawl to be named in the will. I, for one, am not going to oblige him, especially if he can't be a little more polite in his letters. I won't dance jigs to the jingle of his money, not I."

"I am afraid he will be disappointed if he wants me to dance," I asserted. "As you know, I have never learned."

My aunt glared at me across the table. "Peter, I never know whether you are being stupid or witty."

"You're sure you won't go?" I demanded of her. "Uncle Tobias will be very disappointed."

"The hell with him," said my aunt.

It is often necessary for me to repudiate her profanity.

I took a plane from Los Angeles to Chicago, intending to make a connection with the Traverse City-bound Père Marquette train Monday night. Having three hours to wait in Chicago, I went to the Newberry Library and there discovered photostatic copies of some little-known letters written by John Wilmot to Wycherley, the Restoration dramatist, six of which I had never seen. When I completed the engrossing task of making notes I found I had missed my train. This created a rather serious dilemma. No train ran until Tuesday night, which was too late, and there was no plane service in that direction. Finally I discovered I could obtain passage on a Greyhound bus leaving Chicago Tuesday afternoon and passing the west side of Crystal Lake (on which my great-uncle's estate was situated) around midnight. This bus I took, but because of the late hour of my approach to the lake and because it was a twenty-five-mile drive over rough roads from the estate to the highway and only four miles by the footpath, I had resolved to come unannounced.

The half-mile gravel road to the lake from the highway was smooth and when, swinging along at a good pace, zipper bag banging against my right knee, I caught my first glimpse of the water, I was surprised to find my breath coming evenly. My physical condition, I thought, must be better than I had imagined.

The lake, however, did make me catch my breath. I hadn't seen it since I was twelve, and I hadn't remembered how beautiful it was. I don't suppose, as a boy, I had an eye for sublimity. The clouds had partially cleared, and in the light of the moon the water, bound by the perfectly circular shore, gleamed like a huge pearl. The moon hung over tall pines across the lake, almost over my great-uncle's house, and toward me, on the calm water, extended a path of silver like a narrow carpet of the glistening stuff women use in evening gowns, called, I believe, silver lamé. The lake was of a dark shade of blue, but back of it, on its sides, the dense forest was even darker; midnight blue, almost pitch black.

I started on the path around the lake but found the going slower. If I relaxed my attention for an instant a wet branch would strike my face or my zipper bag would become entangled in the tall underbrush. Slippery grass grew on the path, and several times I narrowly missed a nasty fall. By the lake the moon and its reflection lighted the ground, and the way was easy to follow, but each time the path veered away from the shore I felt as though I were imprisoned in a pitch-black tunnel.

As I walked I wondered about the Coffin family. We were not a numerous family nor a friendly one. My father and my grandfather had both been archaeologists, and for some reason my great-uncle and the other branch of the family had resented this. My aunt Nineveh had, I believe, seen the two children of my grandfather's other brother once during a visit in New York, but I had never met them. And I hadn't seen Uncle Tobias for twenty years. I wondered if he would recognize me.

My train of thought was broken by a creepy sensation that something was following me. Several times I imagined that I could hear the underbrush being rustled fifty feet or so inland, but when I halted, my breath checked, there was only silence. I realized my nerves were jumpy. Once I stumbled over a small log and sent it tumbling into the water. With the sound of the splash a great bird raced over the surface of the lake away from me and launched itself into the air, uttering a sort of demented cry, halfway between a laugh and a shriek.

My hair stood on end, and I held one hand over my heart, which, though doctors deny it, doubtless trying to hide my real condition from me, is very weak.

Further along I came to a marshy section of the shore. There my ears rang with the voices of, I presume, frogs. I was surprised at their alarmingly human intonation. At first, as I was entering the marsh, I could hear only the higher-pitched voices, saying in chorus: "Take care, take care, take care, take care."

But further along where deeper water covered the marsh the voices changed from tenor to baritone, warning me to "Go round, go round, go round, go round."

At the same time the footpath began to have an unstable feel under my feet, sinking with each step, and I felt a sudden apprehension that the way might lead into a bottomless swamp from which I would never emerge. I have read somewhere that the only way to avoid death in quicksand or in a swamp is to distribute the weight over as large an area as possible by lying down. I slowed my pace and cautiously felt of the ground in front of me before trusting my weight to it, at the same time ready to throw myself flat on my back in case it should yield. Once when I thought I felt the ground give under my advanced right foot I clutched at an overhanging branch and sent a shower of cold water into my face and down the back of my neck. The shock sent me stumbling on a few paces, and to my surprise I found the ground was still solid.

Then the path dipped, and, peering ahead, I could see it ran into a small gully. Enough moonlight sifted through the trees for me to make out a small stream flowing through the gully, and I realized that here was the most likely place for me to lose myself in the bog.

Coarse grass grew in clumps along the stream, and distressingly soft mud made black patches between the clumps. This mud oozed under the soles of my shoes as I neared the stream, but I determined to risk a crossing.

Suddenly a deep bass voice not more than ten feet away commanded: "Go back! Go back! Go back!"

I may as well admit I was frightened. My heart felt as though it was in my throat, blocking my breath. My back felt as though someone had touched it with a piece of ice. I wanted to run, but I couldn't.

Then my mind began to work, and I realized the command was voiced by a frog, probably the biggest frog in all the world. I waited, and in a few seconds the bass voice repeated:

"Go back! Go back! Go back!"

I said angrily, "Go back yourself," and was startled by the sound of my own voice. The frog was startled, too, and made a heavy splash as it landed in a large pool by the further bank of the gully.

I hurried across the stream, which was only a few inches deep and perfectly solid, and climbed the incline on the other side and started at a rapid pace along the path. I was relieved to feel that the footing was firmer and to know that I had left the marsh behind. The clouds were beginning to form again in dark masses against the purple sky, but whenever the moon managed to break through the way became quite clear. I hurried along at a very good pace for more than a mile, thinking with satisfaction of the comfortable bed awaiting me in my great-uncle's house and worried only by repetitions of the noise of something apparently keeping abreast of me through the bushes about a hundred feet inland. I vainly assured myself it was only an over-alert imagination which created the sounds, and several times I halted to listen, but I could hear nothing.

If anything was following me, I finally decided, it was only some small animal, curious as to what I was doing. I was not far enough north to run any danger from bears or wildcats.

At a bend in the path, on a bush-covered slope leading down to the edge of the lake, I imagined I heard the noise again, and I paused abruptly. No sound came from inland, but far ahead of me in the direction the path led I heard a noise of branches being pushed aside and broken. This noise, I knew at once, was real. I waited silently while the sounds approached. They were the sounds of something large passing through under-brush, of bushes being shoved aside, of leaves being trampled on, of twigs being broken. Whatever was making the disturbance was coming directly toward me along the path!

I suspected it was a human being, and ordinarily I would have waited to see who it was. But my nerves had been pretty well jangled by the episode with the frog chorus. I turned from the path on tiptoe and crouched down behind a large clump of bushes.

I was just in time.

Around the bend of the path, full in the moonlight, came one of the strangest figures I have ever seen. It was a man. He was wearing gray cotton trousers, a blue shirt, and his feet were bare. He had no hat, and his face, fat and very pale, was smiling blissfully. He was moving at a jerky gate, as near to a schoolgirl's skip as an adult can come, his arms flapping loose-jointedly from his shoulders and his knees moving in exaggeratedly high steps, like a high-spirited horse.

He came within ten feet of my hiding place, and I could see that his eyes were not looking at the path I had moved over so carefully. They were fixed upon the moon, and his lips were moving in some weird monody. I listened, and at first I was unable to believe my own ears. The man was chanting in a high, shrill voice:

> "*A tisket, a tasket,*
> *A green and yellow basket.*
> *A tisket, a tasket,*
> *A green and yellow bas . . .*"

Quickly he vanished around another curve in the path, and presently the sound of brush being disturbed diminished and was gone.

There was something about the man that froze my blood. I tried to tell myself he was intoxicated, but the explanation didn't satisfy me. There was something terribly unreal about him, something frightfully absurd. I scrambled onto the path and hurried on my way, not even glancing over my shoulder. I was taking no chances of his returning and finding me. I felt a strong desire to reach the security of my great-uncle's house.

I had little more than a mile to go, and I covered it at a trot which would have done credit to a Kentucky woodsman. The forest was even more ominous now. Clouds had again obscured the moon, and a wind breathed through the trees, sending showers of water down on my head. Once I fell over a root and muddied my hands, face and trousers, but I didn't care. My mind was intent upon reaching the house as quickly as possible.

Just as the wind began to blow sort of a half gale,

sending the tall trees into wild gyrations, I reached the path by which my great-uncle's prize Jersey cattle went from the back pasture to the barn. Ahead of me loomed the house, a bulky black mass against the lake, and to the left were two other dark shapes: the barn and the servants' house. The house was even larger than I had remembered it, and its gabled roof, its huge porch, its circular watchtower and its five-sided shape gave it such a fantastic appearance that I should have hesitated to approach it had there not been a light in the library.

I crossed the clay surface of the large court between the servants' house and my great-uncle's house, mounted the stone steps to the side door leading into the library and struck the brass knocker against the wood panel. I could hear a voice talking inside, but no one answered my summons. I waited for several minutes and then pounded the door again.

Someone turned on the porch light. There was a small glass peephole at the top of the door's center panel, and a woman looked through this at me. She was an elderly woman, and her hair hung in two braids over her shoulders. She was wearing what appeared to be a kimono over a nightgown, and her brown eyes were frightened. I could hear her voice faintly through the closed door.

"What do you want?"

"I'd like to get in."

"No."

"No?"

"You can't come in. Please go away."

I was completely bewildered by this reception. The woman was obviously going to send me away. The voice inside was still speaking, and a part of my mind assured me that it must be coming through a radio. At

the same time a sudden apprehension that I had in
some way blundered upon the wrong house flashed
through another part of my mind; an extremely illogi-
cal apprehension, indeed, because I had recognized the
house, but still very real.

"Isn't this the residence of Tobias Coffin?" I asked.

The wind was blowing in angry gusts now, shaking
the trees as a wolf would lambs, and it had begun to
rain. Drops of water blew across the porch, further
drenching my face and hands. It was turning cold.

A tall cadaverous man came up behind the woman at
the peephole and stared out at me. It was my great-
uncle's butler. There were new wrinkles in his gaunt,
hollow-cheeked face and white streaks in his bushy eyebrows and black hair, but otherwise he had changed
little in twenty years.

"He won't go away," I could hear the woman say.

"Bronson," I said, "it's Peter Coffin. For heaven's
sake let me in."

He stared at me without recognition for a time, then
appeared to consult with someone behind him. The
voice on the radio continued to speak in a rapid, excited
tone. Finally, rattling chains and bolts, Bronson unfastened the door and swung it open and hastily stepped
aside. A most amazing sight met my eyes.

A small crowd of men and women were grouped perhaps ten feet from the door, their backs toward a billiard table. Two young men in evening clothes had shotguns leveled at me. A pretty blonde in a gray gown of
some gauzy material brandished a cue, and beside her
stood a small, sharp-featured man with a knobby cane
clutched in his right hand. Another man, about fifty, in
evening clothes like the others and wearing horn-rimmed

glasses which gave him an owl-like appearance, stood apart from the others as though he were planning a flank attack upon me. Near him was a dark-haired girl, who, though unarmed, regarded me with evident apprehension. Back of me, cutting off my retreat, was the woman in the nightgown and the kimono. She had a huge meat cleaver in her hand.

"Now we got you," said the sharp-faced man in a firm tone. "Don't try to escape."

I stood in the doorway, unable for the moment to do more than blink at them.

"Better search him, George," continued the sharp-faced man. "He might be armed."

The man with the horn-rimmed glasses advanced upon me.

"Wait a minute," I said. "I don't understand this. What are you trying to do?" I spoke to the sharp-faced man. "I was invited to come here by Tobias Coffin, and I don't think he will be very pleased by the reception I have received."

"Maybe he's right," observed the man spoken to as George, halting. "I never heard of a madman carrying a zipper bag."

"I'm Peter Coffin," I declared, following up this advantage, "and I'd like to see my great-uncle."

"Have you anything to prove who you are?" asked the sharp-faced man.

I handed him my wallet and some letters. While the others stood in silence he examined these things thoroughly.

"They seem all right," he said at last and added suspiciously, "but you could have stolen them."

I said it was hardly likely I would present myself at

the home of a relative of a man from whom I had stolen a wallet. This seemed to be reasonable, and some of the tension relaxed.

"Have you got the letter from Mr Coffin with you?" asked the sharp-faced man.

"No. I left it home."

"The trouble is," said George, peering at me through his glasses, "that you weren't expected at this time of night, and your aunt was supposed to come with you."

"My aunt didn't like the tone of Uncle Tobias' letter, so she didn't come."

Strangely enough this explanation produced a marked reaction in my favor. Perhaps the others had wished they could have ignored my great-uncle's summons, but hadn't dared.

Suddenly from in back of the first line of defense came a woman's laughter. A small round woman in a black evening gown, with jeweled bracelets and a chain of precious stones, pushed past the others. I hadn't noticed her before.

"He has the Coffin nose," she said, laughing again. "I think we have made a mistake. I cast one vote in favor of Cousin Peter."

The pretty blonde began to laugh, too, and presently everyone was chuckling. The two young men self-consciously lowered their weapons. Finally the laughter died away.

I felt the blood rising to my cheeks. "I fail to see anything of a risible nature in this situation," I asserted.

This produced more laughter. When it died the jeweled woman took hold of my sleeve.

"We're sorry, Peter," she said, "but we were expecting a madman, and it is such a relief to find it is only a relative." She glanced at my face. "Perhaps you'll understand our mistake when you look in a mirror."

"It's your clothes and the mud on your face," explained the larger of the two young men with shotguns.

I turned to my great-uncle's butler. "Bronson, I should think you'd have recognized me. Will you show me to my room? My feet are damp, and I wish to gargle before I apprehend a cold."

Chapter II

FROM MY CORNER windows I could see waves tossing white spray over the black surface of the lake. The wind continued gusty, roaring around the house at intervals and every now and then dashing rain against the panes with an angry violence which made me start. There was an increasing noise of thunder. I congratulated myself on having reached the house ahead of the worst part of the storm.

My great-uncle, despite the fact that he had shut himself away from civilization by secluding himself in a remote part of Michigan, had kept his estate thoroughly modern, and I was able to take a warm shower in the connecting bathroom. As I was drying myself with a huge Turkish towel I heard the noise of the radio downstairs. The man's voice, excited and urgent, continued in some sort of a monologue. I wondered what he could be talking about. It was too late for a political address, and no news broadcast ever lasted more than half an hour. I decided to inquire about it in the morning.

From the minor puzzle of the voice over the radio my mind turned to the much greater puzzle of my strange reception. Someone had explained that they had been expecting a madman in place of me. But does one ever expect a madman? I had to admit to myself that my mud-plastered face, seen in the bathroom mirror when I first reached my room, was rather terrifying, but a short parley should have established my identity. Yet it didn't. As far as I could tell I was Peter Coffin to the others only on an extremely tentative basis.

A bellow of thunder made me jump, and I turned to my customary precautions against colds. I am suscepti-ble to colds (although Aunt Nineveh heatedly denies this), and it is only by a diligent use of gargles, sprays, nose drops, sodium bicarbonate and other remedies that I maintain my precarious health. My constitution is very frail, and I was surprised to feel quite well despite my strenuous walk so many hours past my usual bed-time. Indeed I felt perfectly capable of repeating the journey.

However, I wished to take no risks, and I was just placing a teaspoon of soda in a glass of warm water, the first step in my nightly routine, when there was a knock at my door. I hurriedly put on my pajamas and called, "Enter."

Bronson opened the door and advanced just across the threshold. "Your great-uncle would like to see you, sir," he said.

"What!" I glanced at my wrist watch on the mahog-any dresser. "He wants to see me at two o'clock in the morning?"

"Yes sir."

"Then I have to dress?"

"Oh no, sir. Mister Tobias said you were to come as you are."

Bronson waited while I took my green silk dressing gown and my leather slippers from my zipper bag.

There was a curious lack of expression on his long face. It was wooden.

"You do not appear overjoyed to see me, Bronson," I said, adjusting the cord on my dressing gown.

"I am always pleased to see any of Mister Tobias' guests," he replied guardedly.

I sat on the purple spread over the hand-carved four-poster and pulled on my right slipper. "Bronson, do you remember the time I played Indian and frightened you so badly on the pier that you fell into the lake?"

For an instant Bronson's black eyes met mine. There was some sort of a gleam in them, but I could not interpret it. "No sir," he said. His angular face was severe. "I must say, sir, you have changed considerably since you were a boy. I am unable to recognize you." His voice sounded as though he had no real interest in the matter.

The lights in the room fluttered, faded to a butter yellow, then flared into brilliance again. Seconds later came a heavy rumble of thunder.

"All ready," I said, standing up.

Bronson held the door as I passed into the hall. A chill draft made the flesh on my ankles clammy. "Your great-uncle has the same rooms," Bronson said in a whisper.

He let me lead the way.

Behind a huge walnut desk at the rear of his second-floor library, white light from a green glass-shaded desk lamp reflected from an untidy litter of letters and documents onto his leathery face, sat my great-uncle. He had changed little in twenty years. He sat very erect, his shoulders squared and his round brown wrinkled face tilted upward by a tall stiff collar. His white hair, thick as a wig, covered his entire head, and under his shaggy brows peered out keen blue eyes. He was wearing a velvet smoking jacket over a white silk shirt and a black bow tie. His expression was severe.

"We had given you up," he said sharply.

I started to explain about the missed train and the bus.

"I've heard all about it," he said. "Sit down."

The room looked just as I had remembered it: ceiling-high bookcases, crowded with adventure stories, to the right and left as you entered the study; a speckled marble fireplace with a piece of coal smoldering in the iron grate; the two huge windows in back of the walnut desk with their pulled silk drapes. I felt as though twenty years had been swept away, as though I was again the small boy who used to be brought trembling into the library to explain broken windows, trampled flower beds, the mysterious disappearance of pies and other juvenile misdemeanors.

My great-uncle continued, "I'm surprised you'd go to all that trouble to get here."

"I was very glad to come, Uncle Tobias," I said. "I wanted to show my gratitude for the delightful summers I spent with you as a boy."

My great-uncle thrust a telegram over the desk. "But what is the meaning of this?" On the back of his hand was a network of purple veins.

I accepted the yellow slip. It read:

TOBIAS COFFIN CRYSTAL LAKE MICHIGAN

    NUTS

                              NINEVEH

I repressed a tendency to giggle. I said, "My aunt was—ah—indisposed."

"You mean she didn't want to come, don't you?"

"I believe," I said, "that 'nuts' is a rather vulgar term of—er—defiance."

My great-uncle's voice, suddenly loud, startled me. "Good for her," he boomed out. "She's the only one in the family with any guts." His blue eyes fastened upon me. "I had some hope for you when you were a boy, but I have been disappointed. What do you mean anyway, spending the best years of your life fiddling with the dull records of the English Regency when you should be learning to live?"

"The Restoration," I corrected him, "and the records are far from dull."

"When I was your age," declared my great-uncle, "I'd been around the world three times."

"I've been to London," I said.

"Bah!" My great-uncle struck the desk with his fist. "Your grandfather was the original fool. Had a chance to make a fortune in the importing business and threw it away to dig for broken pots in Asia. Always at me to finance an expedition to Babylon or some other be-nighted spot." He bared his teeth at me. "I never gave him a cent." He ran his fingers around the papers on the desk. "What was it he named your father?"

"Sargon."

"That's it. Sargon. What a name! What names for a pair of children! Sargon and Nineveh!"

"My grandfather was very enthusiastic over the early peoples of the valley of the Tigris and Euphrates," I said. "Perhaps his enthusiasm got the better of his judgment."

My great-uncle snorted. "What about your own father? What did he name you?"

"Peter."

"Peter what?"

"Peter Nebuchadnezzar Coffin."

My uncle said triumphantly. "There! That gives you an idea of the general insanity of your side of the family. If it hadn't been for your mother you'd never even had the name Peter."

"I am not displeased with my name," I said.

My great-uncle moved his papers again, watching me under his heavy eyebrows. Suddenly he asked: "What did he leave you?"

"Who?"

"Your father."

"His principal bequest was a remarkably fine collection of cuneiform tablets, at present on display at the Oriental Institute of the University of Chicago."

"No cash?"

"A few securities from which I derive a small income."

"Could you use more money?"

"Why, no. I am quite comfortable with my salary."

"Then why are you here?"

"I told you," I began. "I felt that this was a way to show my gratitude——"

"Gratitude!" My great-uncle raised his voice. "Bosh! You came here because you hoped I'd leave you some of my money."

"That's not so, Uncle Tobias."

"It is. You want my money." My great-uncle was half leaning over the table, his face crimson with rage. "You're like all those other sycophants. You want my money. You want my money."

"The devil with you and your money," I said, rising from my chair. "You can take your money and . . ."

My great-uncle leaned eagerly over his desk. "Yes?"

"I'm sorry," I said. "I'm afraid I lost my temper. But I meant what I said." I started for the door. "If you will have someone drive me to Traverse City I'll catch the morning train home. I will be dressed in five minutes."

"Wait a minute," said my great-uncle.

"As long as you feel the way you do," I said, "I don't care to spend the night under your roof."

To my surprise my great-uncle was smiling. "By gad!" he said, "I believe there *is* some stuff in you after all, Peter." He sank back in his chair. "I'm sorry to have been so rude, but I wanted to see. I'll explain later." He waved a hand at me. "Now, good night. It's long past my bedtime."

I stood irresolutely in the doorway. I was really quite angry—I had inherited my share of the Coffin temper—but I realized I should humor my relative, particularly in view of his past kindness.

He seemed to sense my inward struggle. He said, "Please, Peter. I shall take it as a very great favor if you will stay here. You must forgive the whims of an old man."

His tone was really penitent, and I said, not very graciously, "Very well, I'll stay. But only because of my sense of gratitude, not because——"

He interrupted me. "Not because of our relationship. Like all the Coffins, you feel that blood is no thicker than water. It is a family characteristic." His smile took some of the sting from his words. "Good night, Peter."

"Good night, Uncle Tobias."

I encountered Bronson in the hall, and he walked back to my room with me. I had an impression he had been waiting outside the door during my interview with my great-uncle.

"What is the meaning of all this?" I asked him.

"Of all what, sir?"

"Of this gathering of Coffins."

"I really can't say, sir."

Bronson's attitude was precisely that he would have taken with any stranger. He had been a footman with Sir Richard Chandos in England, and although he had been with my great-uncle in America for more than twenty years he had never forgotten his early training. I believe it is the custom of the old-school English servant to treat his employer's guests with condescension. He walked behind me to my room, and as I entered he coughed.

"Yes," I said.

"I think it would be advisable, sir, to sleep with your windows closed."

I imagined he was solicitous about my health. "Nonsense, Bronson," I said. "I'm not afraid of fresh air. I am a firm believer in oxygen."

"I wasn't thinking of fresh air, sir. I was thinking it would be safer."

"Safer?" I stared at Bronson. "You mean someone might try to enter the house through my windows?"

"Exactly."

"But what for? Who would . . . ?"

Bronson's voice was lowered impressively. "A madman is loose in this vicinity. He escaped from an automobile near here this afternoon while he was being taken to an institution at Lansing."

"A madman!" I exclaimed. "So that was what they expected when they met me downstairs."

"Yes sir. He had already tried to break in this evening."

"Did you see him, Bronson?"

"Yes. It was I who managed to frighten him away," he said impressively.

I clutched his arm. "Was he barefoot and without a coat?"

The butler's pitch-black eyes widened. "Why, yes."

"Then I met him."

Despite his passive face I could see Bronson was interested in my story of the near encounter with the skipping man. "It was well that you hid from him," he commented when I had finished. "He had been sent up for the murder of his wife and three children. I believe he cut off their heads with a meat cleaver."

I sank down on the bed. "Zounds! A very narrow escape."

Overhead, thunder sounded a fierce barrage. Bronson said, "Yes sir," and turned to go.

"A moment," I said. "I can see how everyone would be alarmed at my knock, but why all the suspicion after I had identified myself? Surely you could see I wasn't the same madman?"

"It occurred to us you might have obtained some other clothes. And then, sir, you did look a bit odd with mud all over your face and clothes."

"Unfortunately there are no facilities for pressing one's clothes on the way around the lake," I said severely

"No sir," said Bronson. "Good night."

Despite his warning I opened both my windows a foot and climbed into bed. Even the rattle of thunder, the roar of wind, the swish of wet branches, the tattoo of heavy rain could not keep me awake.

Chapter III

I AWOKE sitting up in the center of my bed, my arms clutching the blankets to my chest, my eyes vainly trying to penetrate the darkness. I was terribly frightened, as though I had had a very vivid nightmare, but I couldn't remember any dream. It seemed to me I had heard a scream. I held my breath and listened. The curtains, flung inward by the erratic wind, brushed damply against my face, produced goose flesh on my arms and back.

Then from somewhere close to my door came a woman's scream, vibrant with terror. It wasn't a dream! I swung myself out of the bed, snatched one of my military hairbrushes from the dresser in a mad notion it would serve as a weapon, and ran out into the hall. Another scream, shrill, hysterical and terrible, echoed through the corridor. I ran in its direction, toward my great-uncle's rooms.

The door to the upstairs library was open, and a rectangle of cream-colored light made a patch on the opposite wall of the hall. In this patch, huddled in a wheel chair backed against the wall, was a very old woman whom I immediately recognized as Mrs Spotswood, my great-uncle's housekeeper. I halted in consternation at the sight of her face. She was looking in my direction, but her eyes, insane with terror, did not see me. From her open mouth came a weird, inhuman screaming, and her hands, tight yellow flesh making them look like the talons of a bird of prey, clawed the air in a spasm of panic. I am altogether unused to hysteria, and for a moment I considered securing a bucket of cold water and dousing her with it.

While I was hesitating another woman appeared around the bend in the hall just beyond my great-uncle's bedroom door. I recalled her as the pretty dark-haired girl in the group which had met me downstairs. She was wearing pink slippers of a type known, I believe, as mules, and she had on a lacy peachtinted silk robe over her pajamas. I confess that I was frightened by the screams which continued to come from Mrs Spotswood, but the young woman's face showed no trace of fear.

"What are you doing to her?" she cried to me, somewhat unreasonably, I thought. She ran to the wheel chair. "What's the matter, Mrs Spotswood?"

The old lady halted halfway through a scream. Intelligence swept back into her eyes. She tried to reply, but nothing except a convulsive sob came from her wrinkled throat. She turned her head toward the open door of my great-uncle's library, then collapsed in the young woman's arms. I endeavored clumsily to aid in supporting Mrs Spotswood.

"No," said the young woman. "See what frightened her." She shoved me with her left hand. "Don't be such a coward."

"I'm not a coward," I retorted. "I was merely trying to help you." I left the two women and entered the library.

I knew something pretty awful must have happened

to terrify Mrs Spotswood so, and I suppose I was sub-consciously prepared to find my great-uncle dead. But I was in no way ready for the truly horrible sight which checked me in my tracks, caused my heart to fly into my throat and made me feel for the first time in my life that I was going to faint.

Across the walnut desk, over the litter of papers and legal documents, sprawled my great-uncle's body. Blood from a mangled stump where his neck had been had pooled blackly under the desk lamp, and a few drops had oozed over the edge to the soft green Chinese rug. My eyes searched frantically for his head, but it was not in sight. I bent down and examined the floor. It was not there. I turned back to the body, fervently hoping I had been the victim of a hallucination, but my vision was confronted by the gaping wound just above the high stiff collar. Where the head should have been was my great-uncle's right hand, the arm making an awkward circle back to the body. The forefinger on this hand was outstretched, while the three remaining fingers were half opened, as though something had been removed from the hand's grasp. The left arm was stretched backward, parallel to the body.

Someone came up behind me. "Moses!" he exclaimed. "Where's his head?"

I saw it was the larger of the two young men who had trained shotguns on me earlier in the night. "I haven't got it," I replied inanely.

The young man bent over and peered under the desk. He was about twenty-six years old, and he was blond and very muscular. "Gone," he muttered. His vivid scarlet pajamas contrasted with my somber black ones. He glanced at the corpse again.

There were sounds of people in the hall. Hurried footsteps and excited voices echoed through the house. There was also a sound of metal doors being opened and closed and the vibration of an electric motor. The noise was like that of an elevator. People were running toward our door.

"You'd better stand outside and warn everybody," I said to the young man. "The women shouldn't be allowed to come in here."

"That's right," agreed the young man, starting for the corridor.

I went to the desk and picked up the extension telephone. While I was waiting for the operator to answer Bronson came into the room. He had pulled on trousers and a shirt, but he still wore bedroom slippers. He halted, just as I had done, when he caught sight of the body, and sheer horror convulsed his thin features.

"Mister Peter!" he gasped, and I felt surprise that he should so suddenly accept my identity. "Mister Peter! What happened?"

"It looks like murder, Bronson."

"Murder!" He passed the back of his hand across his eyes. "But who . . . ?"

"Possibly our madman."

"No! No!" His voice rose to the breaking point; it was vibrant with horrified negation. For an instant he stared at me, then closed his eyes. "Perhaps you are right," he said.

Just then the operator answered. "This is the Coffin estate," I said. "There's been a murder here. I would like to be connected with the sheriff's office."

A second later a man said, "Hello."

I repeated what I had told the operator.

"This *is* the sheriff's office," said the man. "Who's dead?"

"Tobias Coffin."

"My God!" exclaimed the man. "Who did it?"

"We think the madman who's loose in the neighborhood. Mr Coffin's head has been cut off."

"No!" said the man. "No!"

"Yes," I said.

There was a moment of silence. There was silence in the hall, too, and I looked up and saw a background of faces in the door. Bronson and a new young man were holding the people back. The young man with the scarlet pajamas had disappeared.

"Look," said the man at the sheriff's office. "I'm gong to put in a radio call for the sheriff. He's already out hunting for the madman. He should be over to your place in ten minutes or so, depending where he is. Don't touch anything, and if the madman comes around don't hesitate to shoot him."

I said I wouldn't, and he hung up.

I turned to the crowd at the door and was shocked to see two older women peering over the shoulders of the men. They didn't seem especially affected by the sight of my great-uncle's headless body. "I think everybody had better wait downstairs," I said. "The authorities will be here in ten minutes."

I spoke in the admonitory tone I was accustomed to use on refractory students at Coles, and to my surprise they immediately obeyed me.

"Now, Bronson," I said, encouraged by my success

as a leader, "I think you and the two young men should search the house. It is possible the madman is still lurking about somewhere."

The young man at the door had grown too fast for his weight. He had sandy hair and an alert face, but his build I can only describe as weedy. "Come on," he said with alacrity. "Come on, Bronson. Let's get out of here." I judged his age to be nineteen.

"I'll wait," I said to Bronson, who was hesitating by the door, "until the police come."

For an instant Bronson looked as though he were going to suggest something to me, but finally he said, "Very well, Mister Peter."

It was not pleasant to be left alone in the room. My first move was to peer into my great-uncle's bedroom to make sure no one was lurking there. I was surprised to see that the door leading from the bedroom into the hall was open a crack, and I went over to examine it. There was a lock on the door, one of those snap locks which are turned with a round brass knob, and this was on the safety catch so that the tongue was held back. I closed the door, saw that the regular catch below the knob held, and, stopping only to look into my great-uncle's closet and bathroom, hurried back to the other room.

Over the wood fireplace on the left side of the library, hung head high, was a mirror. In this I caught sight of myself and noticed that I was still carrying my hairbrush in my right hand. Somewhat foolishly I put it on the mantel and looked around for a better weapon. I still felt decidedly apprehensive about the maniac. The only object which looked serviceable, outside of an unabridged edition of Webster's Dictionary, was a heavy metal vase on the mantel. It was a thin vase, made for a single flower, and I found it could easily be grasped in my hand. Moreover the base was weighted, and I decided it made an excellent, if unorthodox weapon. I decided to hold on to it.

Then it occurred to me that if the maniac had broken into the house his feet would have been muddy. I examined the rugs for traces of mud or moisture, but I could find nothing. I was down on my knees, peering nearsightedly at the Chinese rug, when I heard the sound of a footstep. Looking up, I saw a black-haired, middle-aged man regarding me through a pair of horn-rimmed spectacles. He had on slippers and a gray flannel dressing robe, and he was smiling.

I stood up cautiously, grasping the vase in my right hand.

"Sleuth?" asked the man. His eyes were on my great-uncle's body.

"Who are you?" I asked.

"Perhaps a cousin of yours," said the man. "I'm George Coffin."

A remarkable thing about my cousin—if, indeed, he was my cousin—was the lack of expression in his face. There was absolutely no change in it at all when he looked from the corpse to me. It did not even change when he spoke.

"Oh," I said.

"Yes," he said. "Perhaps a cousin." He moved nearer the desk, bent impassively over the pool of blood. "Burton Coffin is my son." There was a faint shade of contempt in his voice.

"The young man in the scarlet pajamas?"

"The young man in the scarlet pajamas." He moved

around in back of my great-uncle's body and looked down at the rug under the chair. It was wrinkled, as though the chair had been moved without having been lifted. "No struggle?"

"No," I said. "The madman must have struck quickly."

There was a noise of footsteps in the hall. The young man in the scarlet pajamas stuck his head in the door. He was carrying a shotgun. "Hello, Dad," he said. "No sign of the guy in the attic or on this floor." He looked derisively at the vase in my hand, then winked at his father. "I guess you'll be safe up here with the professor to guard you," he added. "I'm going downstairs with the others."

His father's face remained frozen. "Some kid," he said to me. "Played fullback on the Princeton team." He ignored his son.

I moved over to my cousin, in back of the desk. "What's that curious odor?" I asked.

He sniffed. "Funny! It's like chloroform." He glanced over the top of the desk. "Maybe some kind of cough medicine."

The odor came from the right side of the desk, about a foot to the right of my great-uncle's bent arm. I smelled the surface of the desk, said, "It was right here, whatever it was."

He peered at me without changing his expression. "What do you make of it, Watson?"

"Nothing," I said. "I was simply curious."

We both examined the room with our eyes. Nothing seemed out of place. On two sides of the room were the warm-colored backs of the volumes my great-uncle had loved so well—the sets of Dickens, Thackeray, Conrad,

Galsworthy, Hardy and other great English authors as well as the tomes of his favorite adventure writers— Stevenson, Conan Doyle, H. Rider Haggard and John Buchan. Not a book was out of place. The oriental scatter rugs, which would have been rumpled by any sort of a struggle because of the slipperiness of the waxed floor, were undisturbed, and, except for the splotches of blood on the pale surface of the Chinese rug, there was nothing of note. I opened the heavy curtains covering the windows and made sure the catches were fastened. It was still raining. I returned to the desk.

George Coffin was looking down at the corpse. "I wonder what he does with them?" he mused.

"Does with what?"

"The heads he cuts off. Do you suppose he reduces them to the size of a potato, like South Sea savages?"

His words brought into my mind a picture of the madman, his pale round face intent, bending over a kettle in which reposed Uncle Tobias' head. I shuddered and said, "I should think a detruncated head would be very unpleasant to carry about."

George Coffin sat down in one of the leather chairs by the fireplace. "Not if you held it by the hair," he said. His voice was perfectly serious, and for the first time there was a note of animation in his manner. "If you had a woman's head, for instance, you could swing it around easily. But a bald-headed man would require a different technique. I don't know exactly——"

A woman was screaming downstairs.

I clutched the vase and started for the hall. George Coffin yelled after me, "I'll stick here."

By the time I had located the kitchen as the source of the sceraming the noise had ceased. Practically everyone in the household was already there, staring at an open window.

"What in the world's the matter?" I asked Bronson.

He pointed to the floor beneath the window. There on the green and gray squares of the linoleum was a cluster of footprints, leading into the dining room. The prints were of bare feet!

The weedy young man, whom I supposed to be another of my cousins, said, "They go round and round, but they don't come out here."

The pretty blonde, whom I had noticed before, giggled. The plumper of the two middle-aged women who had been peering into my great-uncle's room, the one who had observed my Coffin nose, said, "He's still in the house. He must be. I know we'll all be killed." Her voice was shrill.

"Now, Maw," said the weedy young man, "keep your shirt on."

Instead of resenting this vulgarity from her offspring the plump woman subsided. I turned to Bronson.

"Have you completed your search?"

"No sir. We were interrupted when Miss Harvey discovered this open window."

Miss Harvey was the slender blonde. She was very young—about twenty, I thought—and her face was pert. She had on blue pajamas and a blue dressing gown cut in a military fashion at the shoulders.

"I toddled out to get a cold glass of water," she said brightly, "and when I snapped on the light there was the open window. I guess I screamed a little."

"You *guess* you screamed," said the weedy young man scornfully. "You pretty near lifted the roof off the house."

"So what?" queried the blonde, looking at him fiercely.

"So nothing," said the young man.

This appeared to end their conversation, and I spoke to Bronson again. "I think you'd better have everybody go into the living room," I said, "and stand guard over them. We can search the house as soon as the sheriff comes, and in the meantime it will be better not be separated."

"Very well, sir," said Bronson.

I looked about for the dark-haired girl and the young man with the scarlet pajamas, Burton Coffin, but they were not with the others. I walked behind the group to the living room, where a bright fire was burning in the huge stone fireplace, and continued on up the stairs. In the hall, just as I was passing my own door, I saw coming slowly toward me the missing pair. They were in earnest conversation, and I slipped into my room. I did not wish to have the dark-haired girl, whose name was Miss Leslie, think that it was immodesty, rather than necessity, which made me appear in public attired only in pajamas, so I donned my own dressing gown and put on my comfortable slippers. Also I placed the vase on the table beside my bed. I knew that it was almost as absurd a weapon as my hairbrush, and I cared to risk no more jibes from young Coffin.

When I walked out into the hall again I found they were still approaching. They abruptly ceased talking, and Burton Coffin's teeth gleamed in the half light.

"Well, Professor," he said, "I see you're venturing out without a weapon." His tone was mocking. "What would you do if the madman suddenly jumped out at you?"

I glanced at the shotgun under his arm. "I wouldn't be able to shoot him with one of those if I had one," I confessed. "I'd probably run if somebody did jump out at me."

"Or faint," said the young woman. She regarded me with evident contempt. "Come on, Burton," she said, taking his arm. "Let's go downstairs."

They marched past me and turned out of sight at the head of the staircase. I continued down the hall toward my great-uncle's rooms, musing on the unfairness of women. Because I hadn't known what to do to comfort Mrs Spotswood I was taken for an utter poltroon by the girl. Not that I cared what she thought; it was simply the injustice of the matter. How many men would have known what to do with a screaming, hysterical woman? Not many, I thought. And just because I didn't, did that mean I was a coward? Damme, no! Indeed I felt an increasing resentment for the contumely heaped upon me by Miss Leslie. It was an unreasonable feeling, considering that the opinion of the girl was a matter of no concern to me; but it was, nevertheless, quite strong.

Thus immersed in thought, I turned into my great-uncle's room. I was surprised to see George Coffin and the sharp-faced man going through my great-uncle's papers. The man had a disgruntled expression on his face.

"What are you doing?" I demanded peremptorily. "I thought nothing was to be touched until the authorities arrived."

George Coffin's dark face, behind the shell glasses, betrayed neither surprise nor chagrin. "Thaddeus, this is Peter Coffin," he said. "Dr Thaddeus Harvey is married to my sister."

"How do you do?" said the sharp-faced man. He came over and shook my hand, and I noticed a smear of blood on his thumb and index finger. "Off the table," he said, noticing my eye on the blood. "We were looking for the new will." His hand grasped mine firmly.

"The new will?"

"Yes. Didn't you know he"—he indicated the corpse with a long thumb—"had made a new will?" He didn't bother to lower his voice in the presence of the dead.

"I didn't know he had made any will," I said.

He shook his head. "Well, we just thought we'd see what it said." He turned back to the desk.

I said, "I think it would be advisable to wait for the police."

George Coffin added, "It *is* considered good manners to wait for the police, Thaddeus. They will not thank you for a breach of etiquette."

"Oh, very well." Thaddeus Harvey moved away from the desk and sat in a chair on the further side of the fireplace. He crossed his knees. "Damn funny the maniac should have picked Uncle Tobias, of all the people in the house."

"Why?" I asked.

He looked meaningly at me. "He's the only person in this house whose death would be of advantage to anyone."

"Of advantage?" I echoed. "How do you mean?"

"The will." Thaddeus Harvey was leaning forward, his small eyes staring directly into mine. "The new will."

I suppose my expression was blank, because George

Coffin, one arm resting on the mantel, said, "He is endeavoring to intimate you will benefit by your great-uncle's demise."

"I?"

Thaddeus Harvey's body was absolutely motionless. "Then you really don't know anything about the new will? Your great-uncle didn't tell you?"

"He told me only that he was disappointed in my choice of a career," I said. "He seemed to think it was not rugged enough for a Coffin."

Dr Harvey appeared to ponder my answer and find it satisfactory. "The new will is supposed to have named you part beneficiary in the estate," he explained. "Your great-uncle told George and me that much yesterday afternoon."

"That and a lot more," said George Coffin. His eyes twinkled.

I didn't feel especially excited. A bequest of a few hundred or even thousand dollars would not alter my mode of living. "It will all come out after the police clean up this mess," I said, indicating the mass of blood-stained papers.

We were silent for a time. George Coffin found a package of cigarettes in his dressing gown and offered me one. I refused. "You don't mind if I smoke?" he asked. I thought I detected a note of mockery in his voice and replied, "I am quite used to tobacco. My aunt Nineveh smokes a great deal."

George Coffin's eyes twinkled behind the glasses. I could see he was making a mental note of my reply for a future anecdote. "These women," he said, lighting his cigarette.

Actually I smoke and am very fond of a pipe.

Thaddeus Harvey was looking at me again. He had a habit of fixing your eye with his before he spoke. "Did you go through your great-uncle's pockets, Peter?" he asked.

"No. Why should I? I don't generally pilfer cadavers."

His eyes remained on mine. "I thought you might have looked there for the will." He suddenly gazed up at the mantel. "Whose hairbrush?"

"Why, it's mine." I picked it up and put it in my pocket. "It was the only weapon I could find when I heard Mrs Spotswood scream."

George Coffin had moved to a position beside the corpse. "If it was Tobias' hairbrush," he said to Mr Harvey, "it wouldn't be here."

"Why?"

"The madman would have taken it to keep Tobias' hair neat."

Dr Harvey grunted to show his disapproval of such levity. George Coffin was bending over the severed neck. "Nice job," he said. "The knife must have been good and sharp."

I tried not to look, but my eyes kept turning to the corpse.

"Hello!" said George Coffin. "He had on a dirty collar."

I glanced down at the stiff white collar my great-uncle invariably wore. There was a black spot on it at about the point under the right ear. The top of the collar, above the spot, had turned brown.

Thaddeus Harvey was standing beside me. "Maybe that's where the murderer held him," he suggested. "It looks like a smear from a dirty hand."

"It might be," said George Coffin. "Or it might be soot from the fireplace."

"Where did the silver vase that was on the mantel go?" asked Dr Harvey.

I felt sensitive enough about my choice of weapons to lie. "I don't know," I said.

George Coffin shrugged his shoulders. "What's a vase beside a missing head?" he asked.

Our conversation was interrupted by the appearance of Bronson. "The sheriff," he announced.

Chapter IV

THE SHERIFF was a nervous little man in a black suit, and his name was Albert Wilson. He had been a seed merchant for thirty-five years, I was informed, and had been elected to his office on a reform ticket. Nothing could induce him to look at Tobias Coffin's body. He even refused to enter the room. His increasing agitation as the story was unfolded was manifested by frequent repetitions of "I declare!" and "That beats the dickens!" After a nervous tour of the house he returned to the living room, there perching uneasily on the edge of a straight-backed chair while Bronson and the two deputies went through the grounds. He had evidently been informed of my encounter with the madman, and he asked me to repeat the story of my trip around the lake.

The other members of the household, even Miss Leslie and Burton Coffin, who kept persistently by her side, crowded close to listen. I told of my experience in a very matter-of-fact tone.

When I had completed my account the sheriff said, "I bet you was plenty scared."

"I was," I admitted. "Scared rigid."

Everyone found this reply humorous.

41

Fresh birch logs in the great stone fireplace burned with the noise of crackling popcorn, sending agile flames up the chimney. The bright yellow light helped illuminate the room and brought out warm tints in the faces of my relatives. The heat contrasted pleasantly with the dismal sounds of rain and wind outside.

I was surprised to see that there were so many persons in the house. There were, in the half circle of people in front of the blaze, George Coffin, his stately wife, Grace, and their son, Burton; Dr Harvey, his wife, Mary, and their two children: Dan, the weedy boy, and Dorothy, the pretty blonde; all my relatives. And in addition there were the dark-haired Miss Leslie, who was present because she was the only child of Tobias Coffin's late wife's brother; Mrs Bundy, the servant who had first looked through the peephole in the library door at me; her husband, in charge of the Jersey herd; and a tall man wearing a black sweater and a pair of flannel trousers. His name was Karl Norberg, and he was the chauffeur-gardener. He was a good-looking blond Swede about thirty-five years old, with a sunburned face and clear blue eyes.

After another survey of this group I asked, "Where's Mrs Spotswood?"

"She the one who found the body?" demanded the sheriff.

"Yes."

"Then that's just what I'd like to know. Where is she?"

Dr Harvey's bright eyes met those of the sheriff. "She's in bed. She has had a very severe shock, and I gave her some sleeping tablets."

"She won't be getting up then?"

"Not till morning."

"Well, I don't suppose it 'll make much difference if I question her now or in the morning. The thing to do is to get after Elmer Glunt."

"Elmer Glunt?" I inquired.

"The fellow you met. The madman."

Although he had seen them himself the sheriff wanted to know more about the open window and the tracks in the kitchen. Dorothy Harvey, her big blue eyes expressive, told once more how she had discovered the window.

"But the tracks," interrupted the sheriff, "did they just go in?"

Miss Harvey nodded.

"Then he's still in the house," announced the sheriff triumphantly.

Burton Coffin's voice was husky. "Not necessarily," he said. His hand held Miss Leslie's arm. "Walking through the house would have dried his feet. He wouldn't have left any tracks going out."

The sheriff pondered. "There's something in that, son." He turned to me. "We'll get him, though, wherever he's gone. We got men watching every road in the county. He can't get away."

"That's good," I said. "I'd hate to think of his killing any other defenseless people."

Bronson appeared at the front entrance of the house with the two deputies. All three were dripping wet. One of the deputies was wearing a yellow slicker, and he spoke to the sheriff.

"We've looked about everywhere, Sheriff. In the cellar and through the garage and the cattle barns and the boathouse. There ain't a sign of him."

"I reckon that's about all a body can do, Jeff," said

the sheriff. He stood up and looked around at us. "The coroner 'll be here in the morning to get the cadaver. We'll be moving along."

Mrs Harvey raised a plump hand to her throat in dismay. "Oh no! You can't leave us unprotected." Her voice was shrill. "We'll all be killed." There was a diamond ring on her finger.

Dr Harvey moved to her side. "Now, Mary, you'll be all right." His hand patted her plump arm in quick movements.

George Coffin said, "I think it would be an excellent idea, Sheriff Wilson, if you could spare a man to watch the house for the rest of the night."

"Yes, he may attempt to come back," said Mrs Coffin. "It is the duty of the law, is it not, to offer protection?" Her voice was regal.

Sheriff Wilson scratched under his left arm with his right hand. "I reckon I could spare a man if you insist." He looked around at us. "Though you seem to have a lot of able-bodied hands around already."

Jeff, the deputy in the yellow slicker, said, "I'll stay, Sheriff." He moved toward the fireplace. "I got a hunch he's still hanging around somewhere. He ain't going to be lugging a head all over creation."

Mrs Harvey would have screamed, but a warning glance from her husband silenced her. She and Mrs Coffin and young Miss Harvey were huddled together.

The sheriff somewhat reluctantly agreed to allow Jeff to remain with us and departed with the other deputy, assuring us as he left that he'd be back first thing in the morning. "I'll look over them papers then," he added. The deputy borrowed one of the shotguns in the game room and went to the front door.

"I think I'll prowl around outside for a bit," he said. "You folks better try to get some sleep. It's after four o'clock."

A puff of black smoke flew out of the fireplace as he closed the front door. It was still blowing outside, and we could hear the whine of the wind around the house.

"I'm certainly not going to bed," declared Mrs Harvey. "He's not going to come back and find *me* asleep." Her plump face was determined.

"Now, Mary," said Dr Harvey. "You'll regret not going to bed tomorrow." His hand tightened on her arm. "Come on, dear. I'll stay with you."

She allowed herself to be propelled from the room by her husband, who looked, despite his smallness of stature, perfectly confident of his ability to protect her from the assault of a maniac.

Mrs Coffin was quite tall, almost as tall as her husband. She carried herself with aplomb, her head held high and her chest thrust forward, as though she were of royal birth. She spoke to her son. "Burton, I think you should be in bed. It's very late." She took her husband's arm and led him toward the stairs. "We're going."

"I'll be up in a few minutes, Mother," said Burton sulkily. "I'll get plenty of sleep."

Mrs Coffin halted. "Now, Burton. You remember what——"

"Let him alone, Mother," said George Coffin. "He's *supposed* to be of age." He looked over at me. "It might be a good idea if someone watched the upstairs for the rest of the night."

"Yes, it would," I said. "I'll get a chair and sit in the hall by my uncle's door."

"There's no need of watching your uncle's room, Mister Peter," said Bronson, who had remained a respectful distance from the fire. "The deputies locked the door and took the key. They said nothing was to be touched until the coroner came."

"I wasn't thinking so much of my uncle's room, Bronson," I said, "as of acting as a sort of guard."

"I'll be glad to do that, sir."

"That's all right, Bronson. You'll be needing some sleep." I turned my eyes toward George Coffin, waiting with his wife at the foot of the stairs. "I, or someone, will be in the hall."

"Good night, then," he said.

We all said good night.

Mrs Bundy said to me, "I'll just go up to the third floor and stay with Mrs Spotswood. The poor old lady will be frightened if she wakes up all alone." As she mounted the steps the pigtails over her shoulders quivered. "Good night, Mr Bundy," she called to her husband.

A gust of wind crossed the room, blowing the silk bottoms of Miss Leslie's pajama legs. Bronson had opened the front door. "Mr Bundy and Karl and I are going over to the servants' quarters, Mister Peter," he said. "I'll be back at seven o'clock to relieve you, if I may, sir."

"That will be fine, Bronson," I said. "Good night."

"Good night, sir." Bronson waited for the other two men to pass through the door. "I should keep my eyes open, sir." There was a strange expression on his face, urgent and warning. The closing door blotted it out.

Burton Coffin and Miss Leslie were seated on the

couch in front of the fire. Inadvertently I noticed that
Miss Leslie's ankles, exposed by the loose legs of her
pajamas, were brown and slim. "What did he mean by
keep your eyes open?" asked Burton Coffin. He still held
the shotgun in his hands.

"Perhaps he thinks the madman will come back," I
suggested, sitting down in one of the comfortable over-
stuffed chairs at right angles to the couch.

Miss Harvey, who had been lighting a cigarette with
a piece of birch bark, faced her brother. "Look at my
hand wobble, Dan," she said. "Just like a hangover."
She giggled and pretended she could not make the cigarette and the flame meet.

Miss Leslie smiled at her. "May I have one, too,
Dot?" she asked. "I need something for my nerves."

"Why certainly, my dear. How rude of me." Miss
Harvey gave Miss Leslie the cigarette she had lighted,
offered another from the pack to Burton Coffin. He said,
"Thanks," and accepted one and lit it from Miss Leslie's cigarette. Their faces were quite close together as
he did so, and I noticed that they smiled at each other.

Dan Harvey was regarding me. "Well, Professor, do
you think you've got the defense lined up all right?"
he asked. "The enemy may attack at any minute."

There was nothing very friendly in any of their looks.
There was, indeed, in their faces a combination of hostility and amusement. I suddenly felt very lonely, and I
wished I had never come to my great-uncle's house. I
would have liked to remain for a few minutes more before the cheerful fire, but I didn't want to be in anybody's way.

"I hope the enemy is ten miles off by now," I said, rising to my feet. "I hope the sheriff has him in custody."

"But you'll protect us if he should come back?" asked Miss Harvey. "I should like to feel that you are watching over us." Her voice was mocking.

"You can count on the professor," said Burton Coffin. "He'll protect you with his hairbrush."

Miss Harvey and her brother both tittered. I was forced to smile, too, despite an unpleasant feeling that I was being made the butt of an unfair joke. Still, I must have been a remarkably ridiculous figure with that hairbrush in my hand.

"A hairbrush is probably as good a weapon as any for me," I said. "I'm not very handy in matters of violence."

Miss Leslie's eyebrows were delicate arches against the white background of her high forehead. Her eyes were gray and luminous in the firelight. "A coward never is," she said.

I turned away from them and went up the stairs. I took a straight-backed chair from my room and carried it far down the hall to the turn in the corridor. From this point I could watch all the bedrooms on the floor. There were small lights burning at both ends of the hall, and I was not in complete darkness. I sat in the chair and crossed my legs and began to think.

At first I thought about Miss Leslie and her hostility to me. "A coward never is," she had said. It was a very cruel remark, and I felt it was unjustified. I went over the scene with Mrs Spotswood again in my mind. Had I acted as a coward would? A brave man, I supposed, would have rushed to Mrs Spotwood's aid, shouted, "Don't be frightened, I am here," and rushed into the room. I admitted to myself that I had fallen considerably short of the model procedure. But had my failure been the result of cowardice? I examined my conscience. Yes, I had been frightened, badly frightened. But my fright hadn't prevented me from rushing into my great-uncle's room when it became apparent to me that the trouble was there. And it wasn't fright which prevented me from going to Mrs Spotswood's aid. It was a lack of knowledge in dealing with hysterical women. If I was guilty, I decided, I was guilty of stupidity, not of cowardice. Unless, of course, being frightened automatically made you a coward.

I was pondering over these things when the four young people came down the hall. They were smiling, and talking in whispers. Abreast of me, Burton Coffin bent down and asked in a stage whisper, "All quiet on the Potomac, Professor?"

"All quiet," I said.

I didn't look at Miss Leslie until they had gone by me. She halted at the second door on the corridor past the turn. For a moment she and Burton Coffin held a whispered conversation, then she opened the door and went into her room. Burton Coffin came back toward me and entered the first room past the turn. The Harveys walked on to rooms considerably further along the corridor.

I moved my chair against the right angle made by the wall at the turn in the hall and sat down again. I didn't have to worry about anyone coming up behind me. To my right, three doors up, was the locked room in which my great-uncle's body lay. Next was his bedroom and then, next to me, almost by my right arm, was Mrs Spotswood's office. To my left was the long row of guest chambers occupied by the Harveys, the Coffins and Miss Leslie. I felt confident that nobody could get into any of these rooms without my knowledge.

Presently I began to think again. I wondered why the servants and even my relatives accepted my orders. I knew it wasn't because of my dynamic personality; in fact I knew that my personality, except when I was enraged, was more mouselike than dynamic. I wondered if it was because of the will. Was I being left a good share of the estate? Was I to come into control of this house? That would account for the servants. But what about the curious attitude of Dr Harvey? His looks seemed to convey his knowledge of something I had done, almost as if I had a guilty secret which he had uncovered. Of what did he suspect me? I didn't know. Neither did I know the reason for Burton Coffin's open hostility. Was he a disappointed heir? And Miss Leslie. Would my clumsiness earlier in the evening account for her cruelty?

The seat of the chair was hard, and I tilted the back against the wall so that my position was more comfortable. I closed my eyes and thought about Miss Leslie. I thought what different types we were: she, sophisticated, chic, aggressive, accustomed to the ways of the world; I, a man of thought, shy, quiet, diffident, and, in my attire, the antithesis of chic. I did not, however, think of myself as unsophisticated. My study of Restoration times and morals had certainly given me as complete an education as anyone along worldly lines.

The thought of the Restoration made me wonder what my favorite rake, John Wilmot, would have done in circumstances such as I had encountered during the night. I had no doubt that he would have banished the distrust of the younger people with a witty remark or two, and that his elegant attire would have had a profound appeal for Miss Leslie. I leaned my head back against the wall and imagined that I was in reality the gay Earl of Rochester. I could see myself hearing a sound in the night, leaping from bed, grappling with the madman in the hall and triumphantly turning him over to the authorities, not a hair on my head out of place. I could see the surprise on the faces of those who had hitherto distrusted my manhood, the wonderment in Miss Leslie's. . . .

I must have fallen asleep, because the next thing of which I was aware was the presence of Karl Norberg and the deputy, Jeff. They were both standing in front of me, and their faces were excited. Norberg was bending over to touch my arm.

"What is it?" I asked.

"There's someone in your uncle's room," said the tall Swede, a finger over his lips.

"We saw a light up there," supplemented the deputy.

I jumped to my feet and led the way to the door of my uncle's library. Under the crack there was a faint light! I turned to the others. "We'll have to break the door down."

The deputy shook his head. "No." He produced a key. "The sheriff left this with me."

"We better open it quick and all rush in at once," said Norberg. "Then we'll have a chance of surprising him."

We agreed that this was the best plan. The deputy gave the key to me and took his shotgun in both hands. Norberg had a heavy cane.

"All right," said the deputy.

I turned the key and pushed open the door. They rushed into the room past me. It was pitch dark. The deputy cried, "All right, I've got you covered." There was a noise of a scuffle and then a terrific explosion. The deputy had fired the shotgun. Someone tried to push past me at the door, and I said, "Here, where are you going?" Something heavy and solid hit me on the head, and I fell to the floor, my brain filled with shooting sparks and fire.

Chapter V

SOMEONE was putting a damp cloth on my head. The water, which smelled antiseptic, rolled down the sides of my face and along my neck. The water was cold, and my head throbbed unmercifully. I opened my eyes and saw Miss Harvey's blonde head bending over me. Her blue eyes looked into mine.

"You got quite a sock," she said.

"What happened?" I asked.

"You bumped into a blunt object." She wrapped a piece of bandage around my head and said, "Lift up a little." I did, and she tied a knot in back. Her hands were very gentle. "There."

I sat up, and for an instant the room spun dizzily.

"Be careful," said Miss Harvey.

I saw that I was on the leather davenport in my uncle's study and that the entire household had been aroused again. George Coffin, Grace Coffin and Mrs Harvey were talking by one of the windows, while by the door stood Dan Harvey and Burton Coffin. They were examining a splintered place on the wall where the bird shot from the deputy's gun had struck. Miss Leslie was helping Dr Harvey replace bandages and a bottle of alcohol in his handbag.

"Did the intruder get away?" I asked.

Dr Harvey, his sharp face preoccupied, said, "We don't know. The deputy and that chauffeur are still looking for him." He came over to me and looked at my bandage and nodded. "That ought to hold you. It's lucky there's no fracture."

The others, hearing the conversation, grouped themselves around the davenport.

"How did you get hit, Peter?" asked Mrs Coffin.

I told them how the deputy and Norberg had seen the light in my uncle's room and how we burst in on the intruder.

"The fellow must have hit me with some sort of a weapon," I said, "as he was coming out the door."

Dr Harvey said bluntly, "You're lucky to be alive." He thrust an iron poker at me. "Here's what he hit you with. If it hadn't been a glancing blow you wouldn't be here now."

I took the poker from him. It was remarkably heavy. "This once I am thankful for the density of my cranium," I said

Miss Harvey smiled at my poor joke. "Do you think it was the nut who socked you?" she asked.

"I couldn't see anything."

"Why didn't you hand him one?" asked Burton Coffin. "You could have nailed him as he ran out."

"He nailed me first," I said.

As usual my use of slang caused laughter. The women were still giggling when the deputy and Karl Norberg came into the room. Water dripped from their raincoats, and their feet were covered with mud from the court.

"Couldn't find a trace of anybody," Karl reported.

"He must have a hideaway in the house," said the deputy. "We couldn't find a window or a door open."

Mrs Harvey's protruding eyes were alarmed. "You mean the madman's in the house at this very moment?"

"It looks that way, ma'am," said the deputy.

Mrs Harvey took a few jerky steps toward the door. "Come Thaddeus. Come Dan." Her plump body shook under her black silk robe. "We are leaving this place at once."

Dr Harvey hurried to her side. "Nonsense, my dear," he said, grasping her arm firmly. "How could we leave in a pouring rain like this?"

"I am going to leave."

Miss Harvey left my side to go to her mother and was joined by her brother on the way. They both advanced arguments against leaving, citing the weather, the impossibility of catching a train until late in the morning and the foolishness of being frightened.

"Somebody will stay with you all the time, Mother," said Dan Harvey. "Nothing can hurt you then."

"But what if this person does leap out at us?" Mrs Harvey asked the deputy.

"We'll catch him, ma'am."

"But I should die of fright. I should die right in my tracks."

"Now, ma'am," said the deputy.

Dr Harvey took a deep breath. "But, Mary, we can't leave. The deputy won't let us. We're witnesses in a murder case. Isn't that right, Deputy?"

"I reckon the sheriff *would* like to talk to you all in the morning."

"There. That settles it." Dr Harvey nodded as though he was pleased to be under legal restraint.

"We'll have to stay until the sheriff sees us, my dear."

"He'll see us all dead," said Mrs Harvey.

Grace Coffin, her deep voice under perfect control, said, "We'll all stay together in the living room, Mary, if it would make you feel better."

"Oh, it would." Mrs Harvey's round face brightened. "There's safety in numbers."

"A good idea," said Dr Harvey. "You girls can sleep on the two big davenports, and we'll use the easy chairs. It 'll be comfortable in front of the fire."

George Coffin had been looking out the window, but he turned and faced the Harveys. "No need to worry about the madman," he said.

"What do you mean?" asked Dr Harvey.

"Would a madman go rummaging around in this room?"

"I don't know." The doctor's small blue eyes were alert. "Would he?"

"That's just it."

The deputy had been listening with wide eyes. He turned to me. "What does he mean, Mr Coffin?"

"I believe he means that a madman wouldn't return to a room where he had, a few hours before, cut off someone's head."

"Then he thinks someone else was in the room?"

"Perhaps you'd better ask him."

The deputy swung around so that he faced George Coffin. "Do you think someone else was in the room?"

"Like Peter," said George Coffin, "I wouldn't come back if I were a madman."

"Who do you think was in here?"

"A horse of a different color. No idea."

"Well, what would anybody have wanted in here?"

"Dr Harvey can tell you." George Coffin's eyes, behind the shell glasses, were pleased as they regarded the doctor's small red face.

"Why should I be able to tell him?" demanded Dr Harvey.

The deputy looked at me in bewilderment. "I don't make head or tail of this. What would anybody have wanted in here, Mr Coffin?"

I said, "I don't know myself. Perhaps somebody was interested in the papers on my great-uncle's desk. Perhaps he had some money in the desk or some negotiable securities. Perhaps he had some letters someone wished to secure."

"I get the idea," said the deputy.

Burton Coffin, who had been perched on the arm of the chair in which Miss Leslie was seated, asked, "How did the fellow get by you?"

"He must have been hidin' by the door," said the deputy. "He probably heard the key and was waiting. He waits until we come rushin' in and then gives me a terrible shove, and my gun goes off. Then I guess he whales Mr Coffin here and slams the door on us and beats it."

"But how did he have time enough to get away?"

"He had plenty." The deputy grinned. "We got all scrambled up in the room trying to find a light, so it was a couple of minutes before we got the door opened."

Miss Leslie said, "I think I'll try some sleep." She started for the door but halted when Mrs Coffin asked, "Aren't you afraid to sleep alone, dear?"

"Not a bit," said Miss Leslie. "I can take care of myself."

She went out the door, followed by Burton Coffin. The Harvey family also drifted toward the door.

George Coffin said, "Since there is a possibility that someone is interested in these papers suppose you and I, Peter, collect them under the deputy's eye and put them in a safe place."

"That's a splendid idea, George," said Dr Harvey from the doorway. "Provided they are still all there." His voice was satirical. He disappeared down the hall.

"Well, let's do it anyway," said George Coffin. "Then . . ."

"I'll watch 'em," said the deputy. "I'm going to sit right in this room the rest of the night."

"But that's just it," said George Coffin. "If we put them in an envelope and give it to you, then you won't have to sit with the body. You can go down and guard the ladies downstairs."

This seemed to appeal to the deputy. He nodded his head. "I'll collect 'em in an envelope," he said. "You can watch me."

"It's all the same," said George Coffin.

We removed the sheet from my great-uncle's body, and the deputy collected the mass of legal-looking documents strewn over the desk. "Looks like he was doing some business with somebody," said the deputy.

Grace Coffin, who had been standing by the door, took a single glance at the body. "How terrible!" she exclaimed and hurried over to the window.

Some of the papers were stained with blood, and the deputy wiped them off with a soiled handkerchief. "It's only a three-for-a-quarter one," he explained in response to our surprised glances, "and, anyway, I got another."

George Coffin found a manila envelope, and the deputy put the papers in it and fastened the metal prongs on the back. "There! I guess nobody 'll be monkeying with these until the sheriff gets here," he said.

I was pulling the sheet back over the body when Grace Coffin uttered a startled cry. "There's somebody prowling around the lawn!"

Karl Norberg, who had been sitting in a chair by the window, jumped to her side. "By golly!" he exclaimed, his nose flat against the pane. "A feller in white."

The deputy was already running. "Come on, Karl," he called over his shoulder, "let's get him."

George Coffin followed Norberg toward the door.

"George!" his wife called frantically.

"I'll be all right, dear," he shouted and disappeared down the hall.

His wife rushed out after him, calling, "George! George! George!"

I was alone. I got up to go after them, but my head spun so I was forced to sit down again. Sharp pains ran up and down my back; my skull felt as though it was about to split. I could hear the receding voice of Mrs Coffin, still calling, "George! George! George!" I was wondering why she was so terribly alarmed when another wave of pain swept over me.

For a moment I was unable to do anything except sit in my chair with my teeth clenched and my hands pressed to the sides of my head. Then the pain passed, and I said, "Damn it," and leaned against the back.

Miss Leslie was standing in the doorway, looking at me. Her face was alarmed. "What's the matter?" she asked.

I felt my face coloring. "I'm sorry," I said. "I didn't mean to have my dramatics seen. I just had a twinge, but it's gone."

She watched me dubiously. "You're sure you're all right?"

"Yes. My aunt always says I am the worst baby, when it comes to pain, she has ever seen."

She had, I thought, the most remarkable face I had ever seen. It told so little. There was some kind of an expression in her large gray eyes, but I couldn't tell whether she was alarmed for me or afraid I might, as a result of the blow, be out of my mind and therefore dangerous. I couldn't tell whether there was sympathy in those eyes or contempt.

She stared at me without a change in her expression for fully a minute. Then she asked, "What is all the excitement about?"

"Mrs Coffin saw someone on the front lawn."

"A man?"

I nodded, then regretted my action. The movement sent a white flash of pain through my head. I managed to control my features, however.

She walked to the window. "Could she tell who it was?"

"I don't think so. Anyway, she didn't say."

She stood at the window for a long time, and I examined her back. Guiltily, for I am sure no gentleman would have taken advantage of a woman in this way, I noticed that she was slender and graceful, that her bobbed hair was soft and wavy and had a definite luster, and that her neck was small and rounded. She carried herself easily, and her back was straight. She was a bit taller than the average girl.

She turned around and met my eyes. "They're certainly making a thorough search," she said. "I can see half a dozen lights out there."

"I wish they'd catch him," I said. "It is quite a strain, both on my nerves and my head, to have him running around this way."

"It's a strain on everyone's nerves," she said. There were tiny wrinkles on her forehead when she frowned. "Do you think it *was* the madman who hit you?" she asked.

"I don't know. It does seem strange that he would return to the scene of his crime, but who can tell what a madman will do?"

Abruptly she asked, "Do you know anything about your great-uncle's will?"

"Nothing except there seems to be a lot of talk about it."

"And your uncle didn't tell you anything about a will when he talked to you?"

"Not a thing. He contented himself with expressing utter disapproval of my grandfather, my father and myself for our failure to become financiers. I think he was endeavoring to convey the opinion that all the brains and energy in the Coffin family had been centered in himself. He seemed ill pleased with the rest of the family (with the exception of my aunt Nineveh) and especially with me, of whom he had expected better things."

Miss Leslie said, "I can see how he might have felt."

I was trying to think of a good-humored retort when Burton Coffin appeared in the door. He was out of breath, his bathrobe was wet and streaked with mud, his face was damp.

"Did they find him?" I asked.

His eyes were on Miss Leslie. "No," he said. There was a sort of negation in his look, as though he were denying something. "No," he said again and hurried along the corridor. He did not look at me at all. I noticed, just before he passed out of sight, that his slippers were perfectly dry and clean.

Miss Leslie's eyes widened with surprise. She took an involuntary step after him, then glanced somewhat shamefacedly at me.

"I guess they've given up the search," I said. "It's very futile, anyway, on a night such as this."

Miss Leslie was not listening to me. Her eyes were upon the doorway where Burton Coffin had just stood. Her fine brows were knit thoughtfully; her expression was puzzled.

I did not like to sit in my chair and stare at her, but I was afraid to get up for fear I would be taken with another spell of dizziness and further alarm Miss Leslie. So I talked.

"They say rural life is very quiet beside the excitement of a large city," I said, "but I don't believe even New York could excel this evening. Do you think so, Miss Leslie?"

"No, I don't believe it could."

"This excitement is unprecedented for a college professor," I continued. "I think my colleagues will be astounded when I return and tell them my stories of madmen, a walk through a pitch-black forest, midnight alarms, a detruncated relative, a blow on the head, searches through rain-sodden grounds and other small-hour excursions."

She was smiling a little.

"Though I fear I have not played such a heroic part. But then, I am only a scholar."

Her face, when she smiled, lost some of its quality of brooding. "I'm sorry about this evening," she said. "I mean, about the remarks I've been making. I was upset by Mrs Spotswood's screaming, and in some way I held you responsible."

"Anybody would have been upset by my clumsiness. I behaved very badly."

"Then you'll forget what I said?"

"I'd already forgotten it," I lied.

"Thank you." Her oval face was impersonal. "I think I'll go back to bed."

I knew I should escort her to her room, but I was afraid to try my sense of balance by standing. I sat in my chair and watched her move toward the door.

As she neared the hall George Coffin and the deputy appeared in front of her. "No luck," said the deputy. "We found some footprints, but the guy had cleared out."

George Coffin peered solemnly through his horn glasses at Miss Leslie. "Been comforting the sick man?"

"No." Her voice was amused. "I heard the shouting and came out to see what the matter was."

"Oh." My cousin peered at me, then said, "Most of the women, at least my wife and Mrs Harvey and her daughter, are going to spend the rest of the night in front of the living-room fire. Wouldn't you like to join them, Miss Leslie?"

"Thank you, no. I'm not a bit afraid. I'd much prefer to sleep in my room."

The deputy stood aside to let her pass. George Coffin asked, "May I escort you to your room?"

"Yes, I'd be glad to have someone walk with me." Her glance, contemptuous, swept across me, and she was gone.

"How about you, Mr Coffin?" asked the deputy. "Sleep downstairs?"

"I think I'll sleep in my room too."

I got out of my chair. The pain came back with a rush, and I closed my eyes. I must have swayed, too, because the deputy came over and took my arm. "Steady," he said.

After a minute it was all right. My head hurt, but the dizziness was gone. I smiled at the deputy. "The fellow hit me a stout blow."

"I'll say he did." The deputy's blue eyes were shrewd. "I got an idea that your cousin was right when he said somebody beside the madman might be interested in all this business."

"How do you mean?"

"The way that guy hit you, for instance. You stood in the door, your back to the light, and the guy had an easy time hitting your head. He could have tapped you one and got away easy." The deputy wiped a smear of moisture from his sharp chin. "But instead he takes as hard a swipe at you as he could. You'd been dead if he'd connected squarely."

"You mean . . . ?"

"I don't know for sure, but if I had any enemies around here I'd watch my step."

I started to shake my head indignantly but remembered in time. "That's ridiculous. Nobody would have anything to gain by disposing of me." As George Coffin came back into the room I added, "And I haven't been here long enough to make any such violent enemies."

"Enemies?" George Coffin stared at me. "What enemies, Peter?"

"Nothing," said the deputy. "We were just talking." He produced a key. "I'm going to lock this place up and then go downstairs." As he was thrusting the key in the door a thought came to him. "Say! How do you suppose the guy we saw got in here. This door was locked."

I gasped. "By gad! I forgot." I led them into my great-uncle's bedroom and opened the door into the hall. "Here's how he got in."

"The deuce!" The deputy looked inquiringly at me. "He must have come within a few feet of where you were sitting."

"I'm afraid I fell asleep," I confessed.

"I know you did," said the deputy. "You were asleep when we came up after seeing the light." He closed the bedroom door and fastened the catch lock. "Nobody 'll be coming in this way now." Back in the library he added, "Seems to me no intruder would take a chance of prowling down a corridor where a guy was sitting on guard."

"What do you mean?" I asked.

His thin face was solemn. "I mean, couldn't someone who lived in the house walk down the hall? Couldn't they rig up some excuse for being in the hall if you woke up? And if you didn't they could duck in through that bedroom door, couldn't they?"

"That's pretty smart." George Coffin watched the deputy lock the door to my great-uncle's study. "That's pretty smart."

My head was ringing so that there was no room for any of the deputy's ideas. "I'm going to turn in," I said. "We'll see what comes up tomorrow." I walked down the hall with them and opened my door. "Good night."

"Good night," they said.

Chapter VI

A GLOSSY FLY, evidently determined to land on the tip of my nose, awoke me. I aimed a blow at the creature, sending it to the ceiling in a hasty spiral, and sat up in bed. A tawny pelt of sunlight lay across the foot of the bed, and outside my window a breeze rustled green leaves. In the distance I could see Crystal Lake, as brilliant as a perfectly cut jewel, as blue as a cornflower, as cool looking as a cake of cobalt ice. The water, indeed, was so inviting that I decided to have a swim.

I glanced at my wrist watch and was astounded to discover that it was ten minutes past eleven. I had slept all morning! I hastily climbed out of bed and just as hastily halted, remembering that my head had been hurt. I found with my fingers that the place which had received the blow was still sore, but the ache was gone. I could move my head in any direction without the slightest twinge. I went into the bathroom and looked at my face in the mirror. It seemed perfectly normal and not at all the face of one who had encountered madmen, dead men, and had nearly been killed himself during the previous night. I rather admired the calm manner in which my face had withstood the rigors of the night. I felt that many an academician would have had a face filled with wrinkles and hollows and bags under the eyes.

I felt as fresh as a college sophomore, and even the sight of my glass of baking soda and water, untouched, on the sink could not quell my high spirits. I simply poured the soda into the wash basin and let the oversight slip from my mind. Obviously I was not going to catch a cold.

After I had brushed my teeth and combed my hair I put on my swimming trunks, my bathrobe and my slippers. I discovered my hairbrush still in my bathrobe pocket, and in putting it on the bureau I saw the vase I had taken from the mantel in my great-uncle's library. Since my choice of weapons had already caused a great deal of laughter in the household I decided to conceal it until I had a chance to return it quietly to its former resting place. I glanced around for a good hiding place and finally stood it on the window sill in back of one of the muslin curtains. Then I started for the pier.

Downstairs I encountered Bronson. His thin horsey face was pale, and his eyes were red, as though he had not slept much.

"Good morning, Mister Peter," he said.

"Good morning, Bronson," I replied. "What's happened today? And why didn't you wake me?"

"Dr Harvey thought, in view of the blow which you were said to have sustained, that it would be advisable to let you sleep."

"That's right, Bronson, you weren't around when the man struck me with the poker, were you?"

"No sir."

"Where were you?"

"I must have been asleep."

"You didn't hear the report of the shotgun?"

"No sir. I don't believe the sound could have carried to the servants' quarters because of the storm."

"You were all alone in the servants' house?"

"Yes sir." Bronson stared at me with a troubled expression. "But you don't think that I could have struck . . . ?"

"Nothing like that, Bronson. I just wondered where you were. And by the way, where's Mrs Spotswood?"

"She's still in bed, but she's much better."

"Was she alarmed by all the noise last night?"

"No sir. Mrs Bundy, the cook, said Mrs Spotswood slept through it all. Mrs Bundy says she was so frightened that she didn't dare unbolt the door to inquire what was wrong."

"I don't blame her." I glanced around the living room. "Where are the others?"

"The older people are playing croquet in the rear of the house. The others are swimming."

"That's where I'm headed." I started to go to the front door, then paused. "Bronson, what about Uncle Tobias?"

"The coroner came this morning and took the body away."

"And the elusive madman?"

"The police have been unable to apprehend him."

"That's too bad. Bronson, what about lunch?"

"Twelve-thirty, sir. Though if you want a bite . . . ?"

"I'll wait, thank you, Bronson."

On the pier, sunning themselves, were Miss Leslie, Burton Coffin and Dan Harvey. Burton was lying on his face beside Miss Leslie, and his back was brown and muscular. Miss Leslie's back was slender and supple, but she was not so brown. She had on a blue rubber suit which left most of her back bare.

"Hello," I said as I neared the end of the pier.

Dan Harvey and Miss Leslie both said, "Hello," but Burton merely grunted without looking up.

Taking off my bathrobe and slippers, I said, "It's a beautiful day, isn't it?"

No one replied, so I walked out on the end of the springboard and peered down at the water. It was a dark blue, and it looked cold. I decided that I had better not dive because of my head, and I tried to remember the life saver's running jump I had once learned. This jump, by virtue of moving legs and arms, enabled the life saver to leap into the water without submerging his head, and I didn't want to wet my head.

I had learned this dive before I joined the water polo team at the university and had had no occasion to use it for the four years I played this rough but interesting sport, so I had some difficulty in remembering the correct leg and arm motions. I was thinking about these when a feminine voice, far out in the lake, called to me.

"Yoo-hoo! Yoo-hoo! Professor! Come on out."

Miss Harvey was standing on a moored raft two hundred yards out in the lake, her arms waving invitingly. For a hideous instant I had an impression that she was entirely unclad, but at last I made out the lines of a skin-tight suit the exact color of her tan skin. I was about to reply when someone jiggled the diving board, and I lost my balance and tumbled into the lake.

As I sped down through the cold water I decided that Burton Coffin was the perpetrator of this trick, and I determined to have an immediate revenge. I allowed myself to stay below for nearly a minute, and then, beating my arms wildly in the water, I came to the surface and shouted:

"Help! Help! Hel-ubb!"

I could see the assumed expressions of innocence and nonchalance on the faces of the two men and Miss Leslie change to alarm before I went down again. The moment I was far enough below the surface I took five vigorous strokes in the direction of the center of the lake and then appeared again. I assumed a wild expression, beat my hands on the surface and pretended I was unable to shout because of water in my mouth. I did, however, succeed in making some weird animal-like noise which must have been quite alarming.

Burton Coffin was poised on the springboard. He shouted, "Take it easy, Professor, I'm coming," and dove into the water.

Immediately I submerged again and swam rapidly to the right, paralled to the shore. I swam as long as my breath held out, and when I emerged Burton was twenty yards away. I threw up my arms and uttered sounds similar to "Glub-glub-glub."

Burton heard me, swung around and swam toward me with a powerful crawl stroke. I waited, still throwing up spray, until he was ten yards away. Then I sank under the water and swam almost directly under him so that he had passed me when I arrived at the surface. I had intended to keep up this sort of a will-o'-the-wisp proceeding for a considerable time, but my plan was thwarted by Miss Leslie, who had been watching from the pier. She cried:

"Back of you, Burton."

Then she dove into the water, evidently intending to take a part in saving my life.

Immediately I altered my plan. I allowed Burton to come up to me on the surface at almost the same moment Miss Leslie reached me.

"I've got him," Burton called to her. "Better keep away."

He attempted to turn me over on my back so that he could tow me in, at the same time saying, "You're all right, Professor. Take it easy. Take it easy." But I resisted, breaking his grip and moving about with abandon, sometimes allowing an elbow or an arm or a hand to strike his face.

"I can't do anything with him," Burton called to Miss Leslie. "I'm going to have to sock him."

He aimed a terrific blow at my jaw and would doubtless have knocked me senseless if I had not blocked it with my right arm. Then I allowed myself to sink again. He followed me down and grappled with me, and I gave him a brief lesson in the technique of water polo. I caught him under the chin with my shoulder; I grasped his ankles and whirled him around; I turned him upside down, and as a climax I rested both feet on the pit of his stomach and sent him toward the bottom with a tremendous kick. The recoil flung me to the surface almost under the astonished eyes of the Miss Leslie. I floundered about for fifteen seconds until Burton finally reached the surface. He had swallowed a great deal of water, and his face was blue. He could barely swim.

"I'm finished," he managed to say to Miss Leslie.

She swam over to me. "You fool," she said. "If you'll only lie still we'll get you ashore."

I diminished my struggles.

"That's right," she said. "Now let me turn you over on your back."

She rolled me over and hooked an arm under my chin. We started for the shore with Burton following us. He was coughing a great deal, and he seemed barely able to swim. Miss Leslie swam strongly, and I relaxed and looked at a fat cloud in the turquoise sky.

"This is what you should have done in the first place," approved Miss Leslie. "You shouldn't have lost your head."

In a few minutes we were in shallow water. Burton Coffin, some of the color back in his face, was the first to stand up. "Whew!" he exclaimed. "I nearly died out there."

"You can stand up now," said Miss Leslie to me. "You're perfectly safe."

As I stood beside her Dan Harvey came running up to the shore with a life preserver. His face fell as he caught sight of me. "Why didn't you wait until I got this?" he demanded.

"Of all the idiots, you're the worst, Dan Harvey," said Miss Leslie. "He would have drowned a dozen times if we had waited for you."

"Oh, I hardly think a dozen times," I said. "Perhaps not even once." I grinned at Miss Leslie. "Thanks for the nice ride."

I plunged into the water and swam out to the raft, employing the new Japanese crawl with which I had set a university tank record for the hundred yards last January. Miss Harvey was sitting on the raft, her arms about her knees.

"What are you trying to do?" she asked, smiling. "Scare us all to death?"

I explained that I was having my revenge upon the person who forced me to fall off the diving board.

"I saw you were faking when you kept coming up in different places," she said. "A drowning person doesn't move about like that under water."

"I fooled the others, though."

"Yes, but Burton Coffin is a bad enemy. And he's half again as big as you are."

"I'll dive in the lake each time he comes after me. I can handle him in the water."

She giggled. "I'll bring your breakfast out here to the raft if you want me to." Her face, with its bright blue eyes and pert nose, was amused.

I swung myself up on the raft. "I think I'll take a chance and try to have breakfast—or rather, lunch—in the house. Maybe the sheriff will be there to protect me."

"He doesn't look as though he'd hurt a mouse, or save you from one either. I think I'd depend upon my own legs in case of necessity."

"They aren't as nice as yours," I said, "but perhaps they'll do."

Miss Harvey balanced on the edge of the raft. "Professor, I underestimated you," she said. "Let's swim in."

As I paddled along beside her I thought with pride that the Earl of Rochester wouldn't have been too ashamed of me.

Chapter VII

WE ATE LUNCH in the big french-windowed dining room overlooking the verdant lawn and the blue water of the lake. It was a sober meal, and few words were uttered. Burton Coffin and Miss Leslie, sitting at the end of the table opposite me, studiously ignored me. Burton's sullenly handsome face was set in a pout, and once when I encountered Miss Leslie's eyes she apparently failed to recognize me.

I realized I was in—to make use of an expression lately employed by my aunt Nineveh—the doghouse.

The elder Harveys did not speak to me either. Indeed Mrs Harvey spoke but once during the meal and then to her son, urging him to eat all his greens. He wanted to know if she thought he was Popeye the sailor man, a reply which drew a giggle from his sister but passed over my head.

George Coffin, sitting at the head of the table, ate heartily of chicken hash and mashed potatoes and several times peered around his majestic wife to smile at me.

I had ample opportunity to examine the room. One long side was windowed, with lake and grass and crimson and purple heads of tall hollyhocks in the background, while against the wall of the other stood an ornately carved sideboard, backed by a huge silver roast platter and covered with a fine Sheffield tea set. Behind George Coffin was a smaller mahogany table on which reposed two huge candelabra, each holding seven pink candles. Above the sideboard a grim portrait of old Matthew Coffin, miller, church elder, witch hunter and member of the New London town council in 1654, adorned the wall.

Finishing the last bit of his hash, George Coffin addressed me. "I'm the champion croquet player of this shebang," he announced. "I have a small trophy to prove it." He drew a five-dollar bill from his pocket and handed it to me. "You wouldn't believe that rare old bill, just a few minutes ago, was locked in old Doc Harvey's wallet, would you?"

I pretended to examine the bill. "It looks as though it had been kept in good condition," I said. "I expect it's worth nearly three dollars on the open market."

"Three dollars!" George Coffin snatched the bill from me. "Say, any bill that's been taken away from the doc is worth twice its face value. I'll bet this is the first five-dollar bill he's parted with since his honeymoon."

Dr Harvey's red face, really quite angry, looked like that of a great northern pike. He looked as though he'd eaten something bitter. He flashed a furious glance at George Coffin, but he didn't attempt any reply.

"I'm going to frame this bill," continued George Coffin, evidently profoundly pleased with his humor, "and under it I am going to have inscribed: 'Saved from life imprisonment by George Coffin, croquet champion of Crystal Lake.' "

I couldn't help laughing at his extravagance, and I was rewarded by a glare from Dr Harvey. Dorothy Harvey was smiling, too, but when her father's glance turned toward her she quickly assumed an expression of profound vacancy. I imagine the humor was particularly galling to the doctor because of his widespread reputation for parsimony. My aunt Nineveh always described him as "that little doctor who let women pay his luncheon check" after a meeting with him in New York.

On the other hand, Dr Harvey's reputation as a medical man was excellent. He was on the staff of the Belmont Hospital in New York, specializing in the surgical removal of tumors and cancerous growths. He had married Mary Coffin, the daughter of Simon Coffin, my grandfather's and Tobias' other brother, more than twenty-five years ago without the approval of her father, and he had made his way up into the world without help, starting out as a general physician in a small New Jersey town. The Harvey family now lived in a large apartment on Riverside Drive and employed two servants. Perhaps the doctor's early experiences caused him to desire a dollar to go as far as possible.

George Coffin continued in a jocular vein until Bronson appeared with the dessert. It was a creamy custard with caramel sauce. Bronson halted beside my chair and spoke in a low voice:

"The sheriff is waiting in the living room, Mister Peter. He would like to talk with everyone."

"Very well, Bronson," I said. "Did you ask him if he would have lunch?"

"He said he had already eaten."

We ate the custard hurriedly and then moved into the living room. The sheriff and his tall angular deputy, Jeff, were sitting on one of the davenports, talking in whispers. They halted abruptly when they caught sight of us.

"Well, Sheriff," I said, "have you caught Elmer Glunt yet?"

Sheriff Wilson's face was the color, shape and texture of a baked apple: pinkish brown, round, soft skinned and faintly wrinkled. His eyes were mild and tired. He was wearing a black suit, frayed at the cuffs, a blue shirt and a stringy black necktie.

"No sir," he said loudly. "That doggone feller is too slick for us. But we got all the roads blocked, and we'll ketch up to him sooner or later, sure as shootin'." His voice was nasal.

"We hope so," I said.

The sheriff turned to his deputy. "Where do you think we ought to start, Jeff?"

"I reckon we better find out just how the body was discovered." The deputy's large Adam's apple moved up and down when he talked. His blue serge coat, worn shiny, had too short sleeves, and he was continually pulling them down with his fingers in an effort to hide his knobby wrists.

The sheriff nodded. "Then we'll have to speak to the lady who found the body."

"Mrs Spotswood," I said. I glanced at Bronson, who was standing by the dining-room entrance. "Is she able to come down?"

"Yes sir. She's all dressed. Shall I call her?"

"Please, Bronson."

He went into the downstairs library and spoke into a small wall telephone. In a few seconds I heard the purr of an electric motor, the sound which had puzzled me during the night. Presently a panel at the far end of the living room slid open, and Mrs Spotswood's wheel chair emerged. Back of her I could see a small elevator, paneled in a dark wood which matched the walls of the living room.

Mrs Spotswood was old, but just how old I could not tell. A stroke three years before had affected one side of her body and must have considerably aged one side of her face. She was wrinkled, and there were livid pouches under her eyes, and the flesh was puffy over her jawbone. A coil of pure-white hair circled her head. She had violet eyes, and her face was so heavily powdered I could not tell whether her deathly pallor was real or not.

I introduced the sheriff, and he, modulating his tone, asked her to describe the events leading up to her discovery of Tobias Coffin's body. She spoke in a melodious voice pitched so low it was difficult to hear her.

"I was awakened in the night by a noise in the corridor under my room," she began. "I got . . ."

"Just a minute, ma'am," said the sheriff. "What sort of a noise was it?"

"It sounded like something being dropped—something heavy, yet soft, like a watermelon."

The sheriff nodded.

"I climbed out of bed and wheeled my chair to the head of the stairs. There was nothing in the hall below, but I saw the door to Mister Tobias' study was open and that the light was burning. It was very late, and I was afraid he had fallen asleep over a book, so I put on my night robe and took the elevator down to his door."

She paused, and the sheriff said, "Yes?"

"There he was." Her voice caught in her throat. "There he was."

The sheriff frowned thoughtfully while she sat very straight in her chair, twisting a handkerchief in her hands. "You didn't see anybody else?" he finally asked. "Anybody in the hall?"

"Not until Peter Coffin came."

"Thank you, ma'am." The sheriff's blue eyes roved about the room. "Did anyone else hear something before the time the corpse was discovered?"

Nobody replied.

"Well, now," said the sheriff, "it looks as though the madman went on out, because none of you saw him, but even if he didn't I don't think it was likely that he was the prowler who hit Mr Coffin here."

"Why not?" I asked.

"I'll try to show you in a minute." Sheriff Wilson held out a small soft-skinned hand. "Where 're them papers, Jeff?"

The deputy produced the documents he had taken from my great-uncle's desk. The blood on the sheets had turned to dull brown stains, but there was a subdued gasp from the women.

"I understand Mr Coffin was supposed to have made a new will," the sheriff said, rustling the papers. "Do any of you know about it?"

After an interval of silence George Coffin made a noise in his throat. "I think we all heard something about it," he said. "I know Tobias told both Dr Harvey and myself that he was changing the old will."

"Did he show you the new will?"

George Coffin's eyes, behind the thick glasses, turned upon Dr Harvey. "Not to me." Hastily Dr Harvey added, "Not to me either." He glared at George Coffin.

The sheriff appeared not to observe this byplay. He asked me: "How about you, Mr Coffin? What do you know of the new will?"

"Very little. I've only heard the others mention it. Before last evening I did not know of the existence of a new will or of any will, for that matter."

The sheriff frowned, drawing his thin eyebrows together, and gazed in dismay at his deputy. The deputy shrugged his shoulders.

"Then nobody knows for sure there *was* a new will among these papers?" the sheriff demanded.

Finally Bronson, his thin face solemn, moved toward the sheriff from the back of the room. "I do," he announced.

"You!"

"Yes sir. I saw the new will on Mister Tobias' desk. He showed it to me last night before Mister Peter came."

"Ha!" Sheriff Wilson made a washing motion with his hands. "Now we're getting somewhere. What did the new will say?"

Bronson glanced appealingly at me.

"I believe Bronson feels that it would be a breach of confidence to reveal what was in the new will," I said. "Isn't the document Bronson saw still there?"

The sheriff blew out his cheeks, spoke explosively. "That's just it. The darn thing's gone."

If he expected to create a great sensation he was disappointed. I was amazed, and both Mrs Harvey and Mrs Coffin uttered little cries of dismay, but nobody else seemed particularly agitated. Dr Harvey and George Coffin both nodded as though they had already known of its disappearance. Burton Coffin's heavy, handsome face was impassive, while Miss Leslie was perfectly calm.

"That's why I'd like to know what was in the new will," said the sheriff. "I'd like to know how it differs from the old will, which I got here." He held up a group of typewritten pages bound together by staples. "Then maybe I'd get a line on who'd be likely to steal the new will."

Bronson was still looking at me.

Dr Harvey said, "I don't think anybody stole the new will. It wouldn't be worth the effort. More than likely it hadn't even been witnessed." His voice was casual.

"It had been witnessed," said Bronson. "The driver of the grocery truck and the young man who helps him deliver signed their names to it."

The sheriff took from Bronson the name of the grocery, Archer's, and the names of the driver and his helper, Joseph Carter and Edward Thebault. Bronson said they both lived in Traverse City.

"Now, how about the will itself?" asked the sheriff.

"As far as I'm concerned," I said, "I am perfectly willing to have Bronson tell all he knows about the will. But there are other relatives here, and possibly they have some objection to his speaking."

None had, so I told Bronson to go ahead.

"Well, the main bequest," Bronson said, speaking to the sheriff, "is to Mister Peter. He is left the estate here and is given one sixth of the cash residue of Mister Tobias' fortune after certain other bequests are paid."

I stared at Bronson in bewilderment and, I confess, fear. I, a sedentary scholar, had no use for a huge mansion, a model dairy farm and large grounds, and had no desire to own them. Neither did I desire a larger income than I already had. Mine, I felt, was exactly right, allowing me to live comfortably and to travel, but small enough not to be burdensome. Would being a comparatively rich man with a large estate prevent me from carrying out my scholarly activities?

Bronson's voice checked my frantic reverie. "Then Miss Leslie is to have one third the cash residue of the fortune after the bequests are paid, and Mr Burton Coffin and Miss Harvey and her brother are each to have one sixth."

"So," said the sheriff. He was examining the old will. "And the bequests?"

"Dr Harvey and his wife, and Mr George Coffin and his wife are each to receive twelve thousand five hundred dollars, or twenty-five thousand dollars to each family. Mrs Spotswood and I are to receive ten thousand dollars apiece, while Mrs Bundy, the cook, and Mr Bundy and Karl Norberg, the chauffeur, are to receive five thousand dollars apiece."

"Well, well, well." The sheriff waved the old will in the air. "Quite some difference. No wonder somebody wanted to get hold of the new will."

There was indeed quite some difference, as the sheriff went on to explain. In the old will George Coffin and Dr Harvey were the chief beneficiaries, dividing the entire estate, which included "stocks and bonds and cash, as well as the Michigan property." Miss Leslie and my aunt Nineveh and I were each left twenty thousand dollars, while Mrs Spotswood and Bronson were left five thousand apiece. Neither the cook nor her husband nor the chaffeur was named in the old will, which had been drawn up nearly ten years ago.

"Now we begin to see why somebody was prowling through the dead man's room," concluded the sheriff. "Somebody didn't want the new will to be found."

"Are you trying to accuse me or Dr Harvey?" asked George Coffin grimly.

"I'm not accusing anybody. I'm just pointing out the facts. A number of people stood to gain by that will's disappearance."

"I suppose you think that one of us had a hand in Mr Coffin's death too," said Dr Harvey with heavy sarcasm.

The sheriff was genuinely shocked. "Gosh, no! I'm just trying to figure out who would gain by having the new will lost. That's all." His eyes were soft. "I can see a lot of you would benefit a little. I never thought of murder."

"I don't see that a lot of us would benefit," said Dr Harvey. "I think you are speaking of me and Mr George Coffin."

"Not exactly," said the sheriff. "I don't even know how much half the estate, as the old will provides for you two, is. Maybe the twenty-five thousand in the new will is as much as you'd get out of this anyway?"

George Coffin said, "I think Tobias was worth about three hundred thousand plus this property."

The sheriff whistled. "That's pretty good." He thought for a moment. "Then each of you would stand to get about one hundred and fifty thousand by this old will."

"Not quite as much as that," said George Coffin. "You remember seventy thousand dollars in bequests had to be paid first."

"Well, say a hundred thousand dollars apiece." The

sheriff shook his head. "That's a good deal better than twenty-five thousand apiece."

"It is if you look at it one way," said George Coffin, "but it isn't if you look at it another."

"How do you mean?"

"I mean if you figure by families there's not much difference in the two wills. The Harvey family gets twenty-five thousand plus two one-sixth shares in the estate, or about ninety-five thousand dollars. We get twenty-five thousand plus one-sixth, or about sixty thousand dollars."

Sheriff Wilson took a long time to digest this information. At last he said, "One hundred thousand and half this property is better than sixty thousand, isn't it?"

"Yes," agreed George Coffin, "but not enough better to make me take the risk of destroying the will."

"So you say," said the deputy, his lantern jaw thrust forward.

"So I say," agreed George Coffin.

The sheriff leaned forward in his chair. "Well, did you take the will, Mr Coffin?"

Dr Harvey, his face red, moved in front of the sheriff. "He doesn't have to answer any question like that. If you are making a charge he can deny it, but he doesn't have . . ."

"That's all right, Thad," said George Coffin easily. "I don't mind answering his question." He smiled at the sheriff. "The answer is no."

The sheriff's and the deputy's eyes met. The deputy shook his head. "Well, I guess that's all I can do," said the sheriff. "I'll look around a little, both for the madman and the will, if you don't mind."

"I don't mind at all," said Dr Harvey. His small blue eyes moved in my direction for an instant. "And I'm sure Professor Coffin now feels that he is in no position to object."

"I never felt that I was in a position to object to anything," I said. "If I have given any directions in the past twelve hours it was simply because Bronson turned to me."

"I knew it was Mister Tobias' idea to leave the house to Mister Peter," said Bronson. "I was merely following it out." He defiantly faced Dr Harvey. "I shall continue to obey Mister Tobias' wishes."

"Until the new will is discovered the old one goes as the expression of Tobias' wishes, doesn't it, Sheriff?" asked Dr Harvey.

"It seems like it would." The sheriff scratched his head. "But I don't know. A lawyer 'd have to figure that out."

Bronson appeared unconvinced.

"I don't see what difference it makes anyway," I said. "I'll be glad to have Bronson take orders from you, Dr Harvey. I've only filled in, as I said, because Bronson turned to me."

George Coffin was grinning. "What difference does it make who orders the groceries? I suggest we let Mary and Grace and Mrs Spotswood give the orders around the house."

Bronson looked at me. I nodded.

"Hello!" exclaimed the sheriff, whose eyes had been wandering about the room. "Who's this?"

"This" was Mrs Bundy, the cook. Her round face was agitated, and her red hair looked as though she had been out in the wind without a hat. She came directly to me. She was breathing too heavily to speak at first.

"Why, what's the matter, Mrs Bundy?" I asked.

"It's gone," she said.

"What's gone?"

"The thing he done it with. The cleaver."

My face must have been blank, because she continued:

"The meat cleaver that he chopped off poor Mister Tobias' head with. It's gone from the kitchen."

Sheriff Wilson elbowed me aside. "What's all this? What's this about a cleaver?"

"My cleaver has been stolen. It was here yesterday, but when I came to look for it just a moment ago it was gone."

"But how do you know it was the cleaver used to kill Mr Coffin?"

"It isn't likely the madman would be carrying two cleavers, is it?"

Mrs Bundy led the sheriff and most of the others into the kitchen to show them the place where the cleaver had been. I started to go up to my room and was joined on the stairs by George Coffin.

"A funny business," he observed.

"Isn't it?" I said. "It looks as though someone took advantage of the madman's murder of Uncle Tobias to steal the will."

"Maybe and maybe not." He hesitated on the top stair. "Peter, do you think anyone, even a madman, would go very far with a bloody head?"

"I don't know."

"I don't think so. I believe the cleaver and the head are somewhere around here. And possibly the will is with them."

"You don't mean the madman stole the will?"

"I'm not sure what I mean, but I think we should take a look for Tobias' head." He suddenly stared hard at me. "Peter, where would you hide the head of an old man you had just murdered?"

"I!" I blinked my eyes at him. "Why, I suppose I'd throw it in the lake."

"But would it float?" George Coffin's voice was triumphant. "That's the question. Would it float?"

"Why, I shouldn't think it would."

"But are you positive it wouldn't?"

"Well, no."

"That's just it. The man who chopped off the head wouldn't know either. That's the kind of thing nobody would be apt to know."

"I suppose not," I agreed. "Except, possibly, a doctor."

"Aha!" His eyes gleamed. "What made you think of that?"

"Nothing in particular. I simply thought doctors would be more likely to know that sort of thing."

George Coffin seemed disappointed. "I suppose you're right. But I believe we can count out the lake in your search for the head."

"My search?"

"I mean, our search. Where else could a head be hidden?"

"I suppose right here in the house."

"Perhaps. But I believe its presence would sooner or later be given away by—let us say, a certain fragrance."

"The woods?"

"That's better. But there is an excellent possibility that Rob Roy, your great-uncle's collie, would smell it out on one of his hunts for rabbits or other woodland denizens."

"It could be buried in the woods."

"There. I think you've hit it. It's buried and not far from the house." George Coffin's face beamed. "Now we have something to work on."

I followed him along the hall. "I don't exactly follow your reasoning," I objected. "I don't see what would prevent the madman from carrying the head as far as he desired."

"There isn't anything that would have prevented the *madman.*" He halted in front of my great-uncle's door. "But would the madman have taken the will?"

"I don't suppose so."

"Well, then. If the person who took the will cut off Tobias' head, and the madman wouldn't have taken the will, then the madman didn't kill Tobias!"

It took several seconds for me to grasp this. While I thought, George Coffin knelt on the hall carpet and crawled from my great-uncle's room toward the rear of the house. He had his face down a few inches from the carpet.

"You mean that someone in the house killed Tobias?" I gasped.

He spoke without lifting his head from the floor. "I think that's a possibility we should consider." He found a kitchen match in his pocket and lighted it. The yellow light brought out the light and dark green rectangles on the carpet.

"That's ridiculous," I said. "It would be perfectly possible for someone to have found Uncle Tobias after the madman had killed him and taken advantage of the opportunity to take the will."

"Maybe." He advanced on his knees a few feet, then halted abruptly. "Hey! What do you make of this?"

He lighted another match as I bent over. I followed his pointing finger and made out, on the edge of the carpet almost opposite Miss Leslie's door, a brown stain. There were also brown stains on the bottom portion of the papered wall.

"Blood?" I asked.

"Blood. Your great-uncle's blood, Peter."

"Don't be so dramatic," I said. "You make my flesh creep. How in the world did it get out here?"

"This is where the murderer fumbled the head." He peered up at me. "You remember Mrs Spotswood said she was wakened by the noise of something heavy falling in the hall, almost as though somebody had dropped a watermelon?"

"Yes."

"Well, that's probably the way a head would sound."

"I can well believe you. But what good does it do for us to know that?"

"It does us a lot of good." He rose to his feet, using the wall to steady himself. "The stain here signifies that the murderer was going in the direction of the back stairs from your great-uncle's room."

"Yes," I said after a moment's thought.

"But the footprints Miss Harvey discovered in front of the pantry window led in the direction of the dining room and the front stairs."

"That's right."

"Well, then . . . ?"

"I'm afraid I don't follow you," I said. "I don't see why the prints and stains shouldn't be right where they are."

"Let us put ourselves, for a second, in the place of the madman popularly supposed to have entered this house and killed its master." George Coffin leaned back against the wall. "He came in through the pantry window and went into the living room and up the front stairs. He saw the light in Tobias' library and went in and killed him with a cleaver which he had had the forethought to bring with him. Then he took the head and departed.

"But instead of departing by the way which was familiar to him—by the front stairs—our madman goes down a hall which, for all he knows, may be a blind end, and finds the back stairs."

"It does seem a little unusual," I admitted.

"Unusual!" echoed George Coffin. "It's positively bizarre."

Chapter VIII

UNTIL a few minutes after four o'clock I stayed in my room, mostly sleeping and thinking. I secured a copy of *The Exploits of Brigadier Gerard* by Sir Arthur Conan Doyle from my great-uncle's library, but even the boisterous antics of my favorite Napoleonic soldier could not keep my eyes from closing. I put the book on the floor under my bed and rolled over on my side so that my face was toward the wall, but I did not drop off to sleep as soon as I expected. My mind kept turning over the events of the previous night, trying to make logic out of the conflicting elements. I thought about the murder and decided it was obviously the work of a demented person. I thought about the theft of the will. That seemed to fit in well enough if I assumed that someone discovered the body before Mrs Spotswood awakened the household with her screaming.

But I was defeated by the prowler. What did he want in the upstairs library? Had he taken the will? Had he tried to kill me? I thought if he had taken the will there would have been no particular reason for his wishing to kill me. If he knew the old will was to be the only one found my bequest couldn't have mattered. Supposing it was someone who thought that the new will would be found, who could it be? Who would stand to gain by having me put out of the way? The answer to this, of course, was in the list of others named as having been left shares. These included the young Harveys, Miss Leslie and Burton Coffin.

About this point in my cerebration I must have fallen asleep. I was having a wild battle with Burton Coffin in thirty feet of water and had just hit him a fierce blow on the top of the head when I found myself sitting on the edge of the bed. I was fully awake.

Someone was knocking softly on the door.

Taking a shoe in my right hand, I went to the door and opened it a crack. Bronson was standing in the hall. "Could I speak to you, Mister Peter?" he whispered.

"Of course." I opened the door. "Come in."

Bronson's thin face was mysterious. He tiptoed into the room and noiselessly pushed the door shut behind him. "I'm sorry to have wakened you, Mister Peter, but this was the only time I could catch you alone."

"That's all right, Bronson. Sit down."

"I should prefer to stand, thank you. First I wanted to tell you the sheriff said the inquest would be held on the day after tomorrow."

I sat on the bed and somewhat guiltily placed the shoe on the floor. "He's gone, then?"

"He left an hour ago. He said he would let us know who would be requested to testify."

"There isn't much to testify to," I said. "Nobody seems to have seen anything."

Bronson's face, dark and angular, was grim. "Someone must have seen something," he said. "Someone has been lying."

"You mean—about seeing the madman."

Bronson leaned toward me. "Mister Peter, sometimes

I'm inclined to believe the madman did not kill your great-uncle."

"What do you mean?"

"I've seen some things." His thin lips, tightly compressed, were pale. "I've seen some strange things. Some very strange things." He shook his head in bewilderment. "Only I do not understand their significance."

"You mean, things that I don't know about?"

"Things only I and one other know of."

"But, Bronson, why didn't you tell the sheriff? He's supposed to know about things like that."

"I would have, but I didn't want to get an innocent person into trouble." His eyes were suddenly bright. "If the person *is* innocent."

"Well, what is it that you saw?"

Bronson sucked in his cheeks until there were two dark hollows on both sides of his face. "I don't dare tell you, Mister Peter."

I was really amazed. "Why not? I won't tell the police until you give the word."

"I'm afraid to tell you for fear something will happen to you or to both of us, Mister Peter. If what I fear is true we are dealing with a desperate person."

"But, my goodness, Bronson, this is melodramatic. You don't mean to say you have such a dangerous secret that your life is in danger."

"That's exactly it. I'm in no danger at all if what I've seen is unconnected with the murder, but if it is as I suspect, my life hangs by a thread."

"Bronson," I said, "I suspect you are overwrought by my great-uncle's death. Why don't you take the afternoon off and get some sleep? We can manage dinner without you."

His smile was grim. "I know it sounds strange, but murder hangs over this house. I can feel it everywhere." He bent over and whispered in my ear. "If I should die remember the oak in the cow pasture."

With these words ringing in my ears like a prophecy of the Delphic oracle, he left my room. I was thoroughly awake now, and my mind was skittering about like a frightened brook trout. What could he have seen? I hadn't the faintest idea. Of one thing I felt sure: Bronson was protecting someone in the family. He wouldn't have had the slightest compunction about handing anyone else over to the police on mere suspicion, but he was devoted to the Coffin family, or rather to my great-uncle. Remember the oak in the cow pasture. Remember what about the oak? It sounded like Lewis Carroll nonsense. In fact the whole business was extremely odd.

I shrugged my shoulders and glanced at my watch. It was four-thirty. The sun was still bright outside, and I decided that another swim would give me the proper appetite for dinner. I put on my suit and started down to the pier.

Halfway across the lawn I caught sight of a curious figure in a black bathing suit, peering under a lilac bush. It was George Coffin, and the suit hung in creases around his skinny legs and fell away from his hollow chest, making him look like a scarecrow clad for swimming. He would have frightened the most courageous crow. He didn't appear the least bit concerned over the strange appearance he made when I came up to him.

"What in the world are you doing?" I asked.

He crawled slowly on his hands and knees around the bush. "Looking," he said when he had completed the circuit.

He nodded. "Come on."

"For the head?"

He led the way to another bush and indicated by a sweeping motion of his hand that I was to crawl around one side while he went around the other. I got down on my hands and knees and worked my way around the bush, keeping my eyes open for any signs of recent digging. We met head on at the opposite side of the bush.

"Nothing?" he asked.

"Nothing."

He motioned with his head for me to follow and crawled along parallel to the line of rose and other flower bushes in front of the big veranda overlooking the lawn and the lake. I crawled after him with a sort of shambling gait, something like an intoxicated bear. We had covered about three quarters of the length of the veranda when there was a gasp above us.

We looked up and saw Mrs Coffin and Mrs Harvey and Miss Leslie staring at us. Miss Leslie was wearing a bathing suit.

"George Coffin!" exclaimed Mrs Coffin. "Whatever has got into you?"

I felt the blood mounting into my face, but George Coffin carried the situation off with aplomb. "We are trying out Dr Tutmiller's exercise," he asserted boldly. "For the abdomen, you know."

His wife snorted. She was a large woman of impressive aspect, and her face had an expression of outraged disapproval. "Well, I must say it's a very peculiar sort of exercise."

"A very good one, though, my dear," said George Coffin. "Won't you join us?"

Mrs Coffin snorted again and turned away from the railing.

George Coffin resumed his strange means of locomotion, and I, not knowing what else to do and still blushing profoundly, followed him. When we reached a turn in the flower bed which hid us from the veranda I heard a muffled noise coming from my cousin. He was laughing.

"Peter," he said, "my wife is a wonderful woman."

I came to a halt beside him.

"No other woman in the world can convey as much in a snort as Grace. In one snort she can express disapproval of your behavior, intimate that you are a fool, call you a liar, condemn you for making a spectacle of yourself and at the same time disown any responsibility for you whatever. She is a wonderful woman."

"The Dr Tutmiller," I asked. "Did you make him up?"

"A figment of my imagination."

"Well," I said, "where should we look next?"

He sighed and sat on the grass. "I must confess, Peter, that Dr Tutmiller's exercise is a bit hard on the arms and legs of a man my age. I wish we had a few assistants in our search." His eyes, still amused, fastened on me. "Though I feel that we have done a very thorough job of the front of the house and can cross that territory off our list." He massaged one knee with the palms of both hands. "I wonder if we could ask the help of the women. They'd like nothing better than to go on a search for a severed head. A woman is a very barbarous creature."

"I think we'd better leave them out," I said.

"Why?"

"Do you remember what Rochester said to Charles the Second?" He shook his head. "Charles asked the earl why all the bells rang on the birthday anniversary of Queen Elizabeth when none rang on the anniversary of his father.

"Rochester replied, 'Because Elizabeth chose men for her confidants, while Charles whispered his secrets to women.'"

George Coffin nodded. "I guess maybe you're right at that, Peter. Women aren't such good ones to let in on a secret." He struggled to his feet. "What do you say we put off looking at the back of the house until after dinner?"

"That 'll be fine." I stood beside him. "But what makes you think the head won't be out in the woods as we decided after lunch?"

"It may be out there, all right, but I got to thinking about it and decided there was a chance it would be somewhere close to the house. A guy isn't going to go plunging about those woods in the dead of night when there's a madman lurking around, ready to get him. Even if he had the courage to murder your great-uncle, Peter, it doesn't seem likely that he'd have the courage to face the possibility of meeting the madman in those woods."

"It's all too deep for me."

"The thing to do is to keep thinking . . . and to keep looking for that head." He started for the front stairs, then halted. "What about taking another look after dinner tonight?"

"I'll be glad to help you," I said.

His face was mysterious. "You'll be helping yourself, not me." His thin legs passed up the stairs and out of sight through the front door.

I went down to the pier and swam a little way out from the shore. The water was cold, and it sent the blood running through my veins, making me feel very energetic. I swam about on the surface, kicked up spray, rolled over and over, blew water in a stream from my mouth, tried different strokes and then came in to the ladder.

Miss Leslie was lying on the pier in a patch of sunlight, and her gray eyes were amused. She was wearing one of those two-part bathing suits modeled after the costume of the South Seas, and her body was slender and tan and lithe. She was a remarkably attractive girl.

"That was a nice exhibition," she said as I climbed the ladder.

I felt myself blush. "I didn't know I had an audience."

"I wish your college classes could have seen you today," she said. "Their faith in higher education would have been shattered."

"Even a professor has his lighter moments."

"Yes, I can see that." Her teeth were white and regular. "And especially when he is doing the abdomen exercises advocated by Dr Tutwilder or whatever his name was." Her voice was friendly.

"Dr Tutmiller," I said severely. "Dr Gabriel Tutmiller, of Vienna."

Her laughter was musical. "What were you and George Coffin really doing, crawling around the lawn like that?"

I saw it would be useless to lie. "We were looking for Tobias Coffin's head. We had an idea it might have been hidden somewhere around the house."

She nodded, her face suddenly solemn. "That's what Burton said. He thought you were looking for the head."

"How did he guess that?"

"I don't know. He simply said he thought you were looking for the head."

"But there's a missing will. Why didn't he think we were looking for that?"

Frowning made little wrinkles on the smooth surface of her forehead. "I suppose he didn't think his father would be interested in finding the new will."

A light breeze made the pines around the edge of the lake nod, disturbing the placid mirror of the water around the pier. The sun, now fairly low, was warm on my back.

"What are you going to do with the head when you find it?" she asked.

"I don't know." I wondered about that myself. "Put it back with the body, I guess."

Her gray eyes were dubious. "Is that the only reason you're looking for it?"

"Well, there's the exercise."

"You think I'm being unnecessarily inquisitive, don't you?" Her voice had a slight edge to it.

"No. I'm sorry if I seemed facetious. But I really don't know why George Coffin is so anxious to find the head. I'm just his Dr Watson."

At this moment Burton Coffin appeared on the pier. He had on his swimming trunks, and there was a towel over one broad shoulder. His chest was beautifully muscled. He nodded coldly to me and sat down beside Miss Leslie.

"Did you find out what he was doing?" he asked her.

"You were right. They were looking for the head." She talked distinctly, as though I wasn't present. "They want to find it so they can put it with the body."

"Aw nuts," he exclaimed. "They don't expect us to believe they'd waste their time to do that, do they?"

"That's what the professor thinks anyway," she said. "He's just your father's little helper."

"Well, you can bet Dad's got some other idea." His voice was aggrieved. "I don't see why he doesn't ask me to help him."

I put on my bathrobe and tied the cord about my waist. "He thinks you're dumb, that's why," I said. "And so do I, if you have to employ a young lady to get information from me." I bowed to Miss Leslie. "Good afternoon, Mata Hari."

By the time I was back to the house my rage had left me. But still I considered it an unfair trick for Miss Leslie to play upon me. I had admitted that we were looking for the head in reply to her question, but I thought she wanted to know what we had been doing for her own information alone. I didn't like Burton Coffin, and I liked it even less that Miss Leslie should be trying to secure information for him. I wished I was bigger so I could punch him in the eye. I thought maybe I would anyway.

My bare feet were noiseless on the stairs and on the short stretch of carpet between them and my room. I was surprised to discover my door ajar, and I peered in the crack.

Mrs Spotswood, her wrinkled face secretive and purposeful, was going through the drawers of my dresser. She was bending over the bottom drawer, her hands feeling the back section of the container. The position of her bent shoulders, her stiff neck, as she leaned from her wheel chair, gave her the appearance of a hunchback.

I suppose I must have made some sort of a noise, because she suddenly wheeled and faced me, an expression of intense alarm on her face. Curiously this expression changed to one of relief.

"Oh, it's you, Mister Peter," she said.

"Why, yes. This happens to be my room."

She made a clucking noise with her mouth, as though soothing an unreasonable child. "Yes, I know." She came toward me on her way to the door. "I was looking to see if you had anything to go to the wash."

"Why, thank you very much, Mrs Spotswood, but I have nothing at all for the wash." I stood aside to let the wheel chair pass.

She smiled again, allowing her countenance to assume a particularly gentle expression, and pulled the door shut in my face. I went over and sank down on my bed and gave vent to a burst of profanity.

"What the deuce?" I asked myself. "What the deuce?"

Chapter IX

AFTER A DINNER at which I distinguished myself by eating six ears of Golden Bantam corn we went into the great living room for coffee and cigarettes. The sun had not yet gone down, but the air was already chill and we were grateful for the crackling blaze of birch and pine Karl Norberg had started in the stone fireplace. After Bronson, moving noiselessly about the room, had served the coffee George Coffin caught his eye.

"Bronson," he said, "I think Mr Tobias would have thought of one thing more for our comfort on a chill night like this."

"I have it ready," Bronson replied solemnly.

He left the room for a few seconds and returned with a tray on which was a bottle of brandy and a number of bell-shaped glasses.

"Ha!" said George Coffin with infinite pleasure. He took the bottle and began carefully to measure out one fourth of a tumbler of the golden liquor to each person. "This is the climax of a very fine dinner."

I felt amusement at the boyish enthusiasm pictured on his face, and at the same time I experienced a feeling of genuine liking for my cousin. His horn-rimmed spectacles gave him the look of an owl, but the general effect, with the humorous twist of his lips and the friendly gleam in his eyes, was kindly. I thought, as I watched him pour the brandy, how he had made me the butt of two jokes at dinner without hurting my recently sensitive feelings.

The first of these jokes came when I entered the dining room a moment or two after the others had taken their places at the candle-lit table. George Coffin was already telling the group about sitting with me in Uncle Tobias' study. I noticed everyone was present except plump Mrs Harvey, who had a sick headache, and Mrs Spotswood, who was eating in her room.

"I didn't know much about professors," he was saying as I came into the room, "and I wasn't sure whether they approved of smoking or not. So I asked the professor if I could smoke. And what do you think he said?"

Nobody seemed to have an idea.

"He said: 'Go right ahead. I'm used to it. My aunt Nineveh smokes incessantly.' "

I suppose the spectacle of a grown man saying that he can stand smoke because his aunt uses cigarettes is funny. At least everyone laughed.

"The point is," said George Coffin, "that I still don't know whether he was giving me the bird for asking permission to smoke or whether he was telling the truth."

Miss Harvey, her blue eyes bright, said, "I'll bet the professor smokes in secret all the time." She had a youthful tendency to giggle.

"I do," I assured her. "Opium and marihuana."

Then, as we were eating the salad, consisting of tomatoes and lettuce and cucumbers fresh from the garden in back of the servants' house, George Coffin leaned across the table toward Miss Leslie.

"What did you say the professor's middle name was?"

"So you have been talking about me behind my back, my fair Mata Hari," I thought. "All right, talk away," I said to myself, "but sometime my chance for revenge will come."

At least she had the grace to blush. Without looking in my direction she replied, "Nebuchadnezzar. I discovered it in the family Bible."

"Peter Nebuchadnezzar Coffin," said George Coffin while the others laughed.

I laughed too. The name had always amused me: it was so typical of my father. He used to sing me to sleep with Vedic hymns when I was a little boy, and he wrote letters to his colleagues in cuneiform on clay tablets. On his gravestone he had inscribed: "Sargon Coffin —Born 1865 A.D.—Died 736 B.C." He was born an American, but he lived and died a Mede.

George Coffin continued the jest. "I think I'll call you something short for Nebuchadnezzar," he said, peering at me. "Nebuchadnezzar is too long. I think I'll call you Butch for short."

This was funny, because if anybody in the world did not look as though his name would be Butch, it was I. The ridiculousness of the nickname struck everyone at the table, and it was time for dessert before the giggling had stopped.

Then Mrs Coffin asked a question that sent a chill over all of us. "Who's going to guard the house against the madman tonight?" she demanded.

I think this put a shadow of apprehension on the minds of everyone as we moved into the living room.

Even after George Coffin had handed around the brandy inhalers there was no perceptible return to the high spirits of the early part of dinner.

"Karl Norberg and I and possibly Burton could take turns standing guard," I suggested. "We could take three-hour shifts, and none of us would miss the sleep."

This idea was not very well received.

"Guard duty is silly," said Dr Harvey. His small blue eyes moved from one to the other of us. "All we have to do is to lock everything up, and nobody can get in."

"Why won't the police provide us with a guard?" asked Miss Leslie.

"They can't guard every house in the county," explained Burton Coffin.

"Not every house in the county has had someone murdered by the madman," was Miss Leslie's rejoinder.

But it was Mrs Coffin who put her finger squarely on the main objection to my scheme. I had a feeling that she hadn't liked me at all since my association with her husband, and after she spoke I was sure of it.

"I think we should have guards," she said, "but I don't think the idea of Professor Coffin watching over us would cause me to sleep soundly. I can't imagine him subduing a maniac."

I felt that I would do just as well as any of the others, but I acknowledged her the right to an opinion about my puissance. The thing I didn't like was the rather open manner in which she slighted my ability.

Her husband took my part. "I think Butch would be as efficient as anyone," he said. "All anybody could do if the man tried to break in would be to call for help. Nobody would tackle a maniac single handed."

Burton Coffin said, "I would."

His father looked at him wearily. "I meant, no person with any sense." His tone was edged with contempt.

"Perhaps we should let Burton keep guard all night by himself," I said.

Mrs Coffin took me seriously. "Why, the very idea! The very idea. My boy needs sleep as much as anybody. I won't hear of his staying up all night."

Her husband finished his brandy and stood up. "We'll try to think of some way of safeguarding the house," he stated. "Come on, Butch, we have a little tour to make."

I walked to the door with him after excusing myself. I was conscious of Burton Coffin's eyes, angry and yet with a strange glint of apprehension in them, following us.

When we had got around to the back of the house George Coffin took my arm. "You took quite a beating at dinner and afterwards."

"I don't mind," I said. "A college professor is always a ridiculous figure outside of a classroom."

"I don't know. You haven't had a fair chance to prove yourself. A man can't do much when somebody clouts him over the head with a poker."

It was dusk now, but there was enough light to see under bushes and in the flower beds. A few fireflies gleamed intermittently. We searched for signs of recently uncovered earth. We peered under bushes; we examined the soft earth of the tulip beds; I pricked my hands pushing aside a cluster of pink roses; we even moved a small sundial. Our search was utterly fruitless. The back of the house, including the smooth surface of the croquet ground, was as barren as the front.

As we were concluding the search there came to our ears the barking of a dog and the sound of underbrush being broken. Startled, I peered into the forest. Was the madman coming?

Suddenly my eyes caught sight of a cow coming along the path from the back pasture. A bell, fastened by a leather strap about the creature's neck, tinkled softly. Back of this cow were other cows, six in number, the remnant of my great-uncle's prize herd, and back of them danced the estate's brown-and-white collie, Rob Roy. The dog kept them moving at a good pace, barking at them occasionally and now and then pretending to nip their heels.

"Smart fellow," said George Coffin of the dog. "He goes out and brings them in every night. Unlocks the pasture gate with his nose."

As light on his white feet as a ballet dancer, Rob Roy moved the herd past us onto the court between the main house and the barn. Then with a warning bark for his charges to keep moving he came over to speak to us. Recognizing George Coffin as a friend, he paused for a moment to allow his ears to be rubbed, then briefly touched my hand with his cold nose. This bit of politeness having been performed, he raced after the cattle.

I noticed how easily he, and the cattle, too, crossed the surface of the court. "How does it happen that the clay isn't wet after all that rain last night?" I asked George Coffin.

"Karl Norberg rolled it twice today. Your great-uncle always liked to have the surface of the court hard so the cattle wouldn't bog down in the clay. It's like a tennis court."

"Why didn't he put in cobblestones?"

"I don't know, unless he thought they'd be hard on the cows' feet."

I glanced around at the flower beds and grass in back of the house. George Coffin followed my eyes. "I guess the woods are the next item in our search," he said.

Back of the half circle of trees which surrounded the rear of the house was decidedly forbidding gloom. In the half light I could make out oddly distorted stumps, piles of leaves, weird-looking plants.

"We're not going to search there tonight?" I asked in alarm.

George Coffin laughed. "I should say not. I've a healthy dread of Mr Glunt. We'll try it in the morning." He brushed off the knees of his white flannel trousers and caught my arm. "Let's go inside."

As we were rounding the house an automobile came up the driveway and stopped in the clay court between the house and the Jersey barn. It was the sheriff with two strange deputies.

"How do," he said. "Any news?"

"Not a thing," I said. "Have you caught Glunt yet?"

"That feller's a slippery customer. We haven't seen hide nor hair of him all day. But we'll catch up with him, you can bet on that."

George Coffin rested an elbow against the side of the car. "Where do you think he's got to?"

"Can't have got very far," said Sheriff Wilson. "All the roads are being watched."

One of the deputies, a squat dark man with black stubble on his face, spoke. "He's got to come out sometime to eat."

I asked, "What if he comes back to this house for food?"

"Truss him up and send for me," said the sheriff.

"I think it would be a lot better, Sheriff, if you left a man here to truss him up."

"Can't do it." The sheriff's ordinarily mild face was set in obstinate lines. "My men haven't had any sleep for thirty hours, and they've got it coming to them. You got plenty of able-bodied men around the house to stand guard if you think you need one."

"Don't you think there's any chance of his coming back here?" asked George Coffin.

The dark deputy said, "Don't look as though it would be a smart thing to do . . . to come back to the place where you killed somebody."

Sheriff Wilson nodded his head. "That's right, Clark."

George Coffin smiled at them. "Madmen don't do smart things."

"Well, I can't help it." The sheriff stepped on the starter, and the engine roared. "I got a car posted at the crossroad about three miles down the line. If anything happens you telephone me, and I'll have the state police flash the car by radio. It can be over here in three or four minutes."

We watched the automobile swing around the big court and disappear down the drive. It was quite dark by this time, and the sky was pin-pointed with bright stars. There was no sign of the moon. The air was sharp.

George Coffin moved slowly toward the front steps of the house. "I think we ought to stand guard duty tonight anyway."

"There's Karl Norberg and your son Burton and Dan Harvey and me," I suggested. "Perhaps we could watch in pairs."

"That's a good idea. The doctor and I could make the third shift."

By this time we were on the broad veranda by the

door to the living room. I seized George Coffin's arm. "I almost forgot to tell you something," I said. "I caught Mrs Spotswood searching through my bureau just before supper."

"You did!" He eyed me for a moment. "Well, I *am* surprised at that."

"Why would she go through my things?" I asked.

"I don't know." He rubbed the back of his neck. "I don't know at all."

"The funny part is that she didn't seem alarmed when I caught her. You'd think . . ."

"Why didn't you ask her what she was doing in your room?"

"I didn't have to. She said she was seeing if I had any clothes that needed washing."

"Well, that's darn funny. I can't think of any possible explanation of her action." He opened the door, ushered me into the living room. "I'll do some worrying about that tonight in bed."

There was an atmosphere of fear about the big room, a tenseness despite the soothing warmth of the wood fire. Dr Harvey, Mrs Coffin, Burton Coffin and Miss Leslie sat in a circle to the left of the fire. They had been talking, and their faces were raised in brief alarm at our entrance. Even the game of double solitaire being played at the other end of the room by Dan and Dot Harvey had a kind of forced ferocity about it, although at the moment the brother was denying with considerable heat his sister's allegation that he was cheating.

"George," said Mrs Coffin as we neared the fire, "wasn't that a car I heard a moment ago?"

"It was the sheriff." George Coffin related the conversation we had had with the sheriff and his deputy and concluded by saying, "So it looks as though you'll have to trust yourself to the Volunteer Night Watchman's League of Crystal Lake."

Dr Harvey was scowling. "What does the sheriff think he's going to do—wait until the madman shows up at a restaurant somewhere for dinner?"

"That's what the sheriff's man said," I declared. "He said they'd catch him as soon as he got hungry."

The doctor laughed bitterly. "Why don't you put a tray on the front steps for him? That would be simplest."

"Not a bad idea at all, Doc," said George Coffin. "Maybe if we did that he wouldn't break into the kitchen as he did last time."

"George!" Mrs Coffin's voice was exasperated. "I don't think that's anything to joke about."

"But I'm not joking."

"Dad would joke on his deathbed," asserted Burton Coffin. His face was sulky.

Dr Harvey's white teeth gleamed. "You mean on somebody else's deathbed."

"My son thinks I have a light mind, unsuited to the serious business of selling life insurance," said George Coffin to me.

Burton sat up in his chair as though he was about to make some sort of a reply, then sank back again without saying anything. He glowered at his father. Mrs Coffin's face, turned toward her son, was sympathetic.

I felt embarrassment at this unnatural antipathy father and son displayed for each other. It was not right. I changed the subject. "How about this watch? Shall we try it in pairs?"

It was decided that this would be the best method of protecting the house. Though I protested, Burton Coffin and Karl Norberg were given the worst shift: that from four o'clock until breakfast. Dan Harvey and I were selected to guard from one o'clock until four, and George Coffin and Dr Harvey took the early duty.

"That's pretty swell," said George Coffin after the hours had been arranged. "A couple of old gaffers like Doc and me would be up that late anyway."

"It's all foolish," muttered the doctor.

I went out to the kitchen to ask Bronson to tell Karl of his guard duty, but I found only Mrs Bundy. She was mopping the porcelain sink with a damp cloth.

"Bronson's gone to the servants' house," she said in reply to my question. "He wasn't feeling well."

I asked her if she'd found the cleaver, and she said she hadn't. She said she was going to spend the night on the third floor with Mrs Spotswood to quiet the old lady's nerves.

"Won't that be very hard on you?" I asked.

"It's not bad at all. There's a studio couch in her sitting room which I use for a bed. It's quite comfortable, thank you."

"And you're not afraid of someone breaking in the house?"

"It isn't someone outside, it's someone inside the house I'm afraid of."

"Why, Mrs Bundy, what do you mean?"

Her face was very red and serious. "Well, it's a funny sort of madman that can break into a house by unlocking a window from the inside, now isn't it?"

"I don't understand. What do you mean, unlocking a window from the inside?"

"I mean that the window in the pantry where the footprints was found had been securely locked when I went to bed. I know, because I locked it myself."

"Well, that certainly is odd." I felt she was telling the truth. "Why didn't you speak to the sheriff about it?"

"I did, but the old fool wouldn't believe me. He said I must have overlooked it and as much as accused me of making up the story of my locking it so's not to be blamed for my neglect. I'd get no blame anyway; it's Bronson's duty to see that the house is locked up at night."

"Do you have any idea who unlocked the window?" I asked.

"None at all. Though I suspect that Bronson had something to do with it; he turned pale as a ghost when I told him about it."

"Well, don't worry tonight. We're going to take turns guarding the house, and there'll be someone up all the time."

"I won't worry," said Mrs Bundy resolutely. She brandished a large carving knife. "I'm taking this up to bed with me, and if anybody should try to come in . . ." She made an unpleasant cutting motion in the air with the knife.

I walked over to the servants' quarters and found Karl and Bronson and Mr Bundy sitting in front of an open fire in the combination library and sitting room my great-uncle had furnished for the servants.

"Don't get up," I said. "I simply wanted to ask Karl if he would take a shift at guard duty tonight."

Karl Norberg's blue eyes were friendly. "Sure, I'll be glad to watch the house."

I explained to him that we were going to watch in pairs and told him that he and Burton Coffin would be on from four o'clock until breakfast. He said he would be ready then.

"How about me and Bronson?" asked Mr Bundy. "We'll be glad to help out." He was a small man with a jolly round crimson face and straw-colored hair. He was smoking Prince Albert in a briar pipe.

I told them we had already arranged the guard duty for the night and said that they could consider themselves reserves, held in readiness for emergencies. I said good night to them and went back to the house.

"You're just in time, Professor," called Miss Harvey as I entered the living room. "We're going to have a game of hearts."

They had a table with five chairs around it in a corner of the room, and with considerable misgiving I noticed that Miss Leslie and Burton Coffin were preparing to play.

"I don't believe I'd better join you," I said. "I'm a very poor card player."

"Aw, come on," begged Miss Harvey. "It's more fun with five." She made her red lips pout.

I could see that Burton Coffin didn't want me to play. Miss Leslie's face was noncommittal. So I played.

I remembered the game fairly well from my college days. The object was to keep from taking hearts and the queen of spades and at the same time to take the jack of diamonds. Or better yet, to take all the counting tricks and thus score the equivalent of a grand slam. The Harveys played intensely, squabbling over the score, exulting when they were able to hand a heart or the black queen to someone and dropping into a slough

of despair when they were forced to take a trick. Miss
Leslie played an alert game without the emotional vir-
tuosity of the Harveys, but Burton Coffin's mind seemed
to wander.

I played carefully, but one or the other of the Harveys continually handed me hearts on the tricks I took,
and I kept going down on the score sheet. I took this as
an unusual run of bad luck until I happened to catch a
covert look flashed by Dan Harvey to his sister. I saw
then that I was being—I think this is the correct word
—"framed" by them. They were undoubtedly doing
things with the cards that the better bridge clubs would
consider unethical. If they were not actually cheating
they were at least in combination against me.

I tried to think of a way which would defeat their
purpose, which was to drive me down to the minus one
hundred point on the score sheet, a position carrying
with it the unenviable title of Dumb Baby. I did not
want to be known as Dumb Baby; it was bad enough
being called Butch.

However, the problem of avoiding this was a neat one.
I have never learned any trick shuffles with a deck, and
I did not know how to palm cards, so there was no way
I could cheat for myself. I needed assistance. I decided
to approach Miss Leslie, whom I had seen glancing curiously at the Harveys on several occasions. It was impossible to speak to her, but on the next hand I devised
a way of letting her know I wanted help. Instead of
passing her the three worst cards in my hand, as is the
custom, I gave her two high diamonds and the deuce of
hearts. When she looked at me in surprise I winked at
her and then let my eyes roll in the direction of the
Harveys.

For a moment her face was blank, but she quickly thought the matter out. My look at the Harveys told her I knew they were cheating, and my gift of valuable cards was a sign that I wished to win her friendship. Her eyes became amused.

After that hand the Harveys suffered the most amazing series of reverses they probably had ever encountered in a heart game. By passing Miss Leslie five and six and sometimes seven and eight of my cards, she would arrange her hand to suit herself and then slip me under the table the cards she thought would be of the greatest advantage to me. Usually one of us kept all the hearts, while the other kept a hand with high diamonds so as to snare the jack. We invariably short-suited ourselves in either clubs or spades so that we would have an opportunity of throwing a heart on one of the Harveys, and we always provided perfect low-card support when we had the dangerous queen of spades.

While Burton Coffin played his hands in stodgy unconcern, we ran the Harveys down from the plus fifties to the minus fifties in a very few minutes. Miss Leslie arranged the cards perfectly, showing rare judgment on several occasions, and I aided her as far as I was able. I suppose the Harveys would have been more wary had they been playing against younger opponents, but it never occurred to them that I could be cheating too. Bewilderment, chagrin and consternation were mirrored on their faces as their scores kept getting lower and lower. It was one of the most painfully disastrous moments in their lives.

Finally we worked them down to the minus eighties, within fourteen points of the ignominious title of Dumb Baby when luck favored me with a remarkable hand. I had six diamonds, including the ace, king, queen and jack; the ace of hearts and a small spade and two small clubs. I passed the spade and both of the clubs to Miss Leslie and received from Burton Coffin the ace of spades, the king and queen of hearts. It was a perfect hand.

Burton led the four of diamonds, and I took the trick with the ace. Then I exhausted diamonds, took four spades with the ace, and took the remaining twelve cards with the three high hearts. The coup not only netted me seventy-two points, but sent both Dan and Dot Harvey over the line into the Dumb Baby class. Their faces were studies in amazement.

"Thank you very much for a nice game," I said, standing up. "It's the first time I've played in ten years, and I'm afraid I was a bit rusty."

"Oh, I think you played very well for the former world's champion hearts player," said Miss Leslie.

"My gosh," said Dan Harvey. "Was he really the world's champion?" His mouth fell open.

"I won the title at Vienna," I said. "I had to play off a tie with Adamec, the Polish champion, but I was lucky enough to hand him the queen on the very first play, and he conceded his defeat."

A telephone had been ringing in the downstairs library, and George Coffin had passed by our table to answer it. He returned and said to me, "A long distance call for you."

I picked up the receiver and said, "Hello," fully expecting to hear the voice of my aunt Nineveh. Instead it was the voice of a man.

"Is this Professor Peter Coffin?" he asked.

"Yes."

"This is Colonel Jarvis Black."

I remembered Colonel Black. He had been going through the Elizabethan chancery records in search of Shakespearean data at the time I was in London investigating court records of the Restoration. We had become quite friendly. I remember thinking he was sort of an elegant dabbler in a number of esoteric fields: the Baconian theory, Rosicrucianism, lycanthropy and the Black Mass being some of the subjects he conversed eruditely upon. He was a sardonic, Mephistophelean man, immaculately dressed and with perfect manners. I was very much surprised when someone told me he was head of a detective agency and one of the world's greatest authorities on ciphers.

"Well, this is a pleasure," I said warmly. "Where are you now, Colonel Black?"

"In New York."

"Oh."

"I telephoned to ask you about the death of your great-uncle," he said.

"Yes . . ."

"I want to know if you believe it was the work of a madman, as the newspapers report."

"I don't know," I said. "There's been a madman loose in the neighborhood. He cut off his wife's head before he was arrested, and now my great-uncle's head has been cut off."

"Yes. Yes. I know that. But I want to know what you suspect."

I glanced around and saw that the room was empty. I was far enough away from the living room so that I could not be heard there. "There have been some curious things about the death I am unable to explain," I admitted, "but I don't know what to suspect."

"What things?"

"One of them is that the window through which the madman was supposed to have entered was locked on the inside."

"And another?"

"The attitude of Bronson, the butler. He informed me this afternoon that he didn't think the madman had anything to do with the tragedy. He said he thought he knew who committed the crime."

"Did he tell you who it was?"

"No, he didn't. But I think he intends to as soon as he satisfies himself it is for the best."

"The story had a fantastic sound when I read it in the *Herald Tribune* this morning," said Colonel Black There was real pleasure in his voice. "I think I'll pay you a visit, Peter."

"I'll be glad to have you. But why are you so interested?"

"Well, you see, the American Insurance Company is one of my clients."

"But I don't see what that has to do with my great-uncle's death?"

"But didn't you know?"

"Know what?"

"That Tobias Coffin took out a policy last year for a hundred thousand dollars and named you and a Miss Leslie, a niece by marriage, I believe, as beneficiaries."

"Why, that's simply incredible!"

"It is also true." His voice had a note of amusement. "The insurance company is naturally a trifle upset about the matter, especially as they will have to pay a double indemnity in case the death was really violent."

His tone became sharper. "Isn't there a relative named Burton Coffin at the house?"

"Why, yes."

"It's curious he didn't say something about the policy."

"How did he know about it?"

"He sold it to your great-uncle."

I gasped.

"I'll see you sometime tomorrow," continued Colonel Black. "Until then, keep your eyes open."

"I will," I promised.

My mind whirling, I slowly took the receiver from my ear. I heard a click as Central disconnected us, and then I heard another far louder click. I ran out into the living room.

"Are there any extensions to the telephone in the house?" I demanded.

"In the upstairs library and in the servants' house," said Dan Harvey.

The others watched me race up the stairs with startled eyes. I ran into my uncle's study, but there was nobody there. I returned to the living room.

"What's the matter?" asked George Coffin.

I looked carefully over the small group of people facing me. Dr Harvey and George Coffin were there, as were Burton Coffin, Miss Leslie and the two young Harveys. Mrs Coffin had apparently gone to bed.

"Somebody was listening to my conversation," I said.

Chapter X

"HAVE YOU EVER READ *The Dolly Dialogues?*"
Miss Leslie asked, moving a trifle nearer the fire.

I looked up from my book. "Oh yes. They're delightful." The shadows thrown by the leaping flames alternately lightened and deepened the gray of her lovely eyes. "I'm surprised you've never read them."

"Oh, I have. I happened to see a copy on the shelf, and I thought I'd read them again. It's been such a long time I've almost forgotten them."

I knew she wasn't talking to me just to give vent to her enthusiasm for Anthony Hope, and I felt a shade of suspicion. Was she trying to secure further information from me? I would see. I continued the conversation. "I remember the suave Mr Carter and how I wanted him to have his Dolly," I said.

"Yes, it was too bad her husband didn't have the courtesy to die."

"I don't imagine Mr Carter would have known how to be a husband. I think he preferred to be on the outside, wistfully looking in."

"Look," she said, abruptly changing the subject, "do you really regard me as an enemy?"

There was no one in the room except George Coffin and Dr Harvey. They were passing their period of guard duty by playing chess. The others had gone to bed.

"Not as bad as that," I replied. "But I don't think it was quite fair of you to pump me for Burton Coffin's benefit."

She avoided this point. "You don't like Burton Coffin, do you?" There were soft hollows under her cheekbones.

"Not very well."

"Why?"

"I don't know . . . unless it's because he doesn't like me."

"You're sure there's nothing more than that? You haven't had any"—she hesitated an instant—"business relations with him?"

"Why, no. I've never had anything to do with him. I never set eyes upon him before I arrived here. It's more like Tom Brown's parody of that little verse of Martial's:

> *"I do not love thee, Doctor Fell,*
> *The reason why I cannot tell;*
> *But this alone I know full well,*
> *I do not love you, Doctor Fell."*

George Coffin, slouched in his chair, his hands in his pockets, was waiting for the doctor to decide upon his next move. He turned his head in our direction. I could see he was pleased about something. "Peter," he said. He was having difficulty keeping his face solemn.

I said, "Yes?"

"I think the verse might go something like this," said my cousin. "It might go:

> *"I do not love you, Burton Coffin,*
> *I hope I do not see you offin."*

I fear I uttered a sound dangerously close to a giggle. Miss Leslie's face was shocked. George Coffin turned to the chessboard, and I heard Dr Harvey grumble, "How can I concentrate with you spouting poetry all over the place?"

Miss Leslie spoke to me severely. "I don't think it's very nice of you to make fun of Burton behind his back."

I heard George Coffin's complacent response to Dr Harvey: "I've got you licked anyway." I smiled at Miss Leslie. "You really can't blame this on me. You started it."

She had lovely dimples. "I suppose I did." Her face was suddenly serious. "I'd like to know the reason you and Burton hate each other."

"Why, I don't hate him. It's nothing——" I halted abruptly and peered into her lovely gray eyes. "Does he hate me?"

I could see she was genuinely agitated. Her hands gripped *The Dolly Dialogues* until the knuckles were white. "I don't know." Her eyes fell away from mine. "It's very curious. I should be on the side of Burton." She paused, and when she spoke again her voice was very low. "He has made some remarks about you. I thought I ought to warn you."

"But, my goodness! What could he have against . . . ?" I felt an overwhelming amazement. "What kind of remarks?"

"Well." The firelight gave her soft skin an attractive flush. "You must promise not to say a word to anyone." She put one hand on my coat sleeve.

"I promise."

She seemed to be trying to collect her thoughts before she spoke. "I couldn't make much out of what he said," she continued finally, "but it was something like this: he said he wasn't going to do any more dirty work for you, that the next time he'd put you out of the way rather than do your dirty work." Her face was bent over so that she seemed to be examining the tip of her green slipper. "I remember he used the phrase 'dirty work' several times."

"Why, this is insane." I half rose to my feet. "He's never done any dirty work for me. I've never even had any dirty work to be done."

"That's what he said." Miss Leslie was examining my face curiously. "Moreover, he said if you didn't clear out pretty soon he'd finish you."

I threw out my arms in a gesture of complete bewilderment. "Didn't you ask him what the 'dirty work' was?" I demanded.

"He wouldn't tell me." Her voice was solemn. "I think he regretted having told me as much as he had. He asked me to forget everything he said."

"Well, thanks for telling me about this." I could see her green slipper moving back and forth in front of the flames. "I appreciate it. But why did you tell me, when you are, as you say, in Burton's camp?"

She couldn't have said anything that would have surprised me more. She said, "I thought maybe you'd stop whatever it is that you're doing."

I felt as though someone had struck me a hard blow in the stomach. I sank back on the davenport and literally struggled to secure air for my lungs. "This is incomprehensible," I said weakly. "Simply incomprehensible." She watched me without expression. "Do you mean to say, Miss Leslie," I asked, "that you believe I'm some sort of a criminal?"

"Perhaps not that." Her face did appear doubtful. "But why would Burton be so bitter about you?"

"I don't know. But I assure you I'm not involved in any evil-doing other than our conspiracy during the card game." A new thought crossed my mind. "What a bewildering person you are, Miss Leslie," I said. "First you think of me as a bungling coward—I admit, with some grounds—and now you regard me as a sort of master villain who has Burton Coffin in his toils." I took a breath. "I am, in reality, a perfectly harmless college professor."

She made a negative movement with her dark head. "You didn't seem so harmless when you had Burton Coffin in the water. You almost drowned him, you know."

"So you haven't forgiven me for that. Don't you think I had some justification when Burton jolted me into the water?"

"But it was Dan Harvey who upset you."

"He did!" To my shame I felt only a mild regret that I had ducked Burton unjustly. "Then I shall have to apologize to Burton." I grinned at her serious face. "And at the same time I'll tell him he is freed from my toils. I will make him do no more of my 'dirty work', whatever it is."

She smiled reluctantly. "I'm not going to worry about it." She rose gracefully to her feet. "I can't imagine what the 'dirty work' could have been either." She placed *The Dolly Dialogues* under her arm. "Aren't you coming to bed?"

"I don't think so. My watch comes so soon that I might as well wait up."

She bent over me and spoke in a whisper. "Then you *are* going to watch them." Her glance drew my eyes to George Coffin and Dr Harvey.

"Watch them?" I rose with my back toward the fire. "I'm not in the habit of spying upon anyone," I said with dignity. "What makes you think I'd want to watch them?"

Her gray eyes were scornful. "Either you're very smart, Peter Coffin, or terribly—the opposite." She turned her back on me and walked toward the stairs. "Good night," she called to the chess players.

They replied abstractedly, and she went on up the stairs without a backward glance. I sank back on the davenport and tried to make some sense out of our conversation. If Burton Coffin's accusing me of forcing him to do my "dirty work" and my spying upon George Coffin and Dr Harvey made sense, I finally concluded, then Miss Leslie was right intimating that I was terribly dumb.

However, in my thinking, I found one ray of light. She had called me Peter Coffin! I liked the way my name sounded on her lips.

Presently Dr Harvey acknowledged that he was defeated, and the chess game was over. The doctor went out in the kitchen to get a glass of ice water, and George Coffin came over to the fire. "You and Miss Leslie had quite a chat," he observed.

I told him what she had said about Burton and also about my watching him and the doctor. His face was genuinely puzzled.

"I can understand why she might think you would

want to watch us," he declared, "but about my son being a member of your criminal syndicate, I am completely in the dark. You're sure she wasn't spoofing you?"

"I don't think so." I got up and pushed some of the red coals further back on the hearth. "She seemed quite serious." The fire was quite hot. "Why would I want to watch you?"

"I suppose on account of the new will. It is quite possible that one of us older members of the family might have it in our possession and would like to have an opportunity to destroy it."

"I'm not worrying about the will. It's the madman who's got me puzzled."

I told him what Mrs Bundy had said about the window.

"Locked from the inside," George Coffin repeated. "That *is* something to think about! Do you suppose he has a friend inside the house?"

"I hope not," I said. "It's bad enough to have to worry about his breaking in, without having to think of his being escorted in."

Dr Harvey returned from the kitchen. He had evidently caught the last part of my sentence. "Who's being escorted in?" His face was alert.

I repeated what I had told George Coffin.

"She's probably confused," said the doctor. "After times of extreme stress, such as occurred last night, people often become confused. Probably she locked the window the night before last."

"Maybe," agreed George Coffin.

"She seemed pretty sure of it," I said.

"She would," said Dr Harvey. "That's the attitude a person in such a condition would take." He looked keenly at me. "Did you open your windows last night, Peter, or did you keep them closed?"

"I opened them."

"Are you sure?" His expression was that of a person who knew me to be wrong.

"Why, fairly sure."

"Would you swear you left your windows open in a court of law if a man's life hung on your testimony?"

"I don't know," I said slowly. "I'm fairly certain I left them open."

"But you're not positive?"

I thought it best to humor him. "No," I said.

"There!" Dr Harvey triumphantly wheeled on George Coffin. "That's the natural response to questions about some minor act. A moderate certainty, but some doubt. That's what the cook should have said had she been telling the truth."

"You think she's lying?" I asked.

"I won't go as far as to say deliberately lying. She probably thinks she's telling the truth."

George Coffin was nodding his head. "You're probably right, Doc. It seems very fantastic, anyway, that someone inside would unlock a window for Mr Glunt's particular use."

"It's impossible." Dr Harvey glanced at his wrist watch. "Five minutes of one. Time for the new shift to take over." He gave me a tight smile without any humor in it. "Think you and my son can protect us all right?"

"You can count on us," I said.

He moved away from the fire. "Come on, George." He grasped my cousin's arm. "I'll send Dan down to you."

"Good night," I said.

They both responded pleasantly and disappeared up the stairs. Three or four minutes later Dan Harvey appeared. He had on his pajamas and a dressing gown, and he was having difficulty keeping his eyes open. "Hi," he said. He sat on one of the davenports and partially hid a yawn behind his hand. "Any attacks yet?"

"Not a one." I put a pine faggot on the fire and watched the tongues of flame curl around the dry wood. "It looks as though we're going to have a peaceful night."

He watched the blaze drowsily. "What are we going to use for weapons?" he asked.

"Bronson told me this afternoon there were loaded shotguns in the library." I went into the library, took two of the guns from the rack and returned to the fire. Dan Harvey was asleep on the davenport. I shook him. "Here." I handed him one of the shotguns. "Now we're ready for anything."

He blinked at the gun and laid it on the couch. "Say, Professor," he demanded, "is it straight stuff that you were once world's hearts champion?"

I confessed that it was not. "I cheated," I admitted.

"I thought there was something phony about the game," he said thoughtfully. "Still, I don't see how you managed to do it all by yourself."

"I didn't. Miss Leslie acted as my accomplice."

"Holy cow! I'd never have suspected that. I thought she had it in for you."

"What made you think that?"

"Well, she called you a coward last night, and this morning after you ducked Burton she said you were a bully. I don't think that's being exactly crazy about someone."

I felt there was considerable reason in what he said. "I was surprised myself when she came to my aid. I think she was aware of certain irregularities in your sister's and your play."

"Irregularities!" He laughed scornfully. "We were cheating as much as we could, but it didn't seem to do any good at all."

I smiled back at him. "The point is that evil-doing prospers when it comes from an unlikely source. You never thought to suspect me and Miss Leslie of cheating."

For an instant Dan Harvey's drowsy blue eyes widened. "Say! Maybe that's an idea for the will. Maybe someone beside the old people got away with it. Maybe someone we don't think would have the least idea of swiping it."

"What reason would anyone have for taking the new will, outside of the Coffins or your parents?" I asked. "What good would it do them?"

"Why, don't you see?" He brandished the shotgun in the air. "They, or he, could sell the will. They could sell it to somebody who would destroy it or to one of us." He was getting his subjects slightly mixed, but his meaning was clear. "He could get people bidding against each other for it and sell it to the highest bidder."

His theory, I saw, made the possible suspects in the theft of the will practically unlimited. Even the deputy, Jeff, might have taken it. Or Mrs Spotswood or Mr Bundy.

"You may be right," I conceded. "We'll know as soon as someone approaches one of us with an offer to sell it."

"If he ever does approach us," Dan Harvey said darkly.

"But you don't think your father would buy the will and destroy it to keep you and your sister from the estate, do you?"

"I don't know." He laid down the shotgun. "But I have a darn good suspicion that he would."

"But why?"

"Dad likes to wear the pants in the family, and he couldn't if Sis and I had the dough."

I walked over to the french window opening on to the veranda and pondered his last remark. I wondered if his father really would go that far to keep his children from inheriting the money. Dan Harvey evidently thought so, but I was extremely dubious. Relatives were notoriously harsh in their opinions of one another. Take George Coffin's contemptuous references to his son's athletic prowess, with their implications of a lack of gray matter. I was willing to grant Burton some intelligence. Perhaps not much, but some. In the same way I was unwilling to agree with Dan Harvey's estimation of his father.

I turned to tell him this and discovered that he had again dropped off to sleep. His head was thrown back against the arm of the davenport, and his thin neck vibrated with each breath. His mouth was slightly open. He looked enviably comfortable.

By this time the moon had risen, coating the lake and the dew-damp lawn with silver, and I half opened the glass door. It was really a lovely night. So soft was the wind that I could hear the murmur of ripples on the shore, the susurrus of a cricket near the front steps, the

distant croaking of frogs. There was an odor of lilac in
the cool air, and of rose. It seemed incredible to me that
this enchanting gray and black nocturne could follow
only a day after the rain, the wind, the hysteria, the
terror of the weird night which saw my great-uncle's
head brutally severed from his body.

With something like anger I closed the door and returned to the fire. What right had anyone, even an
insane person, to take another's life? What had poor
Uncle Tobias done to deserve such an unnatural end?
Yet he had, I reflected, apparently been aware that his
life had run its course. His will was evidence of that, and
the insurance. I sat down on the davenport opposite
Dan Harvey and tried to think.

I went over the murder again in my mind. It seemed
to me no normal person would murder a man by chopping off his head. That was the kind of a thing a Jack
the Ripper or a similar fiend would do. And then there
was the difficulty of concealing the head. In the first
place no murderer would want the head, at least not for
any reason that I could possibly conceive, and in the
second place the necessity of disposing of the head
would add immeasurably to the risk.

This left Mr Glunt, the madman, in possession of the
field.

But what would Mr Glunt want with the new will? I
could see how he might treasure the head, since he had
already begun the collection with his wife and children,
but I couldn't believe he was also making a similar
hobby of final testaments. No, there was only one way
out of that. Someone had come upon the corpse after
Mr Glunt had left and before Mrs Spotswood had

screamed, and had taken the will. Naturally this person, to avoid suspicion of theft, had returned to bed without giving the alarm.

This was fine, I thought, but it still didn't tell me who had the will (doubtless it had already been destroyed) or who had struck me an obviously murderous blow on the head in the upstairs library. Nor was there in this line of reasoning any motive for the search or for the blow either. Then as a final complication there was the window in the pantry. Despite Dr Harvey I believed that Mrs Bundy had, as she said, locked it. Who had opened it and why?

For an instant I thought I had the answer to the window. It occurred to me that the person who had stolen the will might have gone out through the window to hide the will outside. But on second thought I decided this surmise was absurd. There was no reason for taking the will out of the house: it could be hidden or destroyed quite easily indoors.

By this time my brain was terribly confused by these unanswered questions, and I determined to give myself a recess in the form of a tour of the house. Everything was utterly quiet, even the fire having died to a bed of rose-colored coals, but I wanted to make certain that none of the doors and windows had been opened since Bronson had made his final inspection. Cautiously picking up the shotgun, I left the fire and walked to the staircase, then halted. Of course there could be nobody in the house, but perhaps it was just as well to take precautions. It would be easy for a prowler to dispose of one person but difficult for him to surprise two. I went back and woke up Dan Harvey.

"I'm going to take a tour of the house," I said after

he rubbed his eyes with his fists. "Want to come along?"

"Sure." He grasped his gun firmly and got to his feet. "Did you hear something?"

"No. I just thought it would be a good idea to see if everything's all right."

His mouth drooped in disappointment. "I'd like to get a shot at that old madman." He pretended he was wiping out a battalion of madmen coming down the stairs. "Pop-pop-pop-pop. That's the way I'd give it to him." I saw he was younger than I had thought.

We went up the stairs and along the hall. A single bulb was burning in the corner where I had sat and inexcusably fallen asleep last night, and our advancing bodies threw grotesque shadows on the wall. Our feet fell noiselessly on the thick carpet.

"Spooky, isn't it?" whispered Dan Harvey.

We had rounded the corner and were starting down the hall toward the back stairs when I laid a hand on his arm. "What's that?"

We halted abruptly, and he said, "I don't hear anything."

"Wait."

It was a breathing noise, but unlike any I had ever heard before. It was sort of an agonized gasping, as though the throat had become clogged in a particularly painful manner. It was the hoarse breathing of someone fighting for air and for life. It made my lungs throb in sympathetic pain to hear each gasp. It was horrible.

"Gosh!" Dan Harvey's face was yellow pale. "It's in Burton's room."

I tried the door and found that it was locked. It resisted my efforts to shake the catch free.

"Here," said Dan Harvey, holding out his shotgun.

"Let me shoot the lock out like they do in the gangster movies."

"No. You'll scare everybody in the house to death. Let's hit it with our shoulders together. That ought to get it."

We hit the door together, and it flew open with a bang. I groped along the wall and finally found the light switch. When my eyes adjusted themselves to the glare I saw Burton Coffin stretched out on his bed, his hands and feet bound with brown cord, his mouth covered with a gag of blue cloth, a thick smear of blood on the side of his head. There was blood all over his pillow. His eyes were agonized.

With fingers that seemed all thumbs I unfastened the gag, which I found to have been improvised from a blue shirt. At the same time I told Dan Harvey to bring me a wet towel from the bathroom. Then I undid the cord, and when Dan returned with the towel I washed the blood from Burton's head. I found he had a nasty cut over the left temple. He was still breathing heavily.

"Don't talk until you feel all right," I warned him.

He nodded and lay back on the pillow. I could see that he was not badly hurt, but at the same time he had suffered a violent nervous shock.

The commotion we had caused in breaking down the door had evidently wakened nearly everyone else in the house. George Coffin and his wife arrived first, and on their heels were Dr and Mrs Harvey. Mrs Coffin uttered a cry at the sight of her son's towel-wrapped head and threw herself down beside the bed.

"What have they done to you, Burton?" she wailed.

"I'm all right, Mother," he said. "I'm all right." He sat up in the bed and blinked at us.

"I think you'd better look at his head, Dr Harvey," I said. "He has some sort of a cut." To reassure Mrs Coffin I added, "It's not deep."

I saw Miss Leslie and Miss Harvey arrive at the door as the doctor bent over the wound. "It's just a nasty scratch," he said. "A little iodine 'll fix it."

George Coffin was still by the door. "How did it happen?" he asked me.

"I don't know. Dan and I were taking an inspection trip over the house, and we heard a strange noise in here. We broke in and found Burton bound and gagged and with this cut on his temple."

Burton regarded me with interest. "The door was locked?"

"I'll say it was," said Dan Harvey. "We had to bust it down."

"That's funny." Burton spoke solemnly. "When I went to bed the door was unlocked."

George Coffin blew out his lips in irritation. "But what happened?" he demanded of his son.

"I don't know any more than Dan and the professor." Burton accepted another damp towel from Dr Harvey and placed it over his forehead. "I went to sleep, and when I woke up I was all tied and gagged." There was a kind of horror in his eyes. "I darn near died with that gag. I have a cold, and I can't breathe through my nose very well. And I couldn't breathe through the gag at all. I thought I was going to suffocate."

"How terrible!" exclaimed Mrs Coffin.

"Well, whoever it was," observed George Coffin, "was interested in your private possessions."

I had noticed a certain disorder about the room, but

it had not made an impression on my mind. Now as I looked I could see that it had been thoroughly ransacked. The bureau draws had been opened, and their contents—shirts, pajamas, underwear, handkerchiefs and socks—had been dumped on the carpet. A suitcase, opened, lay on its side in one corner of the room, and by it was an empty golf bag, its clubs lying in a fan-shaped figure at the foot of the silver radiator. Immediately a thought flashed into my mind. I glanced at George Coffin and saw reflected in his eyes a similar spark of interest.

We were both thinking of Mrs Spotswood.

Dr Harvey spoke in a loud voice. "I'm going to get some bandages, and I think it would be a good idea if everybody but Grace cleared out. The boy has had a bad shock."

As everyone moved toward the door Burton said to me: "Thanks, Prof. If you and Dan hadn't come I might have kicked off."

"Oh, not that," I said. "But it must have been devilish uncomfortable."

Out in the corridor George Coffin pulled me aside. "We have to check on Mrs Spotswood," he declared.

I nodded.

"We'd better get Miss Leslie to do it, so's not to alarm her," he continued. "Don't you think that's the best way?"

I said I did, and my cousin signaled Miss Leslie to come over to us. She was pale, but her skin had a luminous quality about it that made me think of the advertisements for cold creams in the smooth-paper magazines. I had a difficult time keeping my eyes from her skin and the soft curve of her jaw.

"Burton's all right," George Coffin assured her, irrelevantly as far as I was concerned, "and how about doing something for us?"

"I'm glad he's not terribly hurt," she said. "It must have been a ghastly experience." Her eyes, with the gray iris so dark that they were almost violet, were wide. "What do you want me to do?"

"Just see if Mrs Spotswood is all right. She and Mrs Bundy seem to be the only ones not aroused by the noise. We would talk to her, only we're afraid it might alarm her."

"Of course I'll see." She moved swiftly down the hall, having never once looked at me during the conversation.

We watched from the stairs while Miss Leslie held a brief conversation with Mrs Bundy, whose head, festooned with curlpapers, timidly appeared from the door to Mrs Spotswood's room on the floor above. In another group, at the opposite end of the second-floor hall, stood talking Miss Harvey, her mother and her brother, who was evidently describing his part in the freeing of Burton Coffin. I could hear him saying: "So I said to the professor, 'If it's the madman let me have the first shot. I can bring him down if anybody can.'"

"Aw," replied Miss Harvey, "I'll bet you were hiding under the hall rug."

Miss Leslie returned. "Mrs Bundy says Mrs Spotswood is asleep. She says the noise woke her up, but she was afraid to leave Mrs Spotswood alone in the room while she investigated."

"Did she wake Mrs Spotswood?" asked George Coffin.

"No. Mrs Spotswood is still asleep."

George Coffin looked at me, then thrust out his lower lip. "Well, that seems to be that."

Miss Leslie's eyes were upon Dr Harvey, coming out of Burton's room with his medicine case. "What is the meaning of all this, Mr Coffin?" she asked in a low tone. "Why would anyone attack your son?"

"I'm completely in the dark, Joan." Cousin George was also watching Dr Harvey. "I can't imagine what's behind all these mysterious events, but I'm inclined to doubt that it's the work of Mr Glunt."

"So am I," I said. "I think someone in this household is responsible."

Miss Leslie turned her eyes upon me for the first time. "Who?" she asked.

I was about to reply that I didn't know when Dan Harvey, who had just gone into his room, appeared at the door. "Hey!" he shouted. "Look what's happened here." He was trembling with excitement.

We hurried to his room and crowded in the doorway. The disorder of the interior surpassed even that of Burton Coffin's room. The prowler had evidently done a thorough job of going through Dan's personal belongings. The floor was littered with clothes.

"My soul!" exclaimed George Coffin. "What in the world is he looking for?"

Miss Leslie was standing out in the hall, and I squeezed past Mrs Harvey and her daughter to reach her side. "Was your room in order when you left it?" I asked.

"Yes," she replied with surprise. "Why?"

"I wondered if he was going through everyone's room."

"But I was in my room."

"So was Burton Coffin."

She smiled a little at me. "I'm not afraid. I've nothing hidden away in my room anyway."

"Nothing except yourself."

"That's not of much value to anyone," she said.

"I don't know. I think you might be very precious to someone."

George Coffin and Dr Harvey came out of Dan's room. Dr Harvey was saying: "I'm going downstairs and get me a shotgun. I'm not going to sit around without any weapon and wait for somebody to bust into my room."

Miss Leslie's laughter was low. "Precious to whom?" She had just a trace of dimples.

"To me, for one," I said.

George Coffin called to the doctor. "Bring me up a gun, too, will you, Doc?" He came over to us.

I may be flattering myself, but I am sure there was a touch of color in Miss Leslie's cheeks. "Is this a declaration, Professor?" she asked.

"Not exactly," I said with a lack of gallantry which would have shamed the Earl of Rochester. "I was thinking of the insurance."

"The insurance?" There was genuine wonder in her voice.

George Coffin said, "Is this a private conversation, or can anybody join in?"

"Anybody," I said. "I was simply speaking of Uncle Tobias' life insurance."

"His life insurance?" repeated George Coffin in almost the same intonation as Miss Leslie.

"Don't either of you know about the life insurance?" I demanded. "The hundred thousand dollars worth?"

"Whew!" George Coffin blinked in amazement. "No." Miss Leslie shook her head.

"Well, he did leave that much insurance in addition to the estate," I said. "That's why I was telling Miss Leslie she might regard herself as precious."

"But why?" asked Miss Leslie.

"Because half of that insurance goes to you."

Surprise and consternation showed on her expressive oval face. "To me? But why did he leave it to me? I'm not even in the family." There was complete dismay in her tone.

George Coffin was blinking at me. "But I don't see how that makes her precious."

"You will," I said. "The other half goes to me." I paused to give them time to digest this. "And if either Miss Leslie or I die the other has complete control of the hundred thousand." I found I was peering into Miss Leslie's gray eyes, and while this did not appear to embarrass her, I turned my head. "In other words she could be worth fifty thousand dollars to me."

"You mean, if you killed her?" asked my cousin.

"Yes."

"Oh!" Miss Leslie appeared shocked, but not frightened. "Please don't talk like that."

"I simply wanted you to know about it," I said. "I only found out tonight."

George Coffin's eyes were amused. "You know, Peter, that you're also worth fifty thousand dollars dead, to Miss Leslie?"

It was my turn to be shocked. "Why that's utterly ridiculous." I scowled at him. "You might just as well come out and accuse Miss Leslie of murder."

Surprisingly Miss Leslie found this funny. "You just

warned me about yourself," she said. "I might as well
warn you, now that I know about the insurance."

"Say, this is nutty," complained George Coffin.
"You two each warning the other to beware. I suppose
you're going back to your rooms now and write notes,
saying: 'If my body is found under strange circumstances please question Miss Leslie (or Peter Coffin).'"

I was forced to laugh. "It's nothing like that. I was
trying to tell Miss Leslie about the insurance, and I
guess I did it in my customary clumsy manner." I saw
she was smiling too. "I don't believe she's terrified of
me."

"I'm not," she smiled. "Are you of me?"

"No."

Mrs Coffin came out of Burton's room and paused a
moment beside us. "Burton's asleep," she said. "Are you
coming back to bed, George?"

"In just a second." He waited until she had gone into
their room, then asked, "How in the world did you find
out about the insurance, Peter?"

I didn't know whether it was advisable to mention my
conversation with the insurance company's detective, so
I pretended it was a mystery. "Oh, I have ways of finding out things," I said nonchalantly.

Chapter XI

I TOOK my customary late morning swim alone. I felt a bit shaken by the mental and nervous strain I had been under when I woke up at quarter past twelve, but the tingling, ice-cold water made me feel quite fit again. I splashed about vigorously, swam out to the raft and back, tried out a few dives and returned to my room. I felt very hungry.

Bronson was waiting for me when I reached the dining room, his thin face solemn. After we had exchanged greetings I asked him where everyone was.

"They've all had breakfast, or rather lunch," he said. "The elder Coffins and Dr Harvey have taken one of the cars to Traverse City. Mrs Harvey is still indisposed, and the young people have gone for a walk."

"I'm sorry to be so late, Bronson," I said, "but no one called me."

"That's quite all right, sir. What would you like to eat?"

I started out breakfast-fashion with orange juice and a heaping dish of fresh blueberries and rich cream and then completed my meal with a cup of coffee, German fried potatoes and four crisply broiled brook trout.

"Mr Bundy caught them this morning," Bronson explained. "He's a rare hand with a fly rod."

"They're delicious," I declared, squeezing a lemon over the last gold-and-white rectangle of flesh. "I haven't had any fish like these since I used to catch them in the meadow creek with worms and a bamboo pole."

The harsh lines in Bronson's face softened. "We never thought in those days that anything so terrible as this would befall the house, did we, Mister Peter?"

"We certainly never did." I laid my napkin on the table and, encouraged by the softening in Bronson's manner, asked: "Have you found out any more about the person you suspect?"

He glanced quickly around the room, then shook his head.

"Are you going to continue to withhold the information from the police?"

"I don't know, Mister Peter. I should hate to cause trouble and perhaps disgrace for an innocent person." His eyes were as black as jet, and they peered straight into mine. "What would you advise?"

"I have an idea, Bronson," I said. "A private detective is to arrive here today to investigate Mister Tobias' death and the loss of the will. I suggest you tell your story to him. He is quite reliable, and I am sure he will hold anything you tell him confidential until it is necessary to act upon the information."

Bronson's eyes, to my relief, left my face, and he nodded slowly. "I think I shall avail myself of your advice." He pretended to be clearing the dishes from the table, "Did you send for the detective?"

"No. He's coming about the life insurance."

"Oh yes."

"Then you know about the insurance?"

"Only by the reference to it in the will, Mister Peter. It said you and Miss Leslie were to use the money (it didn't say how much it was) to provide scholarships for an equal number of boys and girls in American universities of which you approved."

This put quite a different light on the business. It may seem strange, but I felt a sudden relief. The thought of having fifty or one hundred thousand dollars to spend on myself had actually terrified me, and I was pleased to learn that the direction in which the money was to be spent had been pointed out by Uncle Tobias. I much preferred to live in my obscure but perfectly comfortable way on my own income.

"Why didn't you tell the sheriff about the insurance yesterday?" I inquired.

"To tell you the truth, Mister Peter, it completely slipped my mind. I only just thought of it when you spoke of the detective."

"I don't think there was any harm done."

I stood up, and Bronson started for the kitchen with the empty platter. "What do you make of the prowler who tied up Burton Coffin?" I called after him.

Bronson swung around toward me, his face harsh again. "If you want my opinion, Mister Peter," he said dramatically, "I'll tell you I believe the young gentleman tied himself up."

"Oh, come now, Bronson. How could that be possible?"

He refused to say more than, "He could do it, all right." When I tried to question him, he retreated into the pantry, and I was forced to go out onto the veranda. I took a seat in one of the comfortable chairs made of pine, with seats and backs of bark, and speculated on how soon Colonel Black would arrive. I hoped he would come before nightfall as I had begun (with reason) to dread being in the big house with only such amateur guards as we could provide. Moreover, I was eager to see what he would make of the odd and perplexing incidents which had enlivened my stay in the house. If he could make sense of them, I thought, I would be prepared to believe that he was indeed a great detective as well as an authority on the Elizabethan period. I felt that he would have encountered nothing more confusing, and hardly anything bloodier, in the plays of Will Shakespeare or Christopher Marlowe.

My reflections were broken by the appearance of Miss Leslie on the veranda. She appeared very trim in a brown tweed skirt, a soft green leather jacket, brown sport shoes shaped somewhat like moccasins and an orange-colored silk scarf tied about her neck. She was hatless, and her dark hair was charmingly wind-blown.

"Did I disturb you?" she asked.

"Not at all," I said, springing to my feet. "I was simply looking at the lake."

She seemed slightly embarrassed. "I was out walking with Burton and the Harveys when it began to sprinkle," she said. "They were determined to climb the sand dune as far as the watchtower, but I thought I'd better turn back before the rain came."

"I think you were wise." I saw that the clouds were ominously black at the north end of the lake and that a fresh wind was throwing up whitecaps. "I give it about ten more minutes before it pours."

She smiled. "I'm not hoping that the others will get drenched, but . . ."

I completed the sentence for her. "It will serve them right for not agreeing with your forecast?"

"At least they needn't have been so positive that it couldn't rain."

"Your triumph," I said, "will be even more positive when they return dripping wet and find you sitting comfortably before a nice fire."

Her teeth were small and even, and I could just discern her dimples. She said, "I wanted to thank you for sitting in front of our rooms in the hall for the remainder of last night."

"Karl and I didn't mind, as long as Burton was disabled." I could see no reaction to my thrust, so I continued, "And besides, I thought that if something happened to you I'd be the one they'd blame for it."

"You thought," she repeated musingly. "You mean you don't think so now?"

I told her how the conception of the insurance had been altered by Bronson and added, "I don't see how either of us would benefit by the other's demise now. It would merely mean a different trustee."

She frowned, then smiled. "I think I've been what is known as a plaything of fortune for the last two days," she said. "That's twice I've been a rich woman for a few hours."

"Twice?"

"Yes. The insurance and the will."

"Then you did know something about the new will?"

"Only that there was such a will and that I had, in the words of your great-uncle, a substantial interest in it."

I looked at her smiling face with admiration. "You seem to have borne the loss with fortitude," I said.

"So have you," she replied. "You know you've sustained the same losses as I."

"To speak the utter truth, Miss Leslie, I'm quite well pleased. I don't want the responsibility of being wealthy. The only loss I regret is that of this house. I played here every summer as a boy, and I love it better than any place in the world."

"It is lovely," she agreed.

At that moment a squall of considerable force swept across the yard from the lake, bringing with it a few large drops of water and rush of green and yellow leaves.

"We'd better go inside," I suggested. "The storm is about to break."

"Oh, the wind is cold!" she exclaimed. "I think we could use that fire you spoke about."

"Come on, then. Let's build it."

Birch bark, kindling and larger logs were in the basket beside the fireplace, and in a few moments I had a bright fire started. The wind was blowing steadily now, rattling the windowpanes on the lake side of the house. Waves of cold air poured into the house. I was closing some of the french doors on to the veranda when Bronson arrived to help me.

"I'm afraid we're in for an all-night storm," he said. "It usually lasts twelve hours or more when it comes down from Canada."

"Oh, Bronson," exclaimed Miss Leslie in dismay, "another night like the one before last?"

"I'm afraid so, miss."

Bronson and I finished closing the doors and windows, and he went upstairs to inspect the windows in the rooms along the front of the house. I returned to the fire, by now a crackling blaze of dry wood, and sat down opposite Miss Leslie.

"By the way," I said, "nobody has been searching through your room, has he?"

"No. You asked me that last night. Why?"

"Somebody has gone through Burton's, Dan's and mine, and I was trying to imagine what the motive for the searching was. I thought possibly somebody was looking through all the younger people's rooms."

"They—or he—went through your room too?"

"Yes, last night. I found my room in complete disorder when I went to bed this morning."

"I'm surprised you didn't raise a fuss."

"I didn't think it worth while. I simply picked up my clothes (I didn't bring many) and went to bed."

"Why did you think someone was searching the rooms of all the younger people? What would we have to conceal?"

"It's a pretty wild surmise, Miss Leslie, and I don't know if I should tell you."

"I wish you'd call me Joan. 'Miss Leslie' sounds so formal," she said, smiling. "And I promise not to tell. Not even Burton."

"I wasn't thinking of that," I said quickly. "I was thinking that you'd probably laugh at me." I felt myself blushing. "I don't look very much like the popular conception of a detective."

"I think you look very nice, especially since you've taken off your horn-rimmed glasses."

"Do you really think so?" I was becoming quite red.

"It makes you look five years younger."

"Why, thank you, Miss Les—Joan."

"But what was your reason for thinking the person

would go through the possessions of all the younger people?"

"You understand I am including myself in the category of younger people of course?"

"Of course, especially with your glasses off."

"Thank you. You flatter me."

"Not at all."

"The reason is this: I thought possibly someone was trying to make sure the new will was destroyed. He might have been afraid that one of us, who benefit most in the new will, had taken it into safekeeping until the proper time."

Thinking put small wrinkles in the space between her arched eyebrows. "But I don't see why anybody would think that," she objected. "There's been nothing to make anyone think we could possibly have it."

"One thing could have happened."

"What?"

"The person looked for the will beside Uncle Tobias' body and found that it was gone." I looked at her intently to make sure she would catch the import of my next words. "That person had intended to steal the will and destroy it but believed that somebody who did not want the will destroyed had frustrated him."

Her face was alarmed. "But do you believe that's what really happened?" Her gray eyes were wide. "Do you think one of us has the new will?"

"I don't know," I said. "I'm trying to imagine what the person who's doing the searching might think. I don't know what I think. I'm completely confused."

"You don't believe it's possible that the madman is still prowling around? That's what Burton says."

"What do you think?"

"I don't think he could be."

"I don't either. We'd catch sight of him if he was, or he'd . . ."

Joan shuddered. "That's the only thing I'm afraid of. If he came for me I'd be too scared even to scream."

Above the noise of the wind I heard the whine of the electric motor which ran the elevator. I wondered who was using it.

"That madman's many miles away from us by this time," I assured Miss Leslie. "He would have been caught long ago if he'd stayed in this neighborhood."

The elevator door opened, and Mrs Spotswood glided out in her wheel chair. Her sunken eyes, the deep pupils glowing with inner fire, fastened upon us. She propelled the chair in our direction.

"How nice the fire looks," she said. Her voice was low, but she spoke with an intensity which gave her words a funereal quality.

"Yes, doesn't it," Joan replied.

But for the strange light in her eyes, Mrs Spotswood might have been a wax-museum image created to wear the black silk dress, the long skirt of which shrouded her feet, the violet silk shawl, the white hair, done up in a large bun on the back of her head, the lace cuffs of the Victorian maiden old lady. Even when she spoke no expression troubled the pale and wrinkled mask of her face.

"Where are the others?" she inquired. "Taking naps?"

"I'm afraid everyone will be caught in the storm," I said. "They're still out."

Her voice was difficult to catch above the roar of the wind. "Good. Good," she said, barely moving her purple lips. "They're safe out in the open air, out in the woods."

"For myself," I said, "I should prefer to be right here in front of an open fire."

"You would?" No louder, her voice had suddenly become harsh with scorn. "Don't you know that there's danger in this house, death in this house?" Her hands moved convulsively on her lap. They were pale and wrinkled, like roots just pulled from the earth. "It's all over . . . everywhere . . . the feel of death." She leaned forward in her chair, trembling, and her deep-set eyes blazed. "You'll leave if you want to save yourselves. Leave this house. Leave death behind." Her face became tragic. "It's only us who can't run from death that will have to face it. You're both young; you can run fast. Faster than death. Strong young legs can run faster than death." A rumble of thunder checked her voice; she cocked her head, listened to the sound diminish. Her face was expressionless again. Her voice came to us, low and no longer harsh. "I'm afraid we are in for a bad storm." She turned her chair about and passed swiftly into the dining room and out of our sight.

I turned my startled eyes upon Miss Leslie, partly to see what effect Mrs Spotswood's speech had had upon her, partly to make sure I had been actually hearing this odd warning. Miss Leslie's face reassured me. She was properly alarmed.

"How strange!" she exclaimed. "What does she mean?"

I shook my head. "I don't know." I tried to smile at her, but I felt my effort was a failure. "But don't be frightened. Probably Mrs Spotswood is upset and has been imagining things. The events of the last two nights are enough to upset almost anybody."

"Well, I *am* frightened." Her gray eyes were dark

against the pallor of her face. "I feel as though something hung over this house too." She gave me a wan smile. "It's ridiculous, but I have a definite foreboding of evil."

"It's the tension in the air. We've all been under a strain, and we are all suspecting one another of having had a part in searching the house, of breaking into rooms and going through private possessions. Naturally there's an unpleasant atmosphere."

She drew a long breath. "Perhaps you're right, although my feeling is harder to analyze than that. Don't you have a feeling of apprehension?"

"I don't think so," I said. "Each time something happens I'm surprised."

"Then you aren't frightened?"

"Perhaps I am," I admitted. "At least I'll be glad when Colonel Black, the detective for the insurance company, arrives." I delved again into my sensations and was forced to continue, "I guess I am frightened, at that. I hate to think of another night without proper guards in this house."

"Why is the detective coming?" she asked. "I don't see why the insurance company would want to investigate your great-uncle's death."

I explained how Colonel Black had telephoned me, and I told her what Bronson had hinted at to me. "As soon as Colonel Black arrives," I continued, "Bronson is going to tell him all he knows."

"Somebody in the house killed Mr Coffin?" She was evidently appalled by the idea. "Why, that's incredible! Bronson has been seeing things. It's beyond the realm of possibility."

"That's about what I thought, but I felt obliged to mention it to Colonel Black."

"Why the coincidence itself is beyond anything, even in fiction." She was evidently trying to dismiss completely the possibility that Bronson could be right. "A madman with a fixation for people's heads is loose in the neighborhood. We actually see him at this house. Then your great-uncle's head is cut off. It stands to reason the madman did it."

"That's exactly what I thought," I said, "but perhaps Bronson has seen more than we think. He certainly is mysterious enough about it, whatever it is."

"We'll know, anyway, after the detective arrives," she said, a trifle more composed. "I'm not going to worry about it."

I started to say that it was a difficult matter to keep from thinking about the murder, especially when additional mysteries cropped up from time to time, but my observation was checked by the arrival of Dr Harvey, George Coffin and Mrs Coffin. All three of them looked cheerful, and their faces glowed from the wind.

"What we need is hot tea and some muffins," announced George Coffin with a sly glance at Miss Leslie and me. "And what's more we'll have 'em if the professor hasn't eaten them up."

"We've been waiting for you," I said. "It was an effort to deny ourselves, but we did."

After Bronson had been informed of the immediate need of tea for five persons they went upstairs to change their clothes. I looked at my wrist watch and was surprised to discover that it was five o'clock. The afternoon was nearly gone, and there was no sign of Colonel Black.

I hoped he hadn't been delayed, and I said as much to Miss Leslie.

"You are scared," she said triumphantly.

I was trying to explain, without much success, that it wasn't so much for myself as for the others that I was frightened when Bronson brought in the tea wagon. Mrs Bundy had evidently been prepared for such an emergency, and the tray was heaped with hot muffins, biscuits, small cakes and various conserves. They looked delicious.

Bronson pushed the wagon toward Miss Leslie. "Would you care to serve, miss?" he inquired.

Joan was pouring me a cup of tea when the others came back downstairs. George Coffin sniffed the air, said, "Ah! Can it be English muffins and honey that I smell?" His face was pink with health, and his demeanor was gay.

"I don't see any English muffins, George," said Mrs Coffin severely. "You have the imagination of a child."

Dr Harvey's small foxlike face contracted into a grin. "He may have the imagination of a child," he said, "but he also has the nose of a bloodhound. Look." He pointed to the dining room.

Bronson was emerging with a tray completely hidden by great round English muffins. They gave off a delightful odor of toasted dough, reminding me of the small teashop in Oxford Circus that I used to patronize on my way home from the British Museum.

"Aha!" George Coffin gave a delighted leap in the direction of Bronson and seized one of the muffins and a plate. He presented them to his wife with a courtly gesture. "Here, my dear, eat this. Surely a figment of my imagination will not be fattening."

Mrs Coffin snorted.

We were all eating contentedly and listening to an account of the purchases made on the trip to Traverse City (Mrs Coffin was particularly proud of a patchwork quilt she had bought from a farmer's wife, though I was unable to see how the gaudy object would fit in anything except a stable) when the younger Harveys and Burton came in through the back way. Extra tea was brewed for them while they went upstairs and changed their clothes. Upon their return and between enormous bites of muffins and other delicacies they recounted their adventures. They had reached the forest ranger's cabin on the dune and from this vantage point had watched the progress of the lightning and the storm. They were pleased at having beaten the rain to the house, but Dan Harvey predicted that it would soon arrive.

"The clouds were as black as coal to the north," he said.

After Mrs Coffin had chided a somewhat irritated Burton for having taken such a chance with the rain the conversation, as it always had, turned to the mystery. Dr Harvey wanted to know if there were any new developments.

"Nothing since our rooms were searched," I replied.

"Our rooms?" queried Dr Harvey.

"Mine was searched too," I said, repeating the story I had told Miss Leslie.

There followed much general speculation as to the reason for the assault on Burton and the search through the room. Miss Leslie and Burton were talking with considerable animation, so I ate the last of my muffin, smearing it liberally with honey, and moved over by George Coffin.

He spoke in a low voice. "That about lets Mrs Spotswood out."

I nodded. "Unless she hadn't had time to make a thorough search of my room before I came upon her."

"It's very queer." He frowned good-naturedly. "I think I'll have to take up searching. Maybe I'll stumble upon whatever it is the mysterious prowler is looking for."

At this moment Bronson, taking out some of the tea things, glanced interrogatively at George Coffin, who nodded in reply. He stood up, saying, "Excuse me a minute. Bronson has something he wants to speak to me about."

I listened to an argument between Dan Harvey and his sister as to whether or not lightning would strike swimmers, his sister trying to persuade him to come for a plunge in the rain, when Karl Norberg entered the house through the side door. He came directly to me, his yellow slicker clinging to his legs. There were drops of water on it.

"There's a man outside who's asking for you, Mr Coffin," he announced. "Says his name is Black."

Joan, halting in the midst of a sentence spoken to Burton Coffin, turned her face toward me. There was relief in her eyes. The others were also listening.

"Colonel Black!" I said, making my voice sound surprised. "I never thought he'd make it. Where is he?"

I leaped to my feet and followed Karl to the side door. As we passed the library I noticed Bronson and George Coffin in a corner. Their faces were close together, but I could see that Bronson was talking and George Coffin was listening intently.

Karl held the door for me, and I walked out into the gray afternoon. It had just started to rain.

Chapter XII

IN A NILE–GREEN Chinese robe, decorated with white silk dragons, Colonel Black reclined comfortably on his bed and listened with pleased interest to my story. He had had a hot bath and two large whiskies and soda, and his pink face contrasted with the marvelous blue of his eyes. His expression—tinged with arrogance by the aquiline nose, the high cheekbones, the long jaw line; tinged with benevolence by the kindly wrinkles at the corners of the eyes, the healthy plumpness of his jowls, the humor of his lips—was that of a man hearing an entertaining legend.

At the various high spots of my narrative he somewhat disconcertingly would cry, "Excellent! Oh, by the very gods, excellent!" and his face would beam. When I came to the account of the attack on Burton Coffin he beat his hand upon his thigh and shouted, "Oh, good!"

This surprising sentiment caused me to pause for a moment. "But why good?" I demanded. "You don't even know the young man."

"No. You don't understand." His long, perfectly manicured hands disclaimed with an outward gesture any personal feeling. "It's merely the shape of the story. It's quite Elizabethan. Really."

I finished my account and added that I had not revealed the fact that he was a detective to my relatives.

"By the shades of Shakespeare," he exclaimed excitedly, "this is fine." His voice, ordinarily a trifle high and querulous, deepened. "It reminds me, in a way, of that great scene in *Cymbeline* when Imogen awakes with the cloaked body of Cloten lying beside her. Do you remember how the author adds effect to effect to reach a crescendo of horror?"

I shook my head. "I remember the scene vaguely," I said, "but I don't . . ."

He held out an arm in an arresting gesture. "She sits up, mildly puzzled and saying sleepily, 'But, soft! no bedfellow,' and then, becoming aware that the figure beside her is heaped with sweet flowers, she dreamily picks one of the blossoms and is shocked wide awake by the discovery ('O gods and goddesses!') that there is blood on it.

"Then after she prays it is only a dream and hides her eyes with her hands and looks again and sees the body is still there she recognizes some of the garments and lifts the cloak to examine the face and then ('Murder in heaven?') sees that the corpse is headless and goes stark, raving mad."

He paused, his eyes looking down his nose at me, and said, "Isn't that dandy?"

"Well, no," I said.

"I thought only the Elizabethans could as neatly combine murder and horror," he continued, "but here we have a combination (perhaps not as well suited to a dramatic presentation) quite as grotesque." He locked his hands behind his head and sighed comfortably. "I'm really quite pleased to be here."

The storm was increasing. Around the lake-front corners of the house the wind screamed as though it was enraged by its failure to break through the trembling panes. It moaned and wailed like a hungry tiger; it roared and shouted. At times, in a climax of fury, it shook the house like a terrier with a boot. The rain fell in sheets.

"Is there anything more I can tell you?" I inquired. "If there isn't I think I'll prepare for dinner."

"Your account has been extremely lucid," he said magnanimously. "Extremely lucid." He peered thoughtfully at the tip of his brown slipper. "Has the butler— I recall his name as Bronson—said anything more to you?"

"No. He has agreed to speak to you, but he has refused to add a word to what he has disclosed."

The colonel nodded his head in appreciation of Bronson's wisdom. He looked rather like a benign hawk. "That's the sort of a thing a detective likes—monopoly on all the information. Then when he puts his thumb on the criminal everyone says, 'A prodigy! Indeed, a prodigy!'"

"If you like," I said, "I'll send Bronson up to you now."

"Won't he be busy with dinner?"

"Yes, but I'm sure he will be glad——"

"Oh no." The colonel's blue eyes were alarmed. "I wouldn't want anything to interfere with dinner. And besides, I desire a long chat with him." He turned fiercely upon me. "You haven't told anyone else about Bronson's information, have you?"

I blushed, thinking of Miss Leslie, and lied. "No, I haven't."

"Good. Do we dress for dinner?"

"There was some mention of it, but if you haven't . . ."

"Oh, I have, I have," he said airily. "Even a detective would not appear in a pair of gabardine shorts, you know."

"That's fine then," I said, preparing to leave. At the door I halted. "Colonel, have you any idea at all about this?" I asked.

"Of course not. Do you think I'm a magician?" His bright blue eyes twinkled. "And that's just what makes it such a deuced interesting case. Everything's so gloriously mixed up."

"But have you any theory as to the identity of the prowler? Whom do you suspect of stealing the new will?"

"You, among others."

"Me? Why, what possible motive would I have in stealing it? I would only be depriving myself of a share of my great-uncle's estate and of this house."

"Yes, but you'd gain a hundred thousand dollars."

I stared at him blankly.

"You are to receive a hundred thousand dollars, provided we pay the double indemnity, when the insurance is paid," he said slowly. "If the will 'd not been destroyed you'd have simply been the administrator of that money as part of a fund, as would Miss Leslie. But now the will is gone the money will be yours." He leaned forward and squinted at me. "Many an otherwise honest man would destroy a will for one hundred thousand dollars."

My face must have been the setting for such emotions as surprise, horror and indignation, for he chuckled.

"Don't be downcast, Peter," he said. "I'm just proceeding along the best Scotland Yard principles. The first emotion of the orthodox detective is suspicion, and who am I to be unorthodox?" He stretched, his upheld arms causing the white silk dragon over his chest to creep toward his neck. "Therefore I suspect everyone. I suspect the third footman (if you have one) and the cook and the house's faithful spaniel . . ."

"Collie," I said.

". . . And the groceryman (Oh, most of all the groceryman!) and that pretty young lady . . ."

"Miss Leslie."

He smiled. "I was thinking of Miss Harvey."

"A definite touch, Colonel," I said.

"I watch all of you through narrowed eyes," he continued, "and weigh everything you say. I try to catch you in a lie, because one of the primary principles of detection is that no one ever lies but the criminal." He looked down his long nose at me. "I suspect every action; I am uneasy when any of you are out of my sight; I endeavor to convey the idea that it is only a few hours, yea, a few minutes, before I slip the handcuffs on the guilty party whose identity has been perfectly apparent from the first."

He swung his long legs over the side of the bed.

"You say of certain men that they are filled with the milk of human kindness," he concluded dramatically, "but I am overflowing with the sour white wine of human suspicion."

He blinked at me like a very wise parrot.

I laughed and closed his door and went to my room. I glanced at my watch and saw that it was nearly half past six. I had only fifteen minutes until dinner. While I was disrobing I noticed that the vase which I had taken as a weapon from the mantel in Uncle Tobias' upstairs library was back on the bureau. I felt a blush of mortification at the thought of the ineptitude and near cowardice the vase called up in my mind, and I wondered if Burton Coffin had seen it. I knew it would bring a jibe from him. But I calmed myself by the thought that no one could have seen it except Bronson, who had evidently found it behind the curtain while closing my windows at the inception of the storm. I made up my mind to return it to its proper place as soon as the opportunity offered.

A gale of wind made the house shudder, and I glanced out one of my windows. Between the branches of the frantic trees I could see the lake, its surface covered by gray and white waves. I thought it would be fun to swim in that tumbling, angry water, but I suppressed my impulse. I had only time enough to dress, as it was.

Feeling very clean after a bath and a shave and rather proud of my English dinner clothes, I stopped at Colonel Black's room on my way downstairs. There was no response to my knock, and I was about to go on when I noticed that a light was burning in the study.

To my surprise, when I peered through the door I discovered the colonel seated on the floor, his legs crossed under him, his expression one of peaceful contemplation. He was facing my great-uncle's table, and as I entered he bent forward until his chin was only a few inches from the carpet. He did not appear embarrassed when he caught sight of me. He was also dressed in evening clothes.

"Good for the stomach muscles," he stated, calmly continuing to examine the desk from his odd position.

"What in the world are you doing?" I demanded with astonishment.

"I am obtaining what might be termed a worm's-eye view of the room." His face, as he straightened up, was cherry red. "I like to examine rooms from original vantage points. You've no idea what a difference it makes." He rose to his feet. "Now I've an entirely different conception of this room than, for instance, you. You've seen it only from a standing and, possibly, sitting position. I've seen it from these levels, and I've also seen it from the floor and from a somewhat precarious position on that chair." He was frowning at the desk as he spoke. "If the weather was not so inclement I should like to be suspended outside by a rope from the roof so that I could peer in through the windows, and it would also gratify me to bore a hole through the ceiling and examine the room from above." He glanced quickly at me. "Don't be alarmed. I shan't do either of those things unless it seems absolutely necessary."

"But what do you expect to find?" I gasped.

He shrugged his shoulders. "Who knows? Perhaps nothing; perhaps a great deal." His long fingers were feeling the underside of the desk. "Already I have discovered a wad of gum, but its rocklike rigidity convinces me that it has been there for a period of years. I think we may dismiss it from our compilation of relevant data."

He moved around to the back of the table and dropped face down on the floor, almost completely out of my sight. After a second I heard him exclaim, "Ah!" His face was beaming when he appeared above the desk.

"A triumph for the humble worm," he announced.

I suppose my expression showed a grave suspicion of his sanity, because he chuckled and pointed to where I had first seen him bending down over the carpet.

"Get down there, Peter, and examine this very fine Chinese rug in the direction of the desk," he commanded.

I put my eye close to the floor and looked along the carpet. I noticed that the carpet was, from this angle, a soft gray-green in every place except for a small patch about the size of a book in back of the desk. This patch was blue-green.

"Now go over and smell the spot," he said after I had told him of my discovery.

I did, and immediately my nostrils were filled with a sweet, cloying, medicinal odor. "Chloroform!" I exclaimed.

"Exactly."

"But what does that mean?"

He waved a hand airily, as though the meaning of chloroform on the floor was of negligible interest. "I'm sure I don't know. All I can tell you is that it hasn't been there for more than three or four days. The odor is quite strong."

He turned to the desk again. In reply to his questions I showed him how the body had been stretched over the desk, one arm hanging toward the floor and the other, bent, on the surface of the desk. I told him about the papers, some of them stained with blood, on the desk, and how we had searched for the new will.

"What made everyone so sure the will was among those papers?" the colonel asked.

"I suppose they assumed it was, since everyone but me knew the purpose of our meeting was to hear about it."

"But you've no way of being sure it ever was there, have you?"

"Yes. Bronson saw it earlier in the evening."

"Good." The colonel was apparently struck by another thought. "Has a thorough search been made for the will?"

I told him I thought the sheriff's men had been through all my great-uncle's effects.

His eyes were roaming about the room. "Was the door to the hall wide open when you came upon the old lady screaming?"

"Yes. I could see in here perfectly."

"Do you think she opened it?"

"You'd better ask her. I haven't any idea."

He walked over to the door to my great-uncle's bedroom. "You can get out into the hall through this door, can't you?"

"Yes, and that reminds me of something," I said. "The bedroom door to the hall was unlocked."

He walked through the bedroom and examined the door in question. "Ah! A special lock." He turned a penetrating blue eye upon me. "Didn't Mr Coffin ordinarily keep this door locked?"

"I think he did," I said. "I remember he always used to go to his bedroom through his library."

At this moment Bronson appeared. He stood in the door connecting the library with the bedroom and, after coughing to attract our attention, said, "Dinner is ready, Mister Peter. The others are waiting."

"All right, Bronson," I said, starting for the door.

Colonel Black touched my arm. "Just a second." He looked at Bronson with a friendly expression on his usually arrogant face. "Bronson, this door between your late master's bedroom and the hall was usually locked, wasn't it?"

"Yes sir. He always kept it locked."

"And the will, Bronson. You're sure you saw it among the papers on Mr Coffin's desk the night of the tragedy?"

"I'm quite positive, sir. He showed it to me and then read me extracts from it. He wanted my opinion as to whether it was satisfactory. He was somewhat dubious as to the wisdom of leaving the money to the younger members of the family, although he said he preferred to do that than to let the older members make fools of themselves with it."

"And what was your opinion?"

"That it was best to give the younger people a chance."

We were now back in the library, and the colonel could not resist another question. "Bronson, who cleaned off Mr Coffin's desk?"

"Mrs Spotswood, the housekeeper, sir."

"Wasn't she aware she was destroying all possibility of our securing any fingerprints?"

"I don't believe Mrs Spotswood knows what a fingerprint is, sir."

"Well, it's time she did," said the colonel severely.

We went out into the hall, and I said, "Bronson, after dinner I will bring the colonel over to the servants' house. You can tell him your story then."

"Very good, sir."

Everyone was grouped in front of the great fire in the living room as we came down the stairs, and there seemed to be a great deal of conversation. I noticed that the faces of my relatives were more animated than usual, and I speculated whether or not this was the result of the change in weather or of the dry sherry Dr Harvey was pouring from a crystal decanter.

"Will you have a small glass, Colonel Black?" he asked pleasantly, holding out a tray with two drinks on it. "I know Peter will have one."

"I will indeed," said the colonel. "Sherry is an excellent apéritif, though I have an appetite for two now."

I was surprised to see Mrs Harvey talking to Mrs Coffin, and I took the colonel over to be introduced to her. She had not been out of bed all day, and I commented on the fact.

She replied in a low voice, the monotone of which never varied, "I am feeling better tonight, thank you, Peter." She turned her faded blue eyes upon the colonel. "You know, Colonel Black, my nerves have been terribly upset by the events of the last few nights." Her plump body trembled. "But I feel confident you will see that things become normal again."

"I?" For an instant the colonel's alert eyes rested on me. "I fear you are expecting too much of a humble scholar."

Mrs Harvey decided to take this as a joke. She made a coquettish motion of her arm, as though she were tapping the colonel on the shoulder with a fan, and said, "I don't believe you're really that modest."

Bronson announced dinner at this moment, and the colonel gallantly gave Mrs Harvey his arm. I followed them into the dining room, puzzled as to her meaning. Was she merely, in a flirting manner, trying to convey her impression that the colonel was the sort of a man who could cope with a situation involving violence? Or was she aware that the colonel was a detective?

At the candle-lit table I held Miss Leslie's chair for her, beating Burton Coffin to this pleasant task by a fraction of a second. He scowled at me and retired somewhat sulkily to his place. Miss Leslie looked over her shoulder at me and said, "Thank you." She was wearing a black evening gown, cut low over her tan back, with a striped yellow taffeta sash, the color of a canary bird, about her slender waist. It was a charming costume, but its sophistication lowered my spirits. It was evidence of the gulf between Miss Leslie and me, a symbol of the space between the gay haut monde of New York and the dull respectability of a college town.

I wasn't able to brood about this for long though. By the time the consommé was served and Bronson was passing bits of toasted bread Dan Harvey asked a question which caused me to spill half a glass of water on the linen.

"Colonel Black," he demanded, "what steps do you plan to take to recover the will?"

His sister, her pretty pink-and-white face indicating lively interest, added, "Please tell us how a detective goes about finding out thieves."

The colonel's face was momentarily distressed. "What gave you two the idea I was a detective?"

I glanced at Miss Leslie, half in reproach, half in hopeful interrogation. Her widened gray eyes said quite plainly that she hadn't revealed the secret.

"Why, I think we heard it from George Coffin," said Miss Harvey. "But everybody's been discussing what you're going to do."

"Well, it's very humiliating to be discovered so early in the game," said the colonel good-naturedly. "I suppose now none of you will even talk to me."

"Oh, I will," said Miss Harvey. "I think detectives are cute."

When the laughter had died down I leaned toward George Coffin. "How in the world did you hear about the colonel?" I asked. "I thought I was keeping it a secret."

This was the first time I had looked at him closely during the evening, and I was appalled by his appearance. His face was deathly pale, and his eyes had a haunting expression of fright. I remembered how gay he had been at teatime, and I was even more disturbed. He looked terribly ill.

His voice, answering my question, was steady enough, however. "Bronson mentioned it to me," he said. "I had a little talk with him just after tea."

"Did he tell you what it is he's going to tell the colonel after dinner?" I asked.

"He told me that what he was going to tell Colonel Black would be enough to hang someone in this house," replied George Coffin.

For fully thirty seconds an electric silence hung over the table. Even I, who had known of Bronson's supposed secret, was shocked. And the words had a particularly dreadful effect due to the way in which George Coffin said them. He sounded as though he believed them.

Mrs Coffin was the first to speak. "Why, George, how strange!" she said. "What did he mean?"

Her husband, his face even more haggard, shook his head. "He wouldn't tell me, but I gathered that it was in connection with Tobias' death." His hand, holding the silver soup spoon, trembled.

"My goodness, this is terrible," exclaimed Mrs Harvey. The pitch of her voice indicated jangled nerves. "I won't stay in this house another moment." She glanced around the table to see the effect of her threat.

"Nonsense, my dear." Dr Harvey laid a hand on her arm. "You're perfectly safe here, especially with Colonel Black on the scene."

While Mrs Harvey was allowing herself to be comforted I noticed that the colonel's sharp eyes were examining George Coffin, who was trying to finish his soup. I felt sure the haggard appearance of my cousin had not escaped the colonel.

Miss Harvey was evidently still pondering Bronson's statement, because she asked, "Uncle George, has Bronson told anybody who the person is?"

"No," replied George Coffin. "At least he said he hadn't." He lifted his spoon to his mouth and seemed surprised when he discovered there was no soup in it. "He said he was saving the information for the colonel."

"Well, I think that's ridiculous," exclaimed Mrs Coffin. "If he knows something about someone in this house I think he should be made to come in here and tell us what it is."

"I think he will insist on telling it to the colonel," I said. "I think he hopes that what he has seen is susceptible to some other explanation than the one which will hang someone. That's why he doesn't want to tell it to the police."

Mrs Coffin frowned at me. "Then you've known that Bronson had something to tell all the time?"

"Since yesterday anyway."

"Well!" She agitated her large head furiously. "It seems to me you know almost too much about what is going on in this house." Her tone was definitely hostile.

"Mother!" exclaimed Burton Coffin.

"If people are going around accusing people," she said sharply, "I feel it my duty to point out some things myself."

I was silent under this surprising attack, but Burton Coffin took up the cudgel for me. "I don't think the professor has accused anybody," he said, "and I think he's right about Bronson. We have no power to make Bronson tell us something he prefers to tell to Colonel Black."

George Coffin was regarding his son with a strange look in his horror-ridden eyes; a look resembling awe, but I was unable to think why Burton's remark should summon up awe.

"Very well." Mrs Coffin rang the small silver bell in front of her place angrily, and Bronson appeared. His face showed surprise at the length of time the soup course had taken.

The remainder of the dinner went smoothly. The roast of beef was so good that during the main course nobody cared to do more than make the most perfunctory conversation, and when the salad was served Colonel Black turned another question about detection into a discussion of Shakespeare.

"He is one of the most fascinating men who ever lived," he said, "and his life furnishes a field for detection of a far more acute type than that required by the solution of a simple murder." He cut into the crisp half head of lettuce on his plate, using his knife and fork as do the English. "We have in Shakespeare not the problem of how a man died, but the problem of whether he lived at all."

"But Colonel Black," cried Miss Harvey, "there couldn't be any doubt that Shakespeare lived."

"There could and is that any dramatist by that name ever lived," said the colonel, obviously enjoying the effect he was making. "A number of people maintain with the utmost vehemence that Shakespeare never wrote a play in his life."

Through the salad, dessert and into the black coffee in the living room the colonel pursued the Baconian and Spencerian theories of Shakespeare. His talk was interesting, especially when he quoted from court and coroner's records of the time of Elizabeth, but I don't think any of us listened to him with complete attention. I know my mind was busy speculating on what revelation Bronson had in store for the colonel. I hoped that the old butler would be proved to be harboring some ridiculous notion which his unsettled emotions had built into what he considered proof of someone's criminal guilt.

Finally Mrs Harvey interrupted both my train of thought and the colonel's conversation to say apologetically that she was going upstairs to bed. Her plump face looked tired.

Dr Harvey remonstrated with her, pointing out that it was still light outside and far too early for bed, but when she insisted that she would prefer to retire he acquiesced.

"I'll go up with you," he said. "I want to get my *Atlantic Monthly*."

Everyone else began to move away from the fire. The two Harveys and Miss Leslie directed their steps toward the library and the billiard table. George Coffin, looking at me, said he thought he would go down to the cellar for another bottle of my great-uncle's brandy. He still appeared ill.

I said I thought that would be an excellent plan.

Mrs Coffin cast an angry glance at her husband as he started for the pantry. "You be careful, George Coffin," she warned, "and don't try to drink the cellar dry."

I think she and I were both surprised by his reply, for instead of his usual glib witticism, he said, "Yes, my dear," and continued humbly on through the dining room.

Burton Coffin watched him disappear with a puzzled frown on his handsome face. Suddenly he arose from the chair beside his mother. "I think I'll go down with Dad," he announced. "I've never seen the cellar."

He departed, leaving Mrs Coffin, the colonel and me in front of the fire. The colonel bowed to Mrs Coffin and said, "I wonder if you would excuse Peter and me for a moment. I should like to have him show me where the telephone is."

Mrs Coffin nodded. "I shall remain by the fire for a moment or two. The blaze is very pleasant."

I suggested the extension in the upstairs study, rather than the telephone in the big library, and Colonel Black followed me up the stairs.

Once in the room I asked, "I wonder what made Bronson speak of whatever it is that he has seen and reveal that you are a detective?"

"You have me, Peter." The colonel's heavy lids half veiled his eyes. "Unless he's trying to scare a confession out of someone."

This idea hadn't occurred to me before, but I saw at once that such was obviously Bronson's intention. Either his evidence wasn't conclusive, or he didn't want to be responsible for the arrest of a member of the family he had served so long, if he could possibly avoid it.

While I was thinking the colonel had brought out the

French telephone from its place on one of the book-shelves. "Don't go," he said as I started to leave the room. "I don't mind your hearing what I have to say."

He glanced at a card in his pocket and then asked the operator to get him Samuel Watts in Traverse City. I walked over to the window and looked out at the storm. It was almost dark now, and I could barely make out flashes of white on the wind-whipped lake. The moving air still howled around the house, but the rain had, at least for the moment, let up, although the sky was ominous.

The colonel spoke into the telephone. "Hello. Hello. Mr Watts? . . . The Mr Watts who is an agent for the American Insurance Company? . . . Good. This is Colonel Black speaking. I am representing the company in the death of . . . What's that? Oh, you had a wire from the company. . . . Yes, I would like to have you do something for me. Do you happen to know the coroner? . . . Oh, very fine, Mr Watts. If you've in-sured him you must know him quite well. Now this is what I want. Have him make a complete autopsy on the body of Tobias Coffin. I want special attention centered upon the lungs. If the medical examiner for the county isn't an expert toxicologist have the coroner get one immediately. Have him get one tonight if possible. If necessary, have him get McNally in Chicago. He's one of the best in the country. He can be reached at the Northwestern Crime Detection Laboratory. Tell the coroner we'll pay all the expenses, including airplane fare up here for McNally. I'd like to have a preliminary report tomorrow before the inquest, which is set for the afternoon, so you'll have to hurry, Mr Watts. . . . Yes, there is a tremendous rush, Mr Watts. The autopsy should have been performed yesterday, and another day may make it too late. . . . Thank you, Mr Watts. I'm sure you will succeed. I shall look forward to seeing you in Traverse City tomorrow. . . . Good evening, Mr Watts."

The colonel placed the telephone on its shelf. He came over to me at the window. "Now you are going to ask me . . ." he was beginning when, suddenly, he cocked his head on one side, and demanded, "Peter, what the devil is that tinkling noise?"

Above the noise of the wind I heard the sound of a bell. I laughed. "Are you thinking the elf children are out in the storm, Colonel?" I demanded.

"Well, what is it then? It sounds weird enough to make a man wish for bell, book and candle."

"It's only the cows. They return home from the pasture, escorted by Rob Roy, the collie, each evening at sundown. The leader wears a bell so Rob Roy can find them."

The colonel listened to the bell for several seconds. "It's a pleasant sound when you know what it is," he said. "Think of all that rich cream, to be used with cereal and coffee tomorrow morning, coming in from the pasture under its own power."

He would have continued, but I interrupted him. "Why are you so anxious to have an autopsy on my great-uncle's body?" I inquired.

"That's the very question I thought you were going to ask me, Peter," he replied, "and I shan't answer except to say that my decision was influenced by something you and I discovered in this room before dinner."

"The chloroform," I said.

"Perhaps." He smiled at me. "Shall we go back down-stairs?"

There was nobody in the living room. The colonel took advantage of this fact to pour himself a large glass of port, and I peered into the library. Miss Harvey and her brother were having an exciting game of billiards.

"Where's Miss Leslie?" I called.

"She said she was going upstairs," said Dan Harvey, leaning heavily on a cue. "Didn't you see her?" His question was purely perfunctory, however, because his sister made a shot, and he immediately began to cry, "Missed it, missed it, ha, ha, ha," and paid no more attention to me.

From the library I went to the pantry. Mrs Bundy, a damp cloth in her capable hand, was cleaning the ivory-finished sideboard.

"Bronson left for the servants' house about ten minutes ago," she said in response to my question. "He seemed to be in a dreadful hurry to get through, so I said I'd clean the silver for him tonight."

"Are you going to spend the night in your quarters in the servants' house?" I asked her, "or are you going to keep Mrs Spotswood company again?"

"She wants me to stay with her, poor soul," said Mrs Bundy, "and so I shall, even though my man is raising the roof about it."

"I think that's very good of you, Mrs Bundy. It was a terrible experience for the old lady to find Mister Tobias' body."

"Don't I just know it, Mister Peter. I should have died right there had it been I."

When I reached the living room again I found Colonel Black in conversation with Miss Leslie, Burton

Coffin and George Coffin. A bottle of brandy, dust heavy on its sides, stood on the table beside my cousin.

"It's quite a cellar," Burton Coffin was saying. "I never saw so many different kinds of bottles in my life. Every kind of wine in the great bins and brandy bottles . . ." He halted, his imagination evidently unable to find a comparison which would convey the number and variety of brandy bottles to his auditors.

"It's funny we didn't see each other down there," said George Coffin.

Colonel Black was gazing with an interested eye at the bottle on the table. "Pedro Domecq, Spanish brandy," he read from the time-yellowed label. "More than thirty years old." His tongue involuntarily moistened his lips. "I can almost imagine its bouquet."

"No need to do that," said George Coffin, seizing the bottle and inserting a corkscrew in the neck. "We will test it personally."

I spoke to the colonel. "Bronson has gone over to the servants' house. Don't you think you ought to go over to see him?"

The colonel cast a doleful glance upon the bottle between George Coffin's knees, then looked at me. "I suppose my duty must be done."

At this moment the bottle popped, and George Coffin said, "Wait a second, and I'll pour you a small quantity to sustain you on your trip. It's really dangerous to go out in that rain unfortified."

As glasses were being secured from the pantry Dr Harvey and Mrs Coffin came down the stairs. The doctor's alert eye fell upon the bottle. "Ah! A surprise party."

Mrs Coffin's back, even when she walked downstairs,

was as stiff as a queen's. "I sometimes think," she said
in a loud voice, "that George's veins are filled with
brandy instead of blood."

Instead of replying George Coffin smiled sadly and
poured a small quantity of the golden liquid into each
of the inhalers. He passed glasses to Miss Leslie and his
wife, who pretended to wave her share away but nevertheless took it, and then handed an especially large portion to Colonel Black. "See if you don't think this is
as good as any but the oldest of French cognacs," he
said.

Politely waiting until the rest of us had received
glasses, the colonel raised his inhaler to his nose, cup-
ping the thin glass in the palms of his hands so their
heat would cause evaporation. While we waited in
hushed silence he sniffed once, sniffed again and then
drew a long breath and signified his overwhelming approval of the brandy by ecstatically exhaling, "Ah!"

I, and I think possibly the others, felt relieved, as
though in some way the honor of the house had been vin-
dicated, and I tried a sip of the brandy. It was very fine
indeed, with a mellowness which left a pleasant after-
taste in the mouth.

The others, in varying ways, expressed their pleasure
in the fine old liquor and complimented George Coffin
on his choice of postprandial entertainment. I noticed
as I moved around to speak to Miss Leslie that George
Coffin had poured himself almost half a tumbler of the
brandy. His face looked as though he needed it, and I
wondered again if he were ill.

Miss Leslie smiled at me with her eyes. "Don't you
think this is nice: to be warm and cozy in front of a fire
while the wind blows outside?" she asked.

I was about to reply in the affirmative when with a great crash the front door was flung open. A gust of wind flew into the room, fluttering the silk cover on the table nearest the door and causing the fireplace to spew out a cloud of black smoke. The noise of the storm was loud in our ears.

In the doorway stood Karl Norberg, the tails of his wet slicker flapping wildly in the moving air. His eyes, distended in a wild combination of terror and horror, roved over the persons in the room, finally settled on me.

"What is it, Karl?" I cried.

He moved two jerky steps in my direction. "It's Bronson." Back of him the wind shrieked derisively, almost drowned out his words. "The madman's cut off his head."

Chapter *XIII*

A SILENCE so complete that I could hear the splash of waves on the shore, the crackle of half-consumed wood in the fireplace, held the room. Then Grace Coffin uttered a wail. She sat on the davenport to the left of the fire, her back arched, her large bosom outthrust, her hand still clutching the brandy inhaler, her ordinarily austere face quivering with fear. "Oh, oh, oh," she cried. I felt an impulse to giggle and realized I was near hysteria myself.

Her clamor released the room from this queer spell of terror. Miss Leslie moved swiftly to comfort Mrs Coffin. From the library came the two young Harveys, their billiard cues still in their hands. Simultaneously Burton Coffin, Dr Harvey and I started toward Karl Norberg and the door.

"Where's the body?" Dr Harvey demanded.

"In the servants' sitting room." Courage had begun to return to Karl Norberg, making his blue eyes almost normal. "I found him there when I came in from the barn."

"Let's go," said Burton, starting through the door.

"No!" Colonel Black's voice, loud and authoritative, rang in our ears. "Everyone remains here." He moved to the front door. "Young Mr Harvey, will you please notify the police? At once, please." Dan Harvey gave him a startled glance, then hurried to obey his order. The colonel continued, "Peter, I want you and Miss Harvey to search the house for muddy shoes. Or for shoes that show signs of having recently been wiped off." His eyes swept the room. "Does anyone object to having his room searched?"

There was no objection.

"Very good. The rest of you are to stay in this room until my return." He grasped Karl's arm. "Come on."

The closing of the door was the signal for an excited burst of conversation. Everyone began to talk at once. Mrs Coffin began to weep, and Miss Leslie kept repeating, "There's no danger, no danger at all," to her. George Coffin muttered, "This is terrible," and poured himself a goblet of brandy. From the library came Dan Harvey's high, excited voice communicating news of the new tragedy to the sheriff's office.

"But why does the colonel want all of you to remain in this room?" asked Miss Harvey loudly.

Burton Coffin's face was sullen. "Because he thinks one of us killed Bronson," he replied.

"I don't believe he thinks that," I objected. "I think he just doesn't want to overlook any possibility."

For an instant there was a lull in the conversation. The storm, if anything, had increased. The house, despite its great timbers and rock foundation, trembled under each howling gust of wind. In the intervals of calm the hiss of rain, which had started again, on the lake and through the trees, the slap-slap of waves against the wooden boathouse, the pounding of the miniature surf on the shore, beat against our ears.

Mrs Coffin had detached herself from Miss Leslie and was sitting unsupported on the davenport. "You're not going to do anything so silly as to search our rooms, are you, Peter?" she demanded.

"I am," I said. "I intend to do everything in my power to catch the murderer, madman or otherwise." I felt a trifle pompous saying this, but it seemed to silence Mrs Coffin.

George Coffin finished his brandy and lifted a dazed face to us. "They said he cut off Bronson's head?" he asked.

"Yes, dear," said Mrs Coffin with sarcasm. "Karl mentioned his head had been cut off."

"He said by the madman," added Miss Leslie hopefully. "Maybe he saw him."

"I don't want you bursting into my wife's room," said Dr Harvey to me. "If you have to go in there I'll go with you. I don't want her any more frightened than she is."

"Surely it won't frighten her to have her daughter enter her room," I said.

"The madman cut off his head," mumbled George Coffin. "His head . . . off . . . cut off." Then seeing our eyes upon him, he hastily poured more brandy into his goblet.

"This is outrageous," said Dr Harvey, "preventing us from leaving this room. Does that detective think we're all criminals?"

"You can go upstairs," I said, out of patience. "I won't try to stop you. But it will mean you aren't playing the game."

He shrugged his shoulders ill-naturedly. "Go ahead then. But don't scare Mary. She's sick enough as it is."

Dan Harvey returned from the telephone in the library. "The sheriff says he'll be right over," he reported. "He says everyone better stay inside."

"All right, Dan," I said. "You stay here while your sister and I look around."

We hurried up the stairs and started the search in my room. We found nothing of interest there nor in the colonel's room nor in either the study or Uncle Tobias' bedroom. While we were in the study Miss Harvey asked me if I knew what the colonel suspected.

"I don't think he suspects anything," I replied. "He's just trying to check up on everyone who might not have had an—I think this is the correct word—alibi at the time Bronson was killed." I bent down and looked under the desk. There was nothing there. "You and your brother have alibis because you were together after dinner playing billiards. I have one because I was either with Mrs Bundy or the colonel the entire time."

Her pert face was awed. "Gee, detectives are smart, aren't they?"

I admitted I should be inclined to answer her remark in the affirmative.

Next were the stairs to Mrs Spotswood's third-floor rooms. I felt somewhat hesitant about intruding, and I suggested that Miss Harvey go up under the pretense that she was inquiring after Mrs Spotswood's health. I suggested that she could in this way ascertain whether or not anyone had been in Mrs Spotswood's room after dinner and, if they had, whether they had left any wet clothes with her for the laundry, and so spare Mrs Spotswood and Mrs Bundy needless alarm.

I waited in the hall until Miss Harvey came down the

stairs. In response to my unspoken question she shook her head.

"Nobody except Mrs Bundy has been in her room since dinner," she informed me.

The remainder of the search was equally fruitless. We went through each room with the utmost care, but there weren't any muddy shoes. Both of us were quite disappointed. We went downstairs and discovered that Colonel Black, Karl and Mr Bundy had returned from the servants' house. The colonel glanced at me, and I said, "No luck at all."

Dr Harvey showed his sharp teeth in a grin. "I should 've thought you were intelligent enough to know that before you started searching."

Colonel Black took a position close to the fire. "This is a very strange crime—a very strange crime," he declared, his voice sounding like one of my fellow professors giving a lecture on the ablative absolute. "As I see it there are three possibilities: that the madman killed Bronson; that Karl Norberg or Mr Bundy killed him; or that someone from this house killed him."

He paused to allow our minds to grasp this.

"Chances are the madman committed this second crime as well as the first, but the fact that Bronson was killed almost at the moment he was going to present me with information connected with the first crime is worthy of considerable speculation." The colonel held the palms of his hands to the fire. "Bronson was killed less than ten minutes before Karl found his body. That means, if someone from this house killed him, that the murderer must have gone over to the servants' house and come back here in the short interval between the end of dinner and the time we all met to have a glass of brandy."

There was a general silence during another of his pauses.

"Now between this house and the servants' house is a large court, the surface of which is clay. It is impossible, except by a long walk through the woods, to get from this house to the servants' house without walking across this court. That's why I wanted to make sure there were no muddy shoes in the house."

"I get the idea now," said Dr Harvey with something like admiration in his voice. "You figured that if there were no muddy shoes it would clear everyone in the house."

"In a way, yes," agreed the colonel. "But of course there is a possibility that the shoes had been cleaned. However, I did postulate one thing. I assumed that, in the limited time offered, no one would have been able to reach the servants' house from here without crossing the court. Muddy shoes would have proved that someone did cross, but no muddy shoes does not prove someone didn't."

"But then, not finding any muddy shoes," said Dr Harvey, "it appears that you are out of luck."

"No," said the colonel solemnly. "There is an infallible way of determining whether or not someone did cross the court between the two houses."

"And what is that?" asked Mrs Coffin.

"First I want to know who has crossed that court since it began to rain this afternoon."

"I did," said Karl, his face embarrassed. "I crossed it to come over here to tell you about Bronson."

"Yes, I know about you and Mr Bundy, since you crossed with me. But did anyone else?"

There was no reply.

"Good." The colonel's face brightened. "Then, if there are any tracks on the court beside those of Bronson, Karl, Mr Bundy and myself, they will be the tracks of the murderer."

"Yes." Dr Harvey nodded. "That sounds reasonable. But how are you going to keep people off the court until morning? The sheriff, for instance, and his men will have to cross it to get to the house."

"Boards," said the colonel. "Boards." He swung around toward Karl. "Any boards around the house?"

"Sure. There's a pile of one-by-eights under the kitchen porch."

"But you can't board up the entire court," I objected. "It would take enough boards to build a house."

"I don't intend to." Colonel Black's eyes were amused. "I'm not supplying work for Roosevelt's unemployed. I simply intend to board over paths from the point where the driveway enters the court to this house, and from here to the servants' house. Everybody 'll be made to walk on those paths."

"Somebody will have to warn the sheriff before he drives up," I said. "He and his men will make a mess of that court if they're allowed to walk over it."

"Mr Bundy will look out for that. Karl, do you think you and Mr Bundy can lay a path of boards to the driveway? I'd like to have it ready for the sheriff."

Karl glanced at me, and I nodded. "Yes sir," he said. He and Mr Bundy departed in the direction of the kitchen.

Colonel Black paced slowly across the room, came back halfway and halted. "You won't mind if I ask a few questions?" he inquired. "I'd like to be able to straighten things up as much as I can."

"It seems to me you're doing as much as you can to involve us in these horrid crimes," stated Mrs Coffin, "and I see no reason why we should oblige you."

"Perhaps not, madam," said the colonel politely. "But since it is the truth I'm after, I believe everyone who has no connection with the murders should be eager to help me."

To my surprise George Coffin took the colonel's part against his wife. Perhaps it was only habit which led him to disagree with his spouse or perhaps it was because he was feeling better. At least his face looked better. There was color in it now, and his eyes, behind the horn-rimmed spectacles, were steady.

"I don't see why we shouldn't answer any question the colonel has to ask," he said. "Perhaps he will be able to clear us from suspicion, and certainly we will be no worse off than we were before."

Dr Harvey jerked his head up and down in vigorous agreement. "Ask away, Colonel."

The colonel, it appeared at once, was interested in what we all had done in the interval between dinner and brandy in the living room.

"I can eliminate the professor, since he was with me all but a moment or two of the time, and I can, I believe, eliminate the two young Harveys," he said. "And that is all."

"I think you can eliminate Mrs Spotswood and Mrs Bundy," I suggested. "They have been together ever since Mrs Bundy went upstairs."

"That's what they told me," supplemented Miss Harvey.

"All right." The colonel smiled at Miss Harvey. "We'll cross them off the list. Anybody else?"

Considerable questioning showed that everyone else might have had time to cross over from the house and kill Bronson.

Either George Coffin or his son, because they missed each other in the cellar, might have made the murderous trip. Mrs Coffin, upstairs by herself, might have done it, and so might Miss Leslie and Dr Harvey.

"How about Ma?" asked Dan Harvey, entering wholeheartedly into the spirit of the affair. "She could have done it too, couldn't she?"

Colonel Black solemnly wrote Mrs Harvey's name on his list.

I was suggesting Mr Bundy and Karl Norberg when the sheriff and two deputies entered from the pantry. Their faces were alarmed; all three carried shotguns. "What in thunder's goin' on up here?" demanded the sheriff.

"I wish I knew," I replied and introduced him to Colonel Black.

"I heard you was over here," said the sheriff, shaking hands vigorously with the colonel. "The coroner said you wanted some extra work done on the autopsy, though why, I can't make out. It's plain as day he died when his head was cut off."

"You don't mind if I try to assist you, however, do you, Sheriff Wilson?" asked the colonel respectfully. "The insurance company I represent is heavily involved in this matter."

"Glad to have you. Glad to have you." The sheriff looked at his deputies, one of whom was the gawky Jeff, the guard of two nights before. "All I want to do is to clear this business up and get the newspapers off my neck. I ain't had time to turn around in the last two days, much less to tend to my seed business." The second deputy, a heavy-set man with a grim face, nodded approvingly. The sheriff continued, "I want to get my hands on that Glunt as quick as I can."

"The colonel," said Dr Harvey with a trace of sarcasm, "thinks the madman is innocent of these two murders."

"The heck he does!" The sheriff's mouth popped open; he let his hat fall to the floor. "Why, man, that's direct contrary to all common sense." His wide-open eyes were fixed on the colonel.

The colonel smiled at him, "I wouldn't go as far as to say I've cleared the madman, Sheriff Wilson," he said. "But certain facts make me suspect the case may not be as simple as you believe. Suppose we take a look at Bronson's body, and while we're over there I'll tell you all I know. I think Karl has laid the wooden path by this time."

"But why a wooden path?" demanded the sheriff in a bewildered manner. "I got rubbers on."

"I'll explain," said the colonel, a touch of impatience in his voice.

Chapter *XIV*

THE SHERIFF stretched out on the davenport to the right of the fireplace and groaned luxuriously, saying, "I hope that Glunt don't show up around here again tonight."

It was now almost two o'clock, and the storm had passed on to the south, leaving behind a soft wind which moaned and sighed about the house. The lake, subsiding quickly, was so quiet that only an occasional murmur of water reached us from the shore. The rest of the household had gone to bed, but I was too disturbed over the death of Bronson to sleep.

"So you don't believe in Colonel Black's theory that the murders were committed by someone in the house?" I asked.

"I personally don't." The sheriff laid his shotgun on the floor beside him. "It ain't reasonable that a sane man would cut off a couple of heads like that. But as my deputy, Jeff, says, it don't cost us nothing to let him go ahead on his line."

I shifted my chair so that the heat from the bed of glowing coals could reach my shoulders. "What's the program for tomorrow?"

"Well, we got the inquest in the afternoon. I have to be there, I guess. And at dawn we're going to take a look at the court to see if we can find any footprints. And by that time Jeff and Fred will be back from Traverse City with a posse to search the woods. There's no doubt but what Glunt's got a hide-out right near here."

"You'll certainly be busy enough." I paused to wonder what we would find on the sticky surface of the court. Would there be imprinted the evidence of someone's guilt, the solution to both crimes? Or would the surface be bare of information? I spoke to the sheriff. "What will you do if we find someone's footprints leading from the house to the servants' house and back again?"

He had evidently been drowsing. "Huh?"

I repeated the question.

"Pick the fellow up on suspicion, I guess," he replied.

"But you do agree that it would be impossible for anyone to reach the servants' house from here in, say, five minutes without crossing the court, don't you?"

"Yeah. The colonel's right about that. It 'd take half an hour to go by way of the woods, and just about as long if you swam around so's to come up behind the servants' house." He sighed deeply. "There's no doubt that if the murderer did come from this house he'd have to cross the court. The only trouble is that the murderer didn't come from over here. He came from the state asylum's ambulance, and I'm going to stick him right back in there."

"But you'll help the colonel examine the court, won't you?"

"Oh sure. I don't plan to stand in his way."

His tone implied that he was willing to put up with

any nonsense on the part of the colonel, no matter how absurd.

I inquired, "But what makes you so certain that it is Glunt?"

"You."

"Me?"

"Yes, you. You saw him on the path by the lake, didn't you?"

"I'd almost forgotten." I saw with a shock that the sheriff had turned one surprised, dubious eye on me, and I continued hurriedly, "I suppose other people have seen him, haven't they?"

"You're the only one." His eye closed. "Seems sort of funny you'd forget seeing him."

"I didn't forget," I said. "I simply didn't know that the chase hinged on the fact that I saw him that night."

"Well, it does," said the sheriff complacently. "And when Jeff and Fred return from Traverse with the posse we're going to scour the area around this lake cleaner than a dishpan. We'll get him this time, see if we don't."

"Then you think he's still around here?"

Sheriff Wilson sounded irritated. "Well, he must be, dang it, or he wouldn't have killed Bronson."

I remained silent after this outburst, and in a short interval I heard the sheriff's breath assume a deeper quality than usual. While he slept I pondered over the latest developments in this terrible adventure. It seemed to me that the sheriff had developed a rather specious line of reasoning in regard to Bronson's murder. The madman's near here; he cuts off people's heads; therefore he cut off Bronson's head. But how do you know he's near here? Why, dang it, he must be, or he wouldn't have been able to kill Bronson.

I decided this was an evident sophism.

The air in the room had become cold, and I put another pine faggot on the fire. Little tongues of flame, like dancing elves, raced over the dry wood to a brisk sound of crackling. A bright yellow blaze, growing larger every second, sprang up in the center of the fireplace, made moving shadows in the living room.

Why was George Coffin so disturbed this evening? Something had certainly upset him. I went back to my chair and sat down, holding my hands toward the fire. Could it have been what Bronson had said to him? What could Bronson have said to him? Why hadn't Bronson told me, as long as he spoke to George Coffin about it?

Then the question that I had been fighting off, that I had been trying to keep unspoken, even in my own mind, submitted itself. Could George Coffin have murdered Bronson? I shuddered as I asked myself that, but I felt a certain relief in bringing it out in the open. All evening I had been tormented with this fear which I would not allow myself to admit. I was afraid that it must have been George, and I liked him so very much.

But if Bronson was in terror of his life and George Coffin was the man he feared why would he speak to him? It didn't seem possible, if Bronson knew George was a murderer, that he would tell him so. Yet whatever he had divulged had upset George. Another unreasonable thing was the murder itself, if it had been committed by George. He must have known that everyone had seen he was disturbed after talking to Bronson. Would he have dared, then, to kill Bronson? I didn't think so. He wouldn't . . .

What was that?

I sat up on the edge of my chair, my hands gripping

the arm rests. Had I heard a noise in the pantry? I held my breath until my lungs throbbed with pain. My heart, beating wildly, sent blood rushing through my head. I could hear the tinkle of glowing coals in the fireplace, the regular breathing of Sheriff Wilson, the sough of the wind outside, the irregular lapping of the lake.

Then it came again: a faint padding sound, as though someone was crossing the pantry with bare feet. It was a ghostly, subdued sound, almost supernatural, and I felt my flesh crawl. I had a fleeting conviction that the noise was being made by some sort of an animal.

Every inclination bade me sit quietly in my chair until the sounds stopped, but I forced myself to my feet. I knew the sheriff, if I shook him awake, would utter some noise likely to frighten the intruder, whether it was man or beast, and so I crept on toward the pantry alone. I was terribly frightened; I had difficulty breathing through a suddenly constricted throat, and I felt as though I was about to be sick to my stomach, but I was determined to get a glimpse of the thing in the pantry.

I reached the pantry door without a sound and pushed it open noiselessly. A gust of cold wind beat against my face. The pantry window was open, and outside on the lawn I caught a glimpse of something white moving away from the house in the direction of the lake. It was gone in half a second, and I almost believed it had been a product of my imagination, already highly charged.

I slipped through the window and dropped to the grass. Wind ruffled my hair, and water from a branch of an oak tree I had grasped to steady myself wet the back of my neck. I started for the lake, walking in an Indian crouch to keep my body as near the dark ground as possible. To the north a corner of the sky had cleared, and a few pale stars were visible. They looked unusually small. The grass was very wet, and I nearly fell several times. My feet made a low sloshing noise which I found impossible to stop, but I comforted myself by the thought that the wind, now blowing off the lake, would carry the sound back toward the house.

All of a sudden I saw the flash of white again, almost at the edge of the lake. It was a man, barefooted and wearing a white shirt and black trousers. He had several objects clasped in his arms. I circled cautiously behind a clump of rosebushes and made my way on hands and knees behind this protection until I was less than twenty feet from him. Slowly I lifted my head above the last bush and peered at him.

It was George Coffin.

I was so startled that I nearly overbalanced into the roses. What was he doing out here? I looked at his face. He had left his glasses somewhere, and there was mud on his forehead and on his cheeks. But his eyes were what shocked me. They had a haunting quality about them, a mixture of horror and fear and determination. He looked like a priest of the ancient god Baal about to perform one of those weird inhuman rites in which the ancients were accustomed to sacrifice their virgins and children for divine protection.

The object he carried in his arms did nothing to lessen this nightmare impression. It appeared to be some sort of a small naked creature, and I was prepared to hear from it a shrill wail. So fast did my imagination race that I even wondered where he had been able to secure a baby. Did Mrs Bundy have one?

Then he took the object in his right hand and held it

away from him, and I became at once relieved and more
amazed than ever. It was a broiled chicken! He hurled
it far out into the lake. At his bare feet were other objects. As he picked each one up and threw it into the
lake I identified them. Two apples, a loaf of bread, a
half a pie and a covered metal container filled with a
white liquid which leaked out as it flew through the
air.

"There," he muttered to the lake, "eat that."

Then he turned quickly, so quickly he nearly surprised me, and started for the house at a rapid trot. In
three seconds he was out of sight.

I couldn't begin to separate all the emotions, the con-
jectures, the violent disbeliefs which filled me as I followed him. It must be a dream, I told myself. It must
be! But there was a smell of roses and buttercups in my
nostrils and the feel of the east wind on my back and the
damp grass under my feet and the small pale stars in
the north. They were real, too real for any dream. Could
I be mad?

I climbed through the pantry window and groped
my way into the living room. The sheriff was still asleep,
his breath perfectly regular. The bed of small coals still
gleamed on the hearth, and the ashes of the faggot I
had put on the fire lay on them, gray-white and shaped
like a small fossil. I sat down and debated what I should
do. I knew the conventional thing would be to arouse
Sheriff Wilson and tell him of my experience. But I had
several reasons for not wanting to do this. In the first
place he wouldn't believe my story. In the second, he
would want to know why I hadn't called him when I
heard the noise in the pantry. And finally I didn't want
to get George Coffin into any trouble until I was certain

he was responsible for the murders at Graymere, the official name of my great-uncle's estate.

But what in the world would make George Coffin throw a broiled chicken in the lake?

I tossed two pieces of wood on the fire and watched the bright sparks race up the chimney. The noise woke the sheriff, and he struggled into a half-sitting position on the davenport. "Hello," he said. "You still up?"

"I'm too upset to sleep," I explained. "Bronson was an old friend, almost a relative. . . ."

"Yeah, I know." The sheriff's voice was sympathetic. "I was like that when my sister Sophie died." He rubbed his eyes with the backs of his hands. "Any sign of my posse?"

"Not yet."

The fire seemed to have a hypnotic effect on the sheriff. He blinked his eyes at the yellow blaze several times, sighed heavily and sank back on the couch. "Well, I reckon a body might as . . ."

Upstairs a woman screamed.

"Lordalmighty!" exclaimed the sheriff, sitting up. "What was that?"

The woman screamed again. The sound was terrible. There was a note of utter terror in her voice, a feeling of nerves completely out of control.

"Come on," said the sheriff.

We raced up the stairs and down the corridor. The screaming was coming from Mrs Coffin's room. The sheriff flung open the door. Mrs Coffin was sitting up in her bed, her arms crossed over her breast, her eyes insane. A small reading lamp, on a table beside her bed, cast a milky light over her. She screamed again, almost deafening our ears.

At this moment George Coffin came through the connecting door to his room. "Grace! Grace!" he exclaimed. "What's the matter?" He ran to the bed and caught hold of his wife's shoulders.

His touch broke the nightmare spell she had been under. She looked at his face, and the insanity left her eyes. She shuddered and pulled the covers up to her neck.

Other people were in the room now, behind us. I glanced around and saw Dr Harvey and Miss Leslie. They both appeared frightened. Miss Leslie's face was absolutely white, and her eyes met mine questioningly. I shook my head.

George Coffin was asking his wife, "What happened, dear?"

The fear returned to Mrs Coffin's eyes. "The madman. He was in my room. Bending over my bed." She leaned closer to George Coffin. "He frightened me so."

"The madman!" George Coffin's eyes met the sheriff's. "How could he have gotten in here? Haven't you been guarding downstairs?" He turned back to his wife. "Are you sure it wasn't a bad dream, dear?"

"No. He was in here. I saw him." There was an overwrought, sobbing quality to her voice. "He bent over the bed. His face was horrible. Horrible." She put her hands over her eyes. "I think he was going to kill me."

Somebody pushed past me. It was Burton Coffin. He halted by his mother's bed, on the side opposite his father, and asked, "What's happened?"

"Your mother thinks she has seen the madman," said George Coffin.

I looked closely at George, but I was unable to see any traces of the mud I had noticed on his face when he had thrown the food into the lake. His pajamas, of yellow silk trimmed with green, were clean, and there were no signs on his bare feet of his recent excursion. Moreover, his face expressed only natural concern for his wife. Could it have been someone else I had seen outdoors? Someone resembling George?

Sheriff Wilson was speaking. "I think it would be best if we left Mrs Coffin with her family," he said, "but before I go I'd like to know just what the person you saw, Mrs Coffin, did."

Mrs Coffin had regained most of her customary composure. "There isn't much to tell," she said. "I was awakened by a noise, and I switched on the light. There was a man bending over my bed. His face was covered with mud, and he seemed to be grinning at me. His expression was dreadful." Her right hand clasped Burton's arm tightly.

"Then what, Mrs Coffin?"

"I screamed, and he disappeared."

"Oh, Mother," said Burton. "I think you must have dreamed it."

"No." She shook her head. "It was real."

"Well, thank you, Mrs Coffin." The sheriff moved toward the door. "I suppose Mr Coffin will stay with you?"

"Burton and I both will," replied George Coffin.

In the hall we were met by Dan Harvey. "Sis is with Mother," he told his father. "What happened?"

We told him.

"It must have been a dream. I know I have nightmares sometimes that seem absolutely real to me."

"I think you're right, young man," agreed Sheriff Wilson. "If anybody 'd come out of her room we'd seen him." He peered at Dr Harvey for confirmation. "What do you think, Doc?"

Dr Harvey shrugged his shoulders. "There have been some darn funny things around here."

Joan glanced at me. "Are you going to stay up the remainder of the night, Peter?" she asked.

"Yes. I'm too excited to sleep."

"Then I'm coming downstairs with you if you don't mind. I'm not going to stay alone in that room of mine."

I felt a warm glow in the vicinity of my chest. "I don't mind at all," I replied.

She secured a camel's hair overcoat to put over her kimono; the Harveys went back to their suite of rooms, and we started along the corridor. As we passed the stairs to the third floor, Mrs Bundy's red face peered down at us. She wanted to know what had happened.

"Mrs Coffin had a nightmare," said the sheriff.

"Thank the lord," said Mrs Bundy. "I was thinking it might be another murder."

There was a light in Colonel Black's room, further yet along the hall. The door was ajar, and after knocking I pushed it open. There was nobody in the room.

"Ho," exclaimed the sheriff. "I wonder where he is."

The two logs I had put on the fire had made the living room comfortably warm. The sheriff switched on a lamp at the head of the davenport on which he had been sleeping and said, "I wish that posse would get here."

"Do you suppose Colonel Black saw the madman and has followed him?" asked Joan.

"I don't know," I replied, "but I should think he'd summon help before trying to capture the man."

"The colonel looks as though he'd be quite capable of trying all by himself."

"Perhaps." I smiled at her thoughtful face. "I know I'd be scared to death if I encountered Mr Glunt by myself."

Her teeth were small and very white. "So would I," she admitted.

Our conversation apparently made the sheriff nervous. "There ain't going to be any question of anybody getting Glunt singlehanded as soon as my posse arrives," he said sharply. "I can't imagine what in tarnation's keeping them." He glanced at me quizzically. "Maybe they stopped to grab a mite of fodder. If they did I wish I was with them."

"Why not have something to eat here?" I suggested as he meant me to. "There's plenty in the kitchen."

"That's a splendid idea," announced Miss Leslie. "I think some coffee and sandwiches would taste very nice."

The sheriff's face brightened, and he led the way to the kitchen. He snapped on the overhead light and halted abruptly in the doorway. "Thunder!" he exclaimed.

The kitchen looked as though some animal had been rooting around in it. The bread- and cake-boxes were turned over on their sides and their contents spilled on the floor. The icebox was open, and in front of it, on the floor, was a pile of vegetables, meats and assorted bottles and jars. Two blueberry pies, in tins on the windowsill, had been crushed, and half the pie in a third tin was gone. A finely granulated substance, either sugar or salt, was spilled all over the chromium sink.

"Why!" Miss Leslie's eyes widened in horror. "What could have done that?"

Sheriff Wilson's face was at once grim and frightened. "Mrs Coffin must have been right."

"You mean . . ." I began.

"I think the madman *has* been in the house."

Joan and the sheriff exchanged glances of consternation. I said, "Maybe."

Chapter XV

THE SUN rose blood red over the lake, and small clouds, like powder puffs, appeared in the clean blue sky. A fresh wind, carrying the odors of flowers and wet grass, of hay and the forest, blew into the living room, fluttering curtains as it passed through the windows. The indigo of the lake changed to turquoise.

Sheriff Wilson sat up stiffly on his davenport, blinked his small eyes in the light. "Another day," he said without enthusiasm.

I nodded politely. I didn't feel weary, although I hadn't had more than three hours sleep all night. The arrival of the sheriff's posse, fifteen strong and now scattered about the lake in parties of three, had interrupted one nap, and a long conversation with Colonel Black and Miss Leslie on a variety of subjects had eliminated about two hours of possible sleeping time. But I felt perfectly fit for anything the day might bring, and I was excited about the courtyard. Would the colonel find footprints there?

The colonel seemed to think he would. He had arrived just after we had discovered the shocking state of the kitchen, completely dressed and carrying a flashlight. He had been out to see that Karl Norberg and Mr Bundy were guarding the court properly, he informed us. He had not heard Mrs Coffin's screams, and he was very obviously puzzled by the events which had just taken place. He had made the sheriff repeat his story twice.

"What in the name of Queen Elizabeth did the madman want in here?" he had demanded, looking around the upset kitchen.

"Food," replied the sheriff.

"But why did he go upstairs and scare Mrs Coffin?"

The sheriff, with an outward gesture of his arms, implied that the motivation for a madman's action was not a subject for rationalization.

Joan, working with an efficiency which drew my admiration, had partially cleaned the kitchen and had produced coffee and chicken sandwiches. We had retired with the food to the living room, and presently the sheriff had fallen asleep. We had then talked for nearly two hours, the colonel entertaining us with stories of his fascinating research work into the lives of the lesser Elizabethan dramatists (and quite scandalous lives they were) and Joan and I displaying a proper interest. Then we had drowsed off in front of the fire.

"You'd better wake the colonel," said the sheriff. "He'll want to be looking at that court of his, though I don't take any stock in his theory now. Not after last night."

I woke the colonel and apparently Joan, too, because she inquired if she could come along. "I'm one of the suspects," she said, "and that should give me the privilege."

We all went out the front door and walked around to the court. I have already said that the court ran between the main house and that occupied by the servants, and, standing on the edge of it, I assured myself the colonel was right in contending that if someone from the main house killed Bronson and returned in a period of approximately ten minutes he must have crossed the court and at the same time left his prints in the soft clay.

It was possible, I saw, to reach the servants' house in two ways, but both would take more than ten minutes for the round trip. One was to leave the main house in a direction exactly opposite that of the servants' quarters, plunge into the woods and circle around to the rear of the servants' house, a distance of half a mile through the heaviest kind of underbrush. The other was to go down to the lake and swim to a point in back of the servants' house. I doubt if even a Weismuller could have made the round trip on a calm day in the time required, and at the moment of the murder the lake was choppy.

The colonel hailed Karl Norberg, who had been seated on the front steps of the servants' house. "Hi, Karl," he called. "Where's Mr Bundy?"

"Gone to tend to the cows," said Karl, approaching us along the planks which had been laid on the court last night. "We thought as long as it's daylight . . ."

"Sure. That's quite all right." The colonel's eyes were roving over the surface of the court. "I wanted to be sure that nobody erased any tracks during the night."

"Well, they didn't," said Karl. "We kept our eyes peeled."

"Let's begin then," said the colonel. "I think we will find it best to start by the lake."

He arranged us in a fan-shaped formation, something like golfers searching for a lost ball, and we started slowly up the court in the direction of the two houses. Karl was on the left end, the sheriff on the right, and Joan, the colonel and I were in the center. The colonel's angular face was excited.

Under our descending feet the clay oozed, then as we lifted each shoe it clung, finally releasing the leather with a wet plop. We moved with our heads bent down, our eyes searching the surface of the court. I was unable to discern a single track of any kind. Finally we came to the wooden planks, thrown across the place directly between the two houses. While we watched, the colonel and Karl lifted the planks and examined the footprints underneath. There were only two different prints, one large and broad and the other long and narrow, and Karl's shoe matched the first and the colonel's the second.

There was a look of disappointment in Colonel Black's blue eyes as we continued. In a few minutes we reached the T part of the court, one end of which led to the barn and the other to the cow pasture in the rear of the woods. The cows were the reason my great-uncle had made the court of clay. It was easier to keep clean than it would have been had it been grass, and while he had often talked of putting in a surface of English bricks, he never had. I halted as we reached the tracks made by the cattle coming in to the barn last evening.

"You're going to have a hard time seeing a footprint in all these tracks," said the sheriff, also halting. "Them cows got everything churned up."

Colonel Black disagreed. "You could certainly see some traces if someone walked across here," he declared. "We'll have to look especially close."

We barely crept along, with the colonel in the lead, but we couldn't find a single mark. As we reached the forest wall marking the end of the court I felt a great surge of relief. Everyone in the main house was cleared. The murders had been committed by the madman after all. I glanced at the others, half smiled at the defeated expression on Colonel Black's face.

"Well, sir," demanded the sheriff, "are you convinced?"

"I guess I'll have to be." The colonel turned around and surveyed the court, now covered with our footprints. "If someone crossed this court on foot last night we would have found his tracks."

"He certainly couldn't have jumped across," commented the sheriff.

Colonel Black shook his head sadly. "No, he couldn't have." He sighed. "I think I'll have a bath and some breakfast." He glanced inquiringly at the sheriff.

"The coroner's coming out pretty quick for Bronson's body," said the sheriff. "I think I'll wait around for him."

I turned to Joan. Her lovely skin, despite a night with practically no sleep, was clear and smooth. She was smiling. "How about a swim before breakfast?" I asked. "I think it might help our appetites."

She said, "I think that would be fun." As I walked beside her toward the house she added, "I'm so glad the suspicion is lifted off all of us."

"The colonel is tenacious," I reminded her.

There was an odor of dust about the circuit courtroom on the second floor of the red brick county courthouse. Dust coated the warped pine floor, clung like talcum to the long rows of varnished pine benches, floated like golden motes in the angular yellow beams of the afternoon sun. The tall windows were glazed with it.

In the judge's leather chair on the judge's bench sat Coroner Lester Hart. He was a gaunt individual with deep hollows under his eyes and uneven yellow teeth, and his blue shirt was frayed at the cuffs. He appeared to be well pleased with the position of authority the inquest into the death of my great-uncle gave him, and he darted quick glances of triumph at the reporters, the crowd of spectators in the room.

Little of interest to me had developed during the early part of the testimony. I sat on one of the wooden spectator benches between George Coffin and Dr Harvey and listened to Deputy Sheriff Jeff Watson describe how he and the sheriff had been notified of the tragedy and relate what they had seen when they arrived at Graymere. The deputy's account was graphic, and he had the undivided attention of the six-man jury, especially when he told how the intruder had been surprised in my great-uncle's room. He made me into something of a hero when he declared that I had tried to stop the intruder but had been stunned by a blow with a poker.

Coroner Hart leaned toward the deputy and asked, "Do you think the intruder was the same person who killed Mr Coffin?"

"No."

I noticed that Sheriff Wilson, who was seated with Colonel Black and Dr McNally, the toxicologist, who had flown down from Chicago in a special plane at dawn, shook his head angrily at the deputy. Apparently he had no desire to have the problem complicated.

The coroner continued, "Who do you think it was?"

"I think it was someone looking for the new will," said the deputy slowly. "I don't think the madman would have been interested in any will."

While he was leaving the stand the jury digested this theory. They had already heard about the missing will from Dr Harvey, and they had been read a deposition by Mrs Spotswood telling of the discovery of the body. They had also heard an account of Mr Glunt's previous feat of chopping off his wife's and children's heads, an attendant's story of his escape while on his way to the asylum and the local coroner's physician's report that death was the result of decapitation.

I really didn't see why the theft of the will was brought out at all, the function of the jury being to turn in a verdict of either murder, suicide or accidental death, not to determine the motive for the crime. I suspected the coroner's questions were the work of Colonel Black.

There was something strange in the colonel's manner anyway. All during the inquest he had been seated at the very rear of the courtroom, holding some sort of a debate with Dr McNally and the sheriff. As far as I could make out he had paid no attention to the testimony.

While the attendant from the asylum was on the stand my curiosity got the better of me. Could there be new evidence in the case? I walked to the back of the room and paused behind the trio. The colonel was speaking:

"If you want blue cardinal flowers, Sheriff, I advise you to get a beehive."

"What in tarnation have bees to do with my bed of blue cardinal flowers?" demanded the sheriff.

"You say you have hummingbirds in your garden. That's why you have plenty of red cardinal flowers. Hummingbirds like red flowers, so yours are more often fertilized than the blue."

"Yes, but what . . ." began the sheriff.

Dr McNally took up the lecture. "Bees like blue and purple flowers. Have lots of bees, and you will have lots of blue cardinal flowers."

"I declare!" The sheriff's voice was awed. "I been selling seed for thirty years and never knew that."

"You should send a beehive along with each package of blue lobelia," said the colonel. "That would assure the buyer of plenty of flowers."

"And a couple of sphinx moths with every orchid," added Dr McNally.

At this moment the sheriff was called to the stand. I followed him to the front of the room, my faith in detectives shaken. Was this the way a detective worked? Talking about bees and flowers?

The sheriff substantiated almost everything his deputy had said, but he asserted that in his opinion the intruder who had struck me was the madman. He admitted he didn't know why the madman had returned to my great-uncle's room, but he scored a point with the jury by demanding if anybody in the world did know why a crazy person did something.

The jurymen—evidently, from their tan faces and ill-fitting black clothes, farmers—nodded at this evident truth.

I went on the stand next, and while I told of my encounter with the madman on my way around the lake the sheriff beamed at the jury. I could see his point of view. If it was understood that the madman was responsible for all the disturbance at Graymere the case would be closed upon his capture, and the sheriff would be spared any further trouble.

"You say you heard the madman mutter something as he passed you?" Coroner Hart asked. "What was it?"

"A tisket, a tasket, a green and yellow basket," I replied.

The jury, to my surprise, guffawed at this.

I completed my story of my first night at Graymere, and the coroner asked:

"Have you any idea who was responsible for the theft of the will from your great-uncle's room, Mr Coffin, or who struck you over the head?"

I said I hadn't and was released from the stand.

"Now," said the coroner to the jury, "you have heard testimony to the effect that the madman was near Graymere on the night of the murder, and you have heard the sheriff's opinion that only the madman could have committed the crime. You have heard of a former and similar crime by the madman, and you have the physician's report. Ordinarily that would be enough, but . . ." He fixed his eyes on the back of the room and raised his voice. "I have been asked to allow another person to testify. I wish you to listen carefully to him, but I do not want anything but facts to sway your findings in this case.

"Dr William McNally."

Both the colonel and the toxicologist came forward.

Dr McNally was a small, pink-and-white, round-faced man. His hands were plump, his skin shone as though it had just been scrubbed, his thin hair was slicked back on his head. He smiled shyly at the jury.

In response to the coroner's questions he gave the following information: his residence was Chicago, Illinois; his present occupation was president of the Northwestern Laboratories; by profession he was a toxicologist. He admitted that he had aided in the autopsies of more than a thousand persons, partly while he was chief medical examiner for the coroner of Cook County.

"But most of these were cases where poisoning was suspected, weren't they?" objected the coroner. "Not murders like this."

"Quite so," agreed Dr McNally with his shy smile.

"Did you perform an autopsy on the body of Tobias Coffin?" asked the coroner.

"Not exactly. I made certain examinations at the request of Colonel Black, representing the American Insurance Company, and with your kind permission."

"Will you tell us what you discovered?"

"I opened the body with one intention. I wished to discover whether or not there was chloroform present in the lungs and blood stream."

"Yes?"

"There was."

The coroner's mouth dropped open, disclosing his gold crowns. "In what quantity, Dr McNally?"

"In a quantity sufficient for me to state that Mr Coffin was unconscious when he met his death."

A murmur of voices rose over the courtroom. The jury eyed the coroner in bewilderment. My mind turned over this new phase of the mystery, but I didn't see that

Dr McNally had made things any clearer. Did the chloroform indicate that Uncle Tobias had been drugged by someone before the madman had chanced upon him? That would account for the absence of an outcry or struggle. But why had someone drugged him? Who would have done that? Certainly the madman couldn't and wouldn't have done it before decapitating Uncle Tobias. No madman would be that considerate of his victim's feelings. Or would he?

The noise of voices had died down, and the coroner was speaking. "But what does the chloroform mean, Dr McNally?" he asked.

"I don't know," said the toxicologist frankly. "I have merely given you my findings and my opinion as to the state of the deceased at the time of death. And even if I did have an idea, to say what it was would exceed my field of authority. I advise you to ask Colonel Black."

Coroner Hart turned to the colonel, who smiled and shrugged his shoulders.

"I haven't any answer ready at this time," he said, "but I would like to point out one more thing to the jury."

"What is that?"

"I should like to have them examine the collar worn by the dead man at the time his body was found."

One of the sheriff's deputies produced my great-uncle's clothes, and the colonel extracted the stiff collar from the bundle. I could see on it the brown stains which I had noticed after the murder on my first night at Graymere. The article was handed from man to man in the jury and finally reached the coroner, who held it up to a beam of light from the afternoon sun.

"What am I supposed to make of it?" he demanded.

"Smell it," ordered Colonel Black.

The coroner held the collar to his nose, inhaled deeply. A surprised expression appeared on his gaunt face; he sniffed again. "Gunpowder!" he exclaimed.

"Thank you," said Colonel Black.

Chapter XVI

I SEIZED THE LADDER and pulled myself out of
the cold water. My skin tingled from the exertion of the
brisk swim to and from the raft. As my head appeared
above the top of the pier Dan Harvey, seated on the
base of the diving board, opened his mouth.

"Is it true what they say . . ." he began, looking at
me.

"Is what true?" I asked.

"Is it true what they say about Dixie?" he repeated,
shaking his body to and fro.

Miss Harvey, lying on the pier with Miss Leslie and
Burton Coffin, giggled. "It's just a popular song, Professor," she called.

"I like a little more swing in my music," I said.

Joan smiled at me. "Sit down," she said, patting the
pier beside her. "The sun feels awfully good."

Burton Coffin scowled at me, so I sat down. "Why
weren't you at the inquest, Burton?" I inquired. "It was
very interesting."

His tone was surly. "I had to stay with Mother."

Dan Harvey moved over to us. His blond hair was
slicked as tight against his head as a skullcap, and water

ran down the bridge of his nose between his alert blue eyes. "What was the verdict anyway, Professor?" he demanded. "Joan tried to tell us, but I don't think she got it right."

Joan shrugged her firmly rounded shoulders. "There were so many whereases and inasmuches in it," she said.

"It was a rather curious verdict," I said. "The jury decided that Uncle Tobias had been murdered by a person or persons unknown, and then recommended that Elmer Glunt be apprehended as soon as possible."

"That is sort of funny," agreed Dan Harvey. "Why didn't they come right out and say Elmer did the murder?"

"I think the coroner wanted to have Glunt's name in the verdict so as to please the sheriff, who wants everyone to think the madman has been responsible for all the trouble up here," I said, "and yet is afraid that the murder might just possibly be the work of somebody else."

"There have been some darn strange things happening here," said Dan Harvey darkly.

His sister smiled at him. "Cheer up, Dan; the worst is over now."

Burton Coffin got to his feet. "How do you know?" he asked Miss Harvey and strode off.

"Good night!" said Miss Harvey in mock alarm. "The way he said that you'd think he knew something more was going to happen." She stared after him with wide blue eyes.

"Boy! I wish we were back in New York," exclaimed Dan Harvey.

Despite their outward appearance of lightheartedness I could see that both the young Harveys were frightened. A certain effort in their gaiety, a certain nervousness in their manner betrayed them. I had also noticed during the past two days how they clung together, as if for protection.

"I think I'll go in and get ready for dinner," announced Miss Harvey. "Coming, Dan?"

"Sure," said Dan. He waved a languid hand at us. "See you later."

Joan and I lay silently in the sun for a time. Out of the corner of my eye I could see the cool, graceful outline of her neck and her bare back. Her bathing suit clung to her body, and I could see she had the sort of a figure I admire in a young woman, boyish, but not stringy. I felt a hollow feeling in the pit of my stomach, and I wondered what was the matter with me. I also felt a strong desire to touch her bare arm, but I resisted this unworthy impulse.

Finally she said, "I believe the Harveys are scared."

"I think so too," I said, "but then, who isn't?"

"Are you scared even now?"

"Yes. I'm worrying about tonight."

She turned her face toward me so that her cheek rested on the pier. "I'm scared too."

I felt a distinct glow inside of me. She wouldn't have confessed that if she didn't feel I was a friend. I yielded to my impulse and took hold of her hand. "I'm not much of a man of action," I said, "but I'll do my best to see that nothing happens to you."

For a moment her gray eyes were tender, and to my surprise she returned the clasp of my hand. "Thanks," she said and released her hand. "I thirk we'd better go in to dress."

My heart was beating a delightful tattoo in my breast

as we walked through the grass to the house. I was suddenly conscious of the perfume of the roses and purple phlox in the air and of the unique gold stripes made by the sunlight in the big oak trees. There seemed to be an idyllic quality about Graymere, about the tall trees and the soft grass and the subtle air, that I had not noticed before.

At the steps leading up to the front veranda we encountered Sheriff Wilson. His small face was at once excited and jubilant. "We found his trail," he called down to us.

"Found whose trail?" I asked.

"Glunt's. We found where he'd built a fire this morning, directly across the lake. We ought to be pickin' him up any minute now."

"That's wonderful!" exclaimed Joan. "That will end all our troubles, won't it?"

The sheriff frowned. "Thare's some that don't think so," he said, "but you mark my words, miss, as soon as that madman's caught there 'll be no more trouble around here."

"How many men have you got on his trail?" I asked.

"Eighteen, and six more are coming out. They're bound to catch him."

I took Joan to her room and then returned to mine. I had a shower and dressed for dinner and then went into Colonel Black's room. He had on his evening clothes and was standing by his window, looking over the gray-green forest of fir trees. His face, which would have been hawklike had it not been for the plump flesh around the jowls and chin, was set in a frown.

"Hello, Peter," he said, turning his head slightly in my direction.

"Hello," I said.

"Been tryin' to figure this deuced thing out," he said, "but I can't seem to make much progress. Too many conflictin' elements. Devilish confusing."

"You mean with the madman——"

"No! No! That fellow's out, no matter what the good sheriff says. Not considering him at all. The problem revolves about the other elements."

"You mean the chloroform?"

"That's one."

"And the gunpowder?"

"Number two."

"What did you make of the gunpowder, Colonel?"

"What did you?"

"Nothing."

"And I, I fear, make too much of it."

I couldn't get him to elaborate on this statement. He smilingly shook his head and said, "Don't want to make a fool of myself, Peter. Tell you later perhaps."

I sat down on the bed and said, "Colonel, I have something which I think I ought to tell you."

His face suddenly alert, the colonel moved away from the window. The late sun put a reddish tinge in his sparse hair. "What is it?"

I told him about my encounter with George Coffin. I told him how I had heard a noise in the kitchen, had followed George to the lake, how he had thrown food into the water and how he had returned to the house.

"Will you repeat what he said when he threw the chicken into the lake?" Colonel Black asked when I had finished the story.

"He said: 'There, eat that.'"

"So!" The colonel's blue eyes, as bright and clear as

a child's, were fixed on mine. "D'you suppose there's a creature livin' in the lake, a naiad subsistin' on broiled chicken and Jersey milk?" he chuckled at my dazed expression. "Maybe your cousin's one of the elect of mankind, before whom nymphs appear and goddesses shine. Do you suppose Graymere's a center for all those elusive sprites, the dryads, the leimoniads, the potamids, the oreads, the Napaea of ancient Greece?"

I shook my head.

"No. I'll give you a better solution, Peter. Your cousin threw that chicken into the lake to get rid of it."

I nodded.

"He wanted to make it appear our friend Mr Glunt had visited the house for sustenance and had carried away the chicken and other viands."

"That's what I thought," I said, "but what about Mrs Coffin?"

"Her scream?"'

"Screams," I corrected him.

"You forget I did not hear them. Still I think they were genuine enough. You say his face was daubed with mud, and you were barely able to recognize him? Then his wife, awakened from sleep, would be even less apt to know him." The colonel was frowning again. "Two answers to her screams are possible. Either your cousin woke her accidentally while he was passing through her bedroom into his, or he frightened her deliberately, to add a witness to the madman's presence in the house."

The colonel went over and stared out the window again. Finally I asked, "What are you going to do about him?"

"After dinner, I think, I shall have him arrested."

"But you can't think he's responsible——" I began.

"I don't think anything, Peter. But I should like to hear his explanation of his actions."

"Can't you just ask him?"

"I think it would be more effective if we frightened him by arresting him."

I got off the bed. "I'll stake my life that he didn't kill Bronson. I know George Coffin well enough to be sure he didn't do that."

The colonel said, "Who knows what a desperate man will do in an emergency?" He came over to me. "Certainly Bronson was afraid of someone in the house. Didn't he tell you that?"

"Yes," I said, remembering Bronson's gloomy words that day in my room. His premonitions of evil had certainly been justified. Suddenly something else he had said came back into my conscious mind. I hit the palm of my hand on my thigh and exclaimed, "Colonel!"

"What?"

"Bronson told me to remember the big oak in the pasture back of the barn in case anything happened to him. I had forgotten all about his telling me that. He said it was important."

"Damme, that was careless of you, Peter." The colonel looked at me reprovingly. "Did he give you an idea why you should remember the oak?"

"Not a hint."

The colonel moved to the door. "Come on. We'll look."

In the living room we encountered Sheriff Wilson. He had been invited for dinner and had evidently just prepared himself for the event. His face shone from a lavish use of soap and water, his hands were scrubbed an angry red, his hair was slicked back damply on his egg-shaped head.

"Where are you going, gentlemen?" he asked with a sort of jocular politeness.

"Mr Coffin has just recalled that Bronson told him to remember the big oak tree in the pasture back of the cow barn in case something happened to him," exclaimed the colonel. "We are about to examine the tree. Would you care to join us?"

We went out the living-room door and down the front steps. The sun was below the tops of the dunes to the west, and while the clouds above were white and the sky a bright blue, there was already a feeling of darkness about the yard. A faint gloom, growing steadily heavier, hung over the two houses and the white barn.

Our feet, crossing the courtyard, sank but did not stick in the damp clay. On the other side we encountered Karl Norberg. He was pushing a heavy roller, such as is employed on tennis courts, over the clay.

"Obliteratin' all my footprints, eh?" said the colonel as we came up to him.

Karl's face was surprised, then defensive. "We always roll the court while it's still damp," he said. "If you rather I let it go I'll——"

"Roll away," said the colonel. "I've had my look."

We went through the barn and into the small pasture in back. The oak tree was almost squarely in the center of the field.

"Where 're the cows?" asked the colonel.

"They use the big pasture about half a mile the other side of the house," I explained. "Don't you remember we heard them passing the house last night after dinner?"

"Oh yes, the tintinnabulation. I'm really quite relieved that they aren't here. Cows are sometimes very unreasonable."

"You said it," agreed the sheriff. "My wife's cow, Bess, takes out after me every time I try to cut across her field to get to the corn patch."

The sheriff was apparently going to continue with a dissertation on the contrariness of bovines when we reached the tree. The dark-leaved branches spread over a wide area, and the trunk, covered at the base by coarse grass, was as thick as a fat man. From a high limb a red squirrel angrily scolded us.

"I don't see anything important," said the colonel, feeling through the grass at the foot of the tree.

The sheriff and I went around to the other side of the trunk and made a similar search. The grass was thick and hard to push aside, and the ground was uneven. The squirrel, convinced we were invading his winter storage vaults, increased his shrill clamor and came down the trunk toward us.

"Nothing important here," said the sheriff at last, "unless acorns are important." He struggled to his feet. "Found anything over there?"

"Yes," came the colonel's voice, low and with an angry rasp. "Something very important to Bronson."

"What is it?" demanded the sheriff. We both moved around the tree.

The colonel pointed to an object half hidden in the grass a foot from the base of the oak. I felt that I was going to be ill. It was Bronson's head, terror and surprise imprinted on his blood-spattered face.

Chapter XVII

DR HARVEY laid his napkin on the linen tablecloth, lighted a cigar and leaned back in his chair. "Bronson told Peter that he would find something important by the tree, and when you looked you discovered Bronson's head." His sharp-featured face was turned toward Colonel Black. "It sounds almost supernatural."

"It does smack slightly of thaumaturgy," agreed the colonel. "Perhaps Oberon is up to his tricks again."

"It sounds more like the secret, black and midnight hags of *Macbeth*," I said.

"Oh! Oh!" exclaimed Mrs Harvey, her face pale. "Please talk of something else."

"But how do you account for it, Colonel?" persisted Dr Harvey.

"I don't," said the colonel with an air of satisfaction.

"Well, I can," announced Sheriff Wilson, who hitherto had paid more attention to the cold consommé, the crisp roast lamb, the garden vegetables and the fresh peach shortcake than to the conversation. "My guess is that the madman put it there."

"You are evidently determined to have Mr Glunt involved in this affair, Sheriff Wilson," said Colonel Black. "I am curious to know just how you arrive at your conclusion."

"I don't mind telling you," said the sheriff. "I figure Bronson saw the madman hide something by that tree— as likely as not Mr Coffin's head. He went out to see what it was, and the madman saw him and followed him back to the servants' house and killed him. Then the madman put Bronson's head in the place of Mr Coffin's and went away."

The colonel nodded. "Not bad, Sheriff. Not a bit bad. What you intend to convey, I believe, is that Mr Glunt had a pronounced affection for Mr Coffin's head and feared that Bronson intended to steal it. Very good indeed. Your solution is quite within the bounds of abnormal psychology."

Well pleased with this praise, the sheriff enlarged on his theory. I turned to Joan and whispered, "I hope he's right."

She nodded, but her face was white, and her eyes were worried. "What's the matter?" I asked. "Aren't you feeling well?"

She said quickly, "I feel all right." Then, noticing what must have been very patent apprehension in my face, she smiled. "Don't worry about me."

"But what is it? Isn't there anything I can do?"

She leaned slightly toward me. Her perfume made me think of jasmine. "It's about Burton."

"Oh."

She appeared not to notice the change in my tone. "He's been so strange all afternoon. And he hasn't touched a thing at dinner. I think he has learned something about the murders which has upset him."

I felt that Burton couldn't be too upset to suit me, but I said, "That's too bad. Why doesn't he speak to Colonel Black?"

"I tried to get him to, but he wouldn't admit there was anything wrong."

"Maybe there isn't anything wrong. Maybe it's your imagination."

"Jut look at him."

I looked. "He does look pretty sick," I confessed. "He's a trifle green around the jowls."

She looked at me suspiciously, but I managed to achieve a sympathetic expression. "I'm afraid for him," she said. "Bronson knew something, and he was killed. Now Burton . . ."

Her beautiful oval face was frightened. I wished I knew whether her alarm was due to affection for Burton or to a natural desire not to have any further murders. I was afraid it was due to affection. I glanced at Burton again and was, I confess, unable to see what there was in his spoiled, sullen, but heavily handsome face to inspire affection. I sighed and said, "I'll do what I can to watch him. Do you think it would be a good idea to mention the matter to the colonel?"

"I wish you would."

For a second her hand touched my arm.

The sheriff had completed a summary of his reasons for believing that Mr Glunt was responsible for all the trouble at Graymere, and he gazed triumphantly at the colonel. "I don't see how you can get around the fact that there were no tracks in the courtyard, anyway, Colonel," he added.

"It is devilish difficult," admitted the colonel. "On the face of most of the evidence it would seem that the murders were the work of either Mr Glunt or of someone living in the servants' house."

Karl Norberg, who had donned one of Bronson's suits

and had been helping Mrs Bundy wait on table, bumped into Mrs Coffin's chair, nearly upsetting over her head the silver platter on which reposed the remains of the shortcake. "Excuse me, ma'am," he said confusedly. His face was suddenly ash pale, and he hurried from the room.

"Hey! What's this?" asked Dr Harvey. "Looks as if your bolt went home, Colonel."

"You might be frightened too," said Mrs Coffin, "if it was said either you or the madman killed Tobias."

Dr Harvey grinned. "I might be, at that."

George Coffin, who had not said a word during the entire meal, rose from his chair. "Shall we adjourn for coffee in the living room?" he asked.

"Coffee?" echoed Dr Harvey. He seemed to be in excellent humor. "I'll wager your coffee begins with a *b.*"

"That's an idea." George Coffin's face brightened. "A little brandy for the soul's sake." He walked into the pantry.

As the rest of us went into the living room there was a sound of bells outside. "Ah!" exclaimed the colonel. "The cows return from their pasture."

"That's a prize herd, ain't it?" Sheriff Wilson asked me.

"Yes," I replied. "They're all pedigreed stock."

"How do they come in from the pasture?" asked the colonel.

"Rob Roy brings them in," said Joan. "He's the collie you've seen around."

"I thought Mrs Bundy's little boy brought them in," objected Mrs Harvey.

"He does when he's here. He rides Lady Cleo out and

back," said Miss Leslie. "But he's away visiting his grandmother."

This was the first I'd heard of the Bundys' child. "How old is he?" I asked.

"Eleven."

"Lady Cleo," said the colonel. "What's Lady Cleo?"

"Lady Cleo," said Miss Leslie, "is a very nice cow."

"Isn't it a bit dangerous for a boy to ride a cow?"

"Depends on the cow," said Sheriff Wilson. "My little girl rides Bess all over the place."

It occurred to me that Bess must be a rather complex character, fierce enough to resent the sheriff's use of her pasture as a short cut to his corn patch and tractable enough to be ridden by the sheriff's daughter.

"Lady Cleo is perfectly gentle," said Miss Leslie.

George Coffin returned with another bottle of Spanish brandy, followed by Karl, bearing a tray laden with large goblets. The colonel's eyes brightened at the sight of the dust on the bottle.

"Fifteen years old?" he asked.

"Fifteen!" George Coffin's voice was indignant. "Why this brandy was of voting age when Admiral Dewey sailed into Manila Bay."

The eleven inhalers nearly exhausted the bottle, although he filled each glass less than one third full. A strong fire burned in the fireplace, and we sat in front of it and rolled the brandy around in the goblets, letting our palms warm the golden liquid until the dry, heady aroma, faintly suggestive of grapes, was released. We sniffed, inhaled, tasted, let the brandy linger in our mouths before swallowing after the manner of fine connoisseurs. Although I have no knowledge of brandy I found the experience agreeable.

"To think," mused the colonel, "that the sun should have burned brightly, that soft rains should have poured down on the Spanish hills fifty years ago solely to produce this bit of pleasure for us."

"You seem to be a bit of an epicurean, Colonel," observed George Coffin, speaking with more of his normal half-mocking, half-humorous tone.

"I believe in a hedonistic world," declared the colonel. "I am convinced that everything in the world is directed toward my pleasure, the difficulty being in finding the exact method of obtaining the proper amount of pleasure from any given event." He took a rather larger swallow of his brandy than a meticulous connoisseur might have approved. "For instance, take the thunderstorm over the Pyrenees fifty years ago. If anyone had told the owner of the vineyard whence these grapes came that the storm was going to give pleasure to a group of people half a century later and three thousand miles away he would have been convinced of his informant's insanity."

"Well, you can't say the thunderstorm last night did you much good," said Dr Harvey with a broad grin. "It certainly didn't help you to any tracks in the courtyard."

"You seem to have touched a weak point in my armor," confessed the colonel, "but again, it is possible that the storm will in the end be the solution of this mystery."

"When we catch the madman the mystery'll be solved," asserted the sheriff, who had finished his brandy. "He's the boy we want."

"Perhaps," said Colonel Black politely, "but don't

you think, Sheriff, that we'd better get down to our business here?"

"All right." The sheriff stood up and put his glass on the tray. "I got to go out and talk to my deputies soon, anyway, so let's get this over with." He faced George Coffin. "Mr Coffin, Colonel Black and I would like to ask you some questions."

George Coffin blinked at him through his thick spectacles. "Questions about what?"

"We'd like to tell you privately," said the sheriff.

George Coffin's jaw set stubbornly. "I think I've answered enough questions already. I don't believe I'll answer any more."

Surprise widened the sheriff's eyes. He rubbed his chin with the palm of his hand. "I'm afraid you'll have to, Mr Coffin," he said firmly. "Either that, or you will be taken into custody."

"Have you got a warrant for my arrest?"

"I have a John Doe warrant."

"What's the charge?"

"Complicity in the murder of Tobias Coffin."

Everyone immediately raised an outcry of protest. Mrs Coffin was especially loud in her protests. "This is ridiculous," she kept insisting. "You can't do a ridiculous thing like this." Dr Harvey shook a finger at Colonel Black. "This is your doing," he stated. "You must be mad to think George had a hand in his uncle's murder."

The sheriff seemed a little dubious himself, and I wondered if his action hadn't been a trifle drastic in view of the fact that I was the only witness he had.

Colonel Black remained cool amid the tumult. "The sheriff hasn't served the warrant," he reminded Dr Har-

vey, "and if Mr Coffin can answer his questions satis-
factorily the chances are he never will."

Mrs Harvey, her face gray and her body trembling
violently, had taken a position beside her brother. They
made a contrasting pair: George Coffin grim and collected, his jaw set and his face inscrutable back of his
horn-rimmed spectacles; Mrs Harvey apparently at
the point of collapse, her eyes wildly searching the sheriff's, the colonel's, mine for a ray of hope.

Dr Harvey glared at Colonel Black. "You've been
staying in this house without my approval," he said,
"and you've done no good as far as I can see. Your silly
meddling has done nothing but upset everyone. The
quicker you get out, the better we'll like it."

"Dr Harvey," I said stiffly, "the colonel is here at
my invitation."

"Your invitation? Bah!" The doctor's face was brick
red; he looked as though he was about to suffer a stroke
of apoplexy. "What right have you to give invitations
in this house? Do you think because there are rumors of
a will, leaving Graymere to you, that you give the orders
here? This house is the property of George Coffin and
my wife, and they'll decide who shall be a guest here."

Small men always seem capable of twice the fury of
large men, and as the doctor seemed on the verge of at-
tacking either me or the colonel, I thought it better not
to reply to him.

Colonel Black, arising with considerable dignity, said,
"I shall be glad to leave at once, Dr Harvey."

To my very great surprise Mrs Harvey held out a
hand toward the colonel. "No." She had regained her
composure, and her eyes were no longer wild. "I wish
you would stay, Colonel. I'm sure my brother's innocent,

and I know we have nothing to fear from you. We'd like to help you get at the truth."

Colonel Black's face relaxed slightly. "Thank you, Mrs Harvey. I, too, would like to get at the truth, and if my methods have been clumsy I should like to apologize. However, unless everyone here is willing to co-operate with me I should prefer not to remain as a guest."

"And you want George to answer the sheriff's questions, Colonel?"

"I think it highly important that he do so."

"Then I think George will answer them."

I was astonished to hear a note of authority in her voice, to see determination mirrored on her face. I had visualized my cousin as a woman of little character, almost devoid of personality and given to collapsing in times of stress. Now I saw I had mistaken ill health for a lack of personality, shattered nerves for cowardice.

George Coffin's face was irresolute for nearly a minute. Then he said, "I suppose I'd better answer the questions. It's either that or go to jail, isn't it, Sheriff?"

The sheriff replied, "One or t'other." He appeared perplexed, as though new ideas were occurring to him.

George Coffin patted his sister's arm. "You always had the better sense, Mary." He regarded the sheriff in a friendlier manner. "Where should we go?"

"Perhaps the library?" suggested the colonel.

Dr Harvey's voice was harsh. "You don't have to go, George. You can wait until I get a lawyer, don't forget that."

"Yes, George," concurred Mrs Coffin. "Let us get Mr Fitzgerald for you." She stared angrily at the sheriff. "He'll make a monkey out of this rustic bumpkin."

A glint of humorous despair came into George Coffin's eyes. "I can't say you are helping me much, Grace," he said. "I'll call Fitzgerald if I think I need him, and in the meantime I do not want to arouse the sheriff."

"Very well." Mrs Coffin drew herself up proudly. "If you prefer me to allow this yokel——"

"I prefer you to be silent, my dear." George Coffin bowed to Colonel Black. "Shall we go to the library?"

The colonel bowed to him. "After you." They started toward the library door.

"Do you want me to come?" I asked.

"You better," said the sheriff hastily. "You're our chief witness."

I could feel the surprised eyes of the others on my back as I followed the sheriff through the door. George Coffin had already seated himself in a straight-backed chair, and the colonel was leaning over the bright green surface of the billiard table, his elbows on the heavy cloth. My cousin gave me an interrogatory glance, but I avoided his eyes. I was wishing heartily, as, indeed, I had been for the past ten minutes, that I had not mentioned George's midnight excursion to the colonel. The enormity of the thing I was doing—bringing an accusation against a member of my own family—was heavy on my conscience. I felt like Benedict Arnold, to whom, by the way, I am related.

George Coffin lit a cigarette with uncertain hands, but when he spoke his voice was firm. "All right, Sheriff; let's hear those questions."

The colonel shook his head as the sheriff turned to him. "You open the show, Sheriff."

"Well, this is what we want to ask you, Mr Coffin," said the sheriff with an air of embarrassment. "We want to know what you mean by taking food out of the kitchen in the middle of the night and throwing it in the lake, why you were sneaking about with your face half covered with mud and why you frightened your wife last night."

George Coffin's face remained immobile, but I thought I detected a trace of sudden terror in his eyes. It was gone immediately, however, if, indeed, it had been there at all.

"Someone must have misinformed you, Sheriff," he said calmly. "I spent last night in bed, sleeping peacefully except for the brief interruption provided by my wife's screams."

"There's no use trying to deny it, Mr Coffin," said the sheriff. "You were seen in the kitchen and out by the lake. You might as well tell us all about it."

"Your witness, Sheriff, is either mistaken or a liar."

Then the sheriff took me by surprise. He swung around in my direction and asked, "What do you say to that, Mr Coffin?"

"I'm sorry," I said, looking at George, "but I saw you throw a chicken and other comestibles into the lake last night and then return to the house." His eyes dropped away from mine. "Moreover, your face was smeared with mud."

There was a long pause before George replied to my accusation. A clock, hung on the wall, seemed to tick a thousand times before he broke the silence.

"You must be mistaken, Peter." His voice was soft. "I didn't leave my bed all night except to go to my wife. You must have seen someone else."

"Is that possible, Peter?" asked the colonel.

"I don't think so. I'm positive it was George Coffin."

George shrugged his shoulders. "It's my word against his." He peered up at the sheriff. "What in the world would I be doing out there anyway? Throwing food to the fish? Is there any sense in that?"

"I don't see none," admitted the sheriff.

"Well, what does my cousin think I was doing there?"

"Only one answer is apparent to me," I said. "You wished to have us believe that the madman had returned to Graymere on the night Bronson was murdered."

Colonel Black nodded approvingly. "That's good reasoning, Peter. My congratulations."

This surprised me, too, as he had previously commended me on this bit of deduction.

"But why would I want to make you think the madman had returned?" demanded George Coffin.

"That's what we want to know," said the sheriff ominously.

George Coffin looked at the sheriff, then at Colonel Black. "There's no use going into the realm of fancy. All I can do is to repeat that I spent the night in my bed."

"What do you say, Colonel?" asked Sheriff Wilson.

The colonel's mouth was grim. "I say, lock him up."

I don't know which of the three of us was the more astonished. The sheriff had evidently been prepared to let him go with a warning that he was not entirely free of suspicion, and I didn't see that we had any case against George anyway. It is not a crime to break into your own kitchen, nor is it one to toss various edibles into water. What George had been thinking I do not

know, but I could see he was badly shaken by the colonel's words.

"What charge?" asked the sheriff, obviously bewildered. "Not the murder charge?"

"Yes, the murder charge," said Colonel Black. "And
you'd better put the handcuffs on him."

George Coffin's face was gray. "But this is inhuman."
He seemed to shrink in his chair. "You haven't anything
against me except the word of Peter. You surely
can't——"

"Put the cuffs on him, Sheriff," said the colonel
harshly.

The sheriff said, "I'll have to get 'em. They're in my
car."

"We'll watch him while you go," said the colonel.

During the absence of the sheriff George Coffin sat in
silence. The only sound was his breathing, loud and
quick, as though he were having difficulty drawing air
into his lungs. The colonel took a cue from the rack and
nonchalantly practiced caroms on the billiard table. I
pretended to be interested in one of the bookcases, but
each agonized breath of my cousin pulled at my heart,
made my lungs throb. I felt as upset as if I had been
accused of the murders.

Presently we heard the sheriff's returning footsteps.
He reached the door, had it half open when we heard
Mrs Coffin ask, "What are you going to do, Sheriff?"

The sheriff clanked the handcuffs together. "We're
going to lock your husband up, ma'am."

Mrs Coffin screamed, and there arose a tumult of
voices, some endeavoring to comfort her, others hurling
angry questions at the sheriff. He opened the door wider
and backed toward us, away from the living room.

Burton Coffin was in front of the others, and in all that confusion the most startling thing to me was the emotion betrayed on his face. His lips quivered, his eyes fluttered, his whole body trembled with an overwhelming perturbation. He seemed utterly beside himself with horror.

"You can't arrest him!" he cried. "You can't arrest him! You mustn't!" His hands clutched at the sheriff.

There was no noise now in the living room. Burton Coffin's voice had silenced everyone, had created an involuntary tableau of all the spectators. I noticed Dr Harvey's awestruck face and, slightly in back of him, Joan, her skin like the petal of a gardenia, her gray eyes luminous with sympathy.

"You can't arrest him," repeated Burton Coffin loudly.

The sheriff had backed all the way into the library, evading Burton's hands. "Why can't we?" he demanded, finally coming to a halt.

His cue held in position for a one-cushion carom, his face politely interested, Colonel Black paused to watch the scene at the door.

Burton awkwardly pushed himself into the room and stood swaying in front of the sheriff. "You can't arrest him," he said, "because I cut off Uncle Tobias' head."

Completely startled, the sheriff took two quick steps backward. Mrs Coffin rushed into the room and seized her son's arm. "Burton, you can't . . ." Her voice fell away to silence. Colonel Black regretfully laid down his cue and asked:

"You mean you murdered Tobias Coffin, Burton?"

"I cut off his head, but he was dead already." He looked across at his father's dead-white face and repeated, "But he was dead already. Dead by his own hand." He drew a gasping, sobbing breath.

His composure regained, the sheriff demanded, "You expect us to believe you cut off his head without killing him?" He added fiercely, "You better get a better story than that."

Colonel Black came around the end of the billiard table. "But Bronson," he said. "Did you kill him?"

Burton's eyes sent another message to his father. I was unable to interpret it, but I thought I detected a note of assurance in it, a sort of a pledge. I had no idea what it meant.

"I don't know," he replied to the colonel's question. "But I must have."

"You don't know?"

"Yes. Yes. I do know." He passed his hand over his eyes. "I killed him. . . ."

Chapter *XVIII*

THE DEPUTY named Jeff and two others of the posse, which was still beating the woods for Mr Glunt, were summoned from the kitchen to take charge of George Coffin. He was removed to the pantry, the handcuffs fastened to his wrists.

"Don't let nobody talk with him," ordered the sheriff, closing the door between the library and the living room.

Burton Coffin, also handcuffed, was seated in the straight-backed chair his father had vacated. Some of the color had returned to his tan face, but he betrayed his nervousness by continually moistening his lips with his tongue. His eyes were half closed, as though the recent emotional strain had exhausted him.

"Now," said Colonel Black, fingering the red billiard ball, "will you tell us your story, or would you rather wait until we take you and your father to the county jail?"

"There's no reason to take my father." The whites of Burton's eyes showed. "He doesn't know anything about this. I'm the only one responsible."

"Then you want to tell us about it now?"

"I guess so." Burton moistened his lips and spoke in a low sullen voice. "I'll be glad to get it off my chest."

His story, told haltingly and with the help of questions from the colonel, seemed utterly incredible to me. I listened with growing amazement as the first part of it was related.

Burton had been awakened, he said, during the night of Uncle Tobias' murder by some sort of a noise. He didn't know what the noise was, but it had, in some mysterious subconscious manner, alarmed him. He had put on his bathrobe, gone out into the hall and had caught sight of the light coming from a crack in Uncle Tobias' door. Filled with wonder that Uncle Tobias should be up so late (it was nearly three o'clock) and desirous of learning whether he, too, had heard the noise, Burton had gone down and tapped on the door. There was no answer, and after half a minute he had tapped again. Still no answer. He had pushed the door open.

For a moment, he told us—his words coming faster now and his voice louder—he had had difficulty in keeping from yelling at the top of his lungs. Uncle Tobias lay dead across his desk, blood oozing from a bullet hole back of his right ear, a pistol grasped in his right hand. A suicide!

"A pistol?" exclaimed the sheriff, his voice rising. "A pistol, you say?"

"Let him continue," said Colonel Black.

Burton had rushed to the desk, he related, and confirmed his impression that Uncle Tobias was dead. His eyes, as he bent over the body, had caught sight of a note on the desk. It was under a bottle bearing a white label marked chloroform.

The colonel dropped the red billiard ball and said, "Damn!" Then he said, "Please go on."

The note had said, as well as he could remember it, that Uncle Tobias was tired with life and old age, that

he foresaw nothing but a gradual diminution of all his
faculties, that he feared his gastric ulcers might turn to
cancer and that he was going to end his life at this
gathering of the Coffin clan with an overdose of chloroform. At the bottom of this note, Burton said, was a
scribbled line which he remembered exactly:

"Chloroform makes me sick, will use gun instead."

After reading the note he had realized, Burton continued, that he must take some measures to prevent
Uncle Tobias' death from being regarded as suicide.

"Why?" demanded the sheriff.

"The insurance," said Burton with an air of surprise. "Didn't you know that the policy became invalid
in case of suicide?"

Colonel Black was frowning. "But what did you care
about the insurance? None of it goes to you."

"Miss Leslie," said Burton Coffin.

Suddenly the explanation of Burton's strange remarks about me to Joan, provided Burton's story was
true, came to me. He had said he was tired of doing my
"dirty work" for me. He had meant by that the removal
of the suicide evidence from Uncle Tobias' room, an act
which had placed him in considerable jeopardy and
which would, if successful, bring me one hundred thousand dollars. He had naturally felt it unfair that I,
whom he did not like, should benefit from an act meant
to help Miss Leslie.

"I don't make nothing of this," the sheriff was saying, "but go on."

He had first thought of removing the pistol, the note
and the chloroform to make it appear that Uncle Tobias
had been shot by someone, Burton proceeded, but he
had abandoned this idea when he saw the powder burns

on the side of Uncle Tobias' head. He knew the burns would make a smart detective think of suicide and in all probability cause the insurance company to hold up payment on the policy.

Then he had remembered the escaped madman and his penchant for chopping off people's heads, he said, and a plan, perfect in all details, had formed in his mind. He had hurried downstairs to the kitchen, taken the cook's meat cleaver, returned to the upstairs library and decapitated Uncle Tobias with it. Then he had made a bundle of the pistol, chloroform, rag and note, wrapped the head in a newspaper, thrust the cleaver under the silk tie cord of his dressing gown and returned to the pantry. The problem was to discover a good hiding place for these articles. He had been unable to think of a safe place in the house; the lake, too, seemed dangerous since the bottom is visible for hundreds of feet out on clear days; thus the only remaining choice was somewhere outside.

He had thought first of the woods, but when he had opened the pantry window and had crossed the lawn on his bare feet the strange, forbidding aspect of the trees, lighted grotesquely and fitfully by occasional flashes of lightning and filled with the mournful noise of the wind, had terrified him. A conviction had assailed him that the real madman was lurking in the woods, waiting for him and his burden. In a blind fright he had wandered out past the cow barn and into the small pasture. The earth, drenched by the heavy rain, had been soft at the foot of the big oak tree, and he had been able there to dig a deep hole with his cleaver. Into this hole he had placed the head, the pistol, the cleaver and the other things and had covered them with the loose earth.

Then he had raced back to the house and had gone to bed.

The sheriff was shaking his head in reluctant admiration. "Some story," he said. "How much do you believe, Colonel?"

"I'd like to believe it all," replied Colonel Black. "It 'd save the insurance company I represent a couple of hundred thousand dollars."

"Could I ask Burton a question?" I inquired of the colonel.

"Go ahead."

"Burton, did you know that the insurance money, under the terms of Uncle Tobias' new will, was given to Miss Leslie and myself to be used for scholarships, not for ourselves?"

"No!" He stared at me with an expression which changed from incredulity to despair. His chin sank down on his chest, his eyelids dropped over his eyes. His voice was hardly above a whisper. "No, I didn't know that. I thought a share was to go to Miss Leslie."

"Yeah," objected the sheriff, "but there ain't a new will. As far as I can see, you two get the money to do with as you please."

"My share of the money will be used as Uncle Tobias desired," I said, "and I believe Miss Leslie will do the same."

The colonel was smiling at me. "You seem to forget one thing. There won't be any money for either you or Miss Leslie if Burton is telling the truth."

"Well, it is the truth," said Burton sullenly.

"Perhaps so," agreed the colonel. "But now tell us how you killed Bronson and why."

"I didn't . . ." began Burton vehemently. Then he

hesitated, said, "I killed him because he knew I had cut off Uncle Tobias' head. I didn't want him to tell you about it."

"How did you know he knew?"

"He told Father that what he was going to tell you would affect me very materially. He wouldn't tell Father any more, and when Father asked me what it was all about I lied and said I didn't know. That's why I killed him."

"Good," said Colonel Black. "Now tell us how you killed him."

"I cut off his head with the cleaver."

"No. I mean how did you go about it? How did you get from this house to the servants' house without making tracks on the court?"

"I just walked over there. You must have overlooked my tracks."

"You'd better think of a better story than that. Even the sheriff will admit we couldn't have overlooked your tracks."

"All right," said Burton savagely. "I swam over then."

"You couldn't have done that," I objected. "Not in the time you were supposed to be down in the cellar." I spoke to the sheriff. "It would take twenty minutes to go down to the lake, take off your clothes, swim around to the servants' house, murder someone, hide the head, swim back, put on your clothes again and come back to the house."

"What's the matter with you?" Sheriff Wilson frowned at Burton. "You seem willing enough to admit you killed Bronson. Why don't you tell us how you got over there?"

"Isn't it enough for me to say I killed him?" retorted Burton angrily. "What do you care how I got over there?"

At this moment someone knocked on the door. It was the deputy, Jeff. His face was excited, and he had to swallow twice before he could speak. "This guy we got here," he began and then swallowed again. "This guy we . . ."

"Go on," said the sheriff.

"This guy we got in the kitchen says he done it."

"What?"

"Yeah, sure enough. He says he wants to confess, says his son is talking just to cover him up, and he won't have it. I thought I better tell you."

The sheriff turned helplessly toward the colonel, who said, "We might as well hear his story."

"All right, Jeff, bring him in," said the sheriff.

The deputy left hurriedly. Burton remained silent, but his eyes were apprehensive. The colonel's face was noncommittal, but the sheriff and I, I imagine, plainly showed the bewilderment we felt. The sheriff, indeed, went so far as to exclaim, "If this ain't the doggonest thing I'll eat my old straw hat!"

When George Coffin, his face composed, but very haggard, was brought into the library, Burton stood up and took two steps toward him.

"Don't say anything, Dad," he said. "Don't talk. I've already told them everything." The high pitch of his voice revealed jangled nerves.

His father faced him sadly. "I'm sorry you thought it necessary to do this, Burton," he said. "I am quite capable of paying the penalty for my crimes." He turned to the colonel, and his words came briskly. "Burton, through a mistaken sense of obligation to his father, has confessed to these murders which I committed. I can't allow him to shield me."

"Very fine of you, indeed, Mr Coffin," declared Colonel Black. "Very fine indeed. If the sheriff will have your son removed to the kitchen guardhouse we should like to hear your story."

Burton started to say something to his father, but the deputy, Jeff, jerked his arm and said, "Come on, buddy." They passed through the door.

In the interval the door was open I could see the rest of the family grouped together in the living room. In particular I noticed Joan's face, pale with sympathy for Burton. Suddenly her eyes met mine, and I was shocked to note a mixture of contempt and resentment in her glance. She stared at me until the door was closed. I realized with something like despair that she was holding me responsible for the arrest of the Coffins. Everything I managed to do, I thought with considerable self-pity, seemed to arouse an unfavorable emotion in Miss Leslie.

"Now, Mr Coffin," said the colonel, "let's have your story. It should be interesting, very interesting. It's not often a sleuth has two confessions for the same set of crimes."

The sheriff led George Coffin to the straight-backed chair. "Don't try nothing," he warned his prisoner.

"You'd better begin with the motive, Mr Coffin," suggested Colonel Black. "Motives are always so interesting."

"The motive is simple enough," replied George Coffin, speaking in a loud, assured voice. "I've lived half my life in the expectation of inheriting a large share of

Tobias' estate. When I heard he was going to make a new will, leaving a much smaller sum to my sister and me, I determined to kill him before he could put his plan into effect."

"You didn't know he had already made a new will, then?" the colonel demanded.

"I still don't," said my cousin. "You haven't seen it, have you?"

The colonel shook his head thoughtfully. "No. You didn't destroy it, did you?"

"Why should I tell you if I did?"

"You shouldn't." The colonel smiled pleasantly. "Now if you will be kind enough to outline your course of action?"

"That was simple too. I got the meat cleaver from the pantry and cut off Tobias' head. . . ."

"What gave you the idea of doing that?"

"The escaped madman. I thought the murder would be blamed on him."

The sheriff made a "tsk" noise with his tongue and teeth. "Everybody seemed to have that idea."

"I cut off Tobias' head. . . ." continued George Coffin.

"Did you notice anything curious about it?" interrupted Colonel Black.

"Why, no."

"How did you manage to cut off his head without arousing his suspicion?"

"He was asleep at his desk, his head lying on a mass of papers. It was an easy matter to creep in and strike him. He never woke."

"And what did you do with his head?"

"I walked down the shore and threw it into the lake. I expect the fish have it by this time."

"I doubt if this lake boasts any fish large enough to swallow a man's head," said the colonel, "but never mind, we can check on that later. Now I'd like to know why you were throwing food into the lake last night."

"I wanted to make it appear that the madman had actually paid the house another visit, so that Bronson's murder would be accounted for."

"That, at least, sounds reasonable enough," said the colonel, "Go on, please."

"Well, next came Bronson."

"Why?"

"He saw me carrying out Tobias' head. He threatened to tell the authorities unless I paid him twenty thousand dollars."

"Is that what you were talking to him about yesterday afternoon?" I asked.

"Yes. I agreed to pay him, but I knew that he would still be in a position to demand more. So I killed him."

"That was a logical way out," approved the colonel. "How did you manage it?"

"I agreed to meet him in the servants' house just before he was supposed to meet you. I was to pay him a thousand dollars as evidence of my good faith. I went over there, crept around to the back entrance and waited until Bronson was seated in a chair. Then I crept up behind him and cut his head off."

"You're a regular walking guillotine," marveled the colonel. "What did you do next?"

"I took his head and buried it by the oak tree in the small pasture and returned to the house."

"Very good," said the colonel. "Now I'm going to ask

you the question that seems to stop these confessions of murder. How did you manage to get from the main house to the servants' house and back without leaving any tracks in the courtyard?"

"That was easy."

"Easy!" exclaimed the colonel. "I don't think it's easy. I've been trying to figure out a way for many long hours."

"I took two boards from the pile in back of the house," explained George Coffin. "I laid one on the court, walked along it to the end, dropped the other, picked up the first board and continued my progress. No tracks and no muddy feet."

"But that's impossible. We would have seen the marks made by the boards."

George Coffin's manner was bored. "You would have if you hadn't laid a trail of boards to the servants' house yourself. You happened to lay them directly over the marks I made with my boards."

The colonel turned to the sheriff in consternation. "D'you suppose we could have done that?"

"I reckon so," admitted the sheriff. "We laid them boards on the most direct path to the servants' house."

"My goodness," said the colonel in a dismayed tone. "I had counted so much on discovering how the crossing was made, and now it doesn't do me any good."

"I don't see why it doesn't," argued the sheriff. "It makes this man's story stand up pretty well."

"It does, indeed, Sheriff Wilson, as far as Bronson's murder goes. But I don't believe Mr Coffin has grasped all the details of his uncle's murder. There's the matter of chloroform, for instance."

"Maybe Mister Tobias was drugged with chloroform

instead of being asleep, as Mr Coffin said," ventured the sheriff.

"I did smell a strong odor of chloroform," said George Coffin. "After the discovery of the body I pointed it out to Peter."

"Yes, he did," I said.

"But the bullet hole in your uncle's head, Mr Coffin? You could hardly have overlooked that?"

"There wasn't any bullet hole," said George Coffin. "You can't catch me with a trick like that."

"Perhaps not," agreed Colonel Black, turning his head toward the sheriff. "I think Mr Coffin might be sequestered somewhere for a time, away from his son. I should like to do some thinking."

The sheriff took George Coffin away. He was gone about ten minutes, and during that time the colonel did not say a word. He leaned against the billiard table, his face absolutely impassive. I leaned back in my chair, my face toward the bookcases, and thought about Joan. I wondered how she had such power to upset my mind and my stomach, to make me feel like a boy suffering from calf love. I was over thirty and too old for such nonsense, I said to myself.

But it didn't help. I was filled with the knowledge that Burton, if his story was true, had done a very courageous thing to save Joan Leslie's share of the insurance for her. I couldn't have done it. Surely she would be grateful to him.

Chapter *XIX*

BACKING HURRIEDLY into the library, the sheriff said, "I can't help it, ma'am. I'm just doing my duty, ma'am." He closed the door on Grace Coffin's angry face and wiped his forehead with a smudgy handkerchief.

"Whew!" he said.

"It's natural she should be agitated," I asserted, "with husband and son locked up."

The sheriff folded his handkerchief and put it in his hip pocket. "I don't blame her." He blinked his eyes at Colonel Black. "I reckon I'd better be taking them two over to the courthouse."

The colonel was staring at the black dot on the white cue ball. "I wish you could wait for a while," he said without raising his head. "I have a feeling I should have the solution to this business right now."

"Then you don't think George Coffin killed them?" asked the sheriff.

"I don't think he killed Tobias Coffin."

"Well, what about his son?"

"I don't think he killed Bronson."

"That seems to complicate things," I observed.

Colonel Black nodded. "It does."

"Look here." The sheriff's pale blue eyes glowed. "Why couldn't this be possible? Why couldn't George Coffin have killed Bronson to cover up his son's having killed Tobias Coffin? It 'd all work out that way."

I realized sickeningly that in all probability his solution was the correct one. It made everything fit into the picture. Bronson could have told George Coffin he knew Burton had murdered Tobias. And George, to protect his son, had killed Bronson, crossing the court by means of boards. He had not known, of course, that Tobias was already dead by his own hand when Burton cut off his head. It was a dreadful solution.

Bright light from the green-shaded lamps above the billiard table made the colonel's face pale. "I'm terribly afraid you're right, Sheriff Wilson," he said.

"You're darn right I am," agreed the sheriff. "And it ain't as terrible as it might be. We'll get George Coffin, all right, but I guess it 'll be hard to pin much on his son. I don't suppose it's much of a crime to cut the head off a person already dead." He rubbed his hands together in triumph. "I don't mind letting him go as long as the chloroform, the gunpowder on the collar and the bullet hole in the head—if we find it—prove he didn't kill his great-uncle."

"Yes, but do they?" asked the colonel.

"Well, I reckon a meat cleaver don't leave a gunpowder mark," said the sheriff with indignation.

The colonel laid down the billiard ball. "It's all very confusing. Very confusing. Yet I suppose it is reasonable to want to lock the two Coffins in your jail, Sheriff."

"Sure it's reasonable. I got their confessions, haven't I?"

"Yes, you have. But in a court two confessions are not better than one; not if they're to the same crime."

While the sheriff was thinking about this someone pounded at the door. I opened it, disclosing the dark, heavy-set deputy who was with the sheriff on the night George Coffin and I had been searching for Uncle Tobias' head.

"We've seen Glunt," he announced excitedly. "You better come, Sheriff."

"Where?" The sheriff jumped for the door. "Where is he?"

"Half a mile down the lake," said the dark deputy. "Come on."

"Tell those other fellows to watch the prisoners," the sheriff called to us. "I'll be back as soon as we get Glunt." He ran off, the deputy on his heels.

The colonel and I walked out into the living room. I felt very apprehensive as to what sort of a reception I would receive from my relatives after my information had caused the arrest of both George and Burton Coffin, but Joan was the only person to meet us.

Her face was worried, but I was relieved to see she showed no contempt for me. "What have you decided?" she asked us.

"The sheriff has decided to lock them up," replied the colonel.

"Yes, but you?"

"Nothing." The colonel shook his head slowly from side to side. "Nothing."

I was peering out the french windows toward the lake. It seemed to me that I could see, far to the right, a light. "I wonder what progress they're making with Glunt," I said.

Joan turned the radio switch. "We'll see. I think the state police are being mobilized."

There was a crackle of static, then a man's voice came from the loud-speaker. "Car 231 proceed to Mann's general store on Highway 22 and watch road for all pedestrians." The voice was loud and high pitched, and the words were spoken rapidly. "Car 231 proceed to Mann's general store on Highway 22 and watch road for all pedestrians."

I recognized the voice as the one which had puzzled me on the night of my arrival. Obviously it was a mobilization of the state police by short wave, for other cars were directed to take up other positions near Crystal Lake. As the voice continued I visualized a huge net of police being thrown about us, with the sheriff and his posse acting as beaters, trying to flush Glunt into the hands of the troopers. The thought was comforting.

The colonel moved restlessly. "Let's go outdoors and see what progress is being made in the hunt," he suggested.

As we went out onto the veranda I asked Joan, "What's happened to everybody?"

"They're upstairs in the study. Dr Harvey is trying to reach an attorney in New York by telephone."

Now from the vantage point of the veranda we could see many lights pin-pointing the darkness to the right. They were spread over a large area in the shape of a semicircle, and they seemed to be moving in our direction. Their effect was artificial, like yellow drops of paint on the purple backdrop of a theater.

I asked Joan, "Why aren't you upstairs with the others?"

"I wanted to see what you and the colonel were going to do."

"The colonel and I!" I exclaimed, amazed. "I don't do anything." I felt strangely gratified.

The reflected light from one of the windows outlined the soft curve of her jaw. "You've found nearly everything of importance in this affair," she said. "And I think you and the colonel will do Mr Coffin and Burton more good than any lawyer."

The colonel spoke. "I wish you were right, Miss Leslie."

"Then you don't think they're . . . ?"

"No, I don't. But proving it is another matter."

"You don't think either of them had anything to do with the murders?" I asked.

"I don't think they're both guilty."

"Oh." Joan's voice was flat. "But you think one of them is guilty?"

"I don't know," said the colonel wearily.

The part of the circle of lights by the lake had been curved in, so that the figure now appeared to be a huge question mark. A soft breeze, blowing from the south, was threaded with the faint sound of voices. Overhead, stars filled the sky.

Colonel Black turned toward me. "How long has your great-uncle raised Jersey cattle?" he asked.

"Why," I said, surprised, "for years. As far back as I can remember. He once had some valuable bulls, too, but he recently gave up breeding."

"Let's take a look at the cows. I'd like to see some fine cattle—that is if there are lights in the barn?"

"There are," I said.

"Won't you come along with us, Miss Leslie?"

"Yes." Her gray eyes were wondering. "But don't you think you ought to——"

"No, I don't." The colonel smiled. "I'd like to look at cows now."

We crossed the lawn and the clay court and entered the barn. There was a sweet odor of hay and clover. I found the light switch. The cows looked at us without surprise through their luminous eyes.

"They live in style, don't they?" observed the colonel. He cautiously approached one of the cows and stroked her dish-shaped face. "So, bossy," he said.

The cow continued to chew her cud.

"The cow's an interesting animal," said the colonel. "It has resisted all efforts to change its productivity for two thousand years."

I was about to say, "Is that so?" when Mr Bundy came in the front entrance of the barn.

"Oh, it's you, Mister Peter," he said. "I was afraid someone was harming my cows." The apprehension left his round pink face.

"We were simply admiring them, Mr Bundy," said the colonel.

"They're a lovely herd," agreed Mr Bundy. "Never seen better markings or better show points."

"Yes, but milk. How much milk do they give, Mr Bundy?"

Mr Bundy's tone showed that he thought milk to be a minor consideration in forming an estimate of a herd of cows. "They give all we can use and then some," he said.

"Well, that's pretty good for seven cows." The colonel's voice had a note of sarcasm. "But how much milk?"

"The best is Lady Cleo here. She produced fourteen thousand pounds of milk last year."

"That's not bad." The colonel glanced admiringly at the silver-dun back of Lady Cleo. "What was the percentage of butterfat?"

"Better than five percent. The whole herd averaged better than five percent."

"Whew!" The colonel moved over to take a closer look at Lady Cleo. "That's remarkable."

"Mr Coffin was always very careful about his sires," said Mr Bundy, following the colonel.

"A wonderful cow," said the colonel. "A wonderful cow. Is she the one your boy is accustomed to ride?"

"Yes sir. He's been around her ever since she was a calf."

"Remarkable." The colonel bent over Lady Cleo and ran his hand along her back. A few loose hairs appeared. The colonel gathered them in his hand. "Do you mind if I keep these, Mr Bundy?"

"Gosh, no." Mr Bundy's eyes were round. "I can get you a lot more if you want them."

"No. These will do very nicely, thank you." The colonel took an envelope from an inside pocket and dropped the hairs in it. "Quite a trophy, don't you think?" he asked me.

"If you care for hair," I said.

"Oh, I do. Definitely." He swung around on Mr Bundy. "What do you think of the Mount Hope Index?"

"Mr Coffin thought it was excellent," said Mr Bundy. "He thinks—I mean, thought—that its use would be a big factor in raising the quantity and quality of milk in this country."

"It is an interesting way of determining the inheritance of milk and butterfat production which a bull transmits to his daughters, if not entirely accurate," said the colonel.

He launched into an involved explanation as to why the index could not be perfectly accurate, throwing scientific terms by the score at the bewildered Mr Bundy.

"Let's go out and see how the hunt is coming along," I whispered to Joan.

As we went out the barn door into the night I heard the colonel saying, "As you know, Mr Bundy, there are nineteen pairs of chromosomes in cattle, and thus the possible number of combinations among chromosomes is almost five hundred and twenty-five thousand. But in addition there are genes in the chromosome, so our possible combinations rise to an . . ."

His voiced faded into silence as we neared the lake. We looked to the right and saw the lights were only slightly closer to the house. The posse was moving slowly.

"He's a strange man," commented Joan. "Why is he so interested in cows at a time like this?"

"I don't know. I'm almost inclined to believe he's a trifle . . ."

"So am I," she said.

We halted by the lake shore. The night was mild, and the wind from the south was soft and fragrant. The moving air caressed our hands and faces and rustled the leaves on the trees over our heads. On the lake, in a patch of still water, were reflected stars.

"Please don't feel too badly toward me because of

George Coffin," I said. "I wish now I hadn't mentioned having seen him throw that food into the lake."

"It was the only thing you could do. It was your duty."

"I don't care so much about duty."

"I'm glad of that. But if Mr Coffin killed your great-uncle, then he deserves to be caught."

"But I don't think he did kill him."

"Then you think Burton . . . ?"

"I almost believe his story."

"You mean that your great-uncle was dead when he found him?"

"Yes. A suicide."

She pondered over my words for a moment. "I hope, for his sake, you're right."

"But don't you believe Burton's story?"

"Yes. Yes, I suppose I do. But it seems such a horrible thing—to cut off even a dead person's head."

"He did it for you, you know."

"I know." Her voice quavered. "But I wish he hadn't. It seems so brutal."

The wind carried to our ears a distant noise of shouting. The lights, flickering as they moved through the trees, were in a half circle again.

"Joan," I said, "do you care very much for Burton?"

"I like him very much."

"Do you love him?"

"Why do you ask?"

Even in the dark my voice trembled. "I ask because —because—well, darn it, because I'm interested in you," I blurted out.

Like a purple cloak of some soft material the night hung over the lake, wound itself about the trees. The

wind uttered a faint sigh. A few dry leaves ran along
the shore. Seconds passed, and I wished with increasing
fervor I had now spoken. What a clumsy dolt I was!
What a bumpkin! This was no way to speak to a girl of
love: to speak of it as though it were an unpleasant confession. What would the Earl of Rochester think of me?

Then she spoke, her voice strangely husky. "I do like
Burton." I could just make out her face in the darkness.
It was like a cameo, heart shaped and cut out of pale
ivory.

I felt relief that she was not angry. But, like a man
who is proceeding in a direction he knows is indiscreet
but is unable, through some quirk of character, to
change his course, I persisted. "And I?" I asked. "Have
I any chance for consideration as a suitor?"

She hesitated, then replied softly, "I have already
considered you." There was the faintest suggestion of
humor in her tone.

"And the result of your consideration?"

"Don't you think it's a bit early for conclusions?"

"It seems as though I had known you all my life instead of three days."

"When we do know each other better, perhaps . . ."

"Perhaps what?" I said eagerly.

"Perhaps"—I knew she must be smiling—"perhaps
you won't like me as well." Suddenly she grasped my
arm. "Who is that?"

She drew me around so that I was facing the house.
The change in her tone, from a mocking note to one of
real terror, made my hair stand on end. I peered into
the darkness. Someone was coming around the house
from the forest side to the front steps. Reflected rays
from the lights in the house dimly outlined the figure,

which moved with a painful hesitancy, shoulders hunched and one leg half dragging, as though from some crippling wound.

I cast a quick glance at the lights of the sheriff's posse. They were still far down the lake. No help there. I started toward the house.

Joan's hand was still on my arm. "Wait," she whispered. "I believe it's Mrs Spotswood."

She was right. The figure came into the shaft of light cast across the lawn by the french windows in the living room, and I saw that it was Mrs Spotswood. "Walking," I breathed. "Walking!"

There was something incomparably sinister, almost evil, in her slow progress up the long stairs. She looked, with her bent body, her frail shoulders covered by a shawl, her weird limp, like the hags I had seen moving about late at night in London's back streets. She finally climbed the last step and pulled an object toward her from the shadowed portion of the veranda. It was her wheel chair. She allowed herself to sink back in its embrace, then, moving quickly, she passed into the house.

"Whew!" I exclaimed.

Joan's hand tightened on my arm. "Peter! Perhaps that's how Bronson was killed."

"How do you mean?"

"Don't you see?" Her voice was excited. "That's the way the court could have been crossed. In the wheel chair. There wouldn't have been any footmarks."

"Gosh!" I pressed her hand. "Maybe you're right." I tried to think what we should do. "We better find the colonel."

"I'll look in the house," she said. "You see if he's still in the barn."

We separated. Hurrying toward the barn, I endeavored to picture Mrs Spotswood as the murderer. Could she have killed Uncle Tobias? She might easily have a motive, I thought. She might want the money left her in the will. Or she might have hated Uncle Tobias. She had lived with him many years. Maybe she thought he should have married her. Or perhaps——

"Peter! Peter! *Peter!*"

My name, uttered in a voice vibrant with fright, resounded in my ears. It was Joan's voice. I turned and raced back toward the front of the house.

Joan was standing in the center of the lawn, slightly nearer the lake than the house. Between her and the house was a man. My heart stopped beating. It was the madman. I couldn't see his face, but the manner in which he held his head tilted toward the sky was unmistakable. There was something round clutched in his arms, and he was advancing slowly upon Joan.

I felt an impulse to shout for help, but my brain warned me a sudden noise might frighten the madman into an attack upon Joan. Besides, the sheriff's posse, still beating the forest at the end of the lake, was beyond the range of a shout.

I hurdled a rosebush and came to a stop by Joan's side. "Oh, Peter," she whispered in terror, "who is it?"

The madman had halted now, and I could see his face. He was frowning, and his lips were moving. "You can't take it," he muttered. "You can't." His arms were wound about the round object.

For an instant Joan's hand rested in mine. Her touch bespoke her confidence in me. I felt a sensation of exultation. She really didn't believe I was a coward. I squeezed her hand and stepped between her and the madman.

"We've been looking for you, Mr Glunt," I said in a conversational tone.

The madman's eyes, which had been raised toward the sky, suddenly bored into mine. There was a glow back of the pupils: they were like those of an animal at night. There was death in his eyes, inexorable and immediate.

Chill terror seized me; my blood turned to water, my bones dissolved, my muscles lost their strength, my stomach seemed to be frozen. I felt a dreadful impulse to run at top speed from this crouching figure. Yet I was unable to move, held in my tracks as if under a hypnotic spell.

For what must have been seconds, but what seemed like minutes, we stood facing each other. I struggled to master my fear. My mind was a tumult of conflicting thoughts and sensations. I could hear the wind in the trees, the murmur of water. I thought thankfully that Joan could not see the fright imprinted on my face. I was conscious of a heavy odor from a bed of tiger lilies. I noticed the night was colder.

Then the madman moved a step in my direction, centering my attention upon him. There could be no doubt he intended to attack me. He had dropped, with his step, the object in his hands, and his arms hung at his sides. He was dressed as he had been the night of my arrival—in a shirt and trousers. His feet were bare and stained with mud; his arms and face were a network of cuts and scratches, sustained going through the underbrush. Under the shreds of his shirt I could see bulky muscles.

He shambled forward another pace. I could hear

Joan catch her breath. His eyes were still fixed on mine; he had assumed a half-crouching posture, like a wrestler; he was waiting for me to move.

Suddenly a sense of inevitability struck me, as it must strike everyone confronted with death, and my confusion vanished. I was still afraid, but who save the very old or the very tired is not afraid in the presence of death? I made up my mind to throw myself upon him and hold him until Joan had time to escape to the house.

He advanced another step. His lips were moving; he was saying, "Oh, my heads. My poor hurting heads." His voice was high.

Something stirred in my memory. The high, absurd voice made me recall what he had been chanting that night on the path, his face joyous.

I spoke slowly, distinctly. "A tisket, a tasket," I said, "a green and yellow basket. A tisket, a tasket, a green and yellow basket." I forced a grin on my face.

What followed was as unreasonable as a nightmare. The expression of watchful concentration faded from the madman's face. He straightened up abruptly. His expression became ecstatic.

"A tisket, a tasket?" he said in an inquiring tone.

"A green and yellow basket," I replied.

With a single bound he was by my side. He grasped my hand, swung my arm, started to skip across the lawn. I followed, also skipping. We chanted as we skipped, "A tisket, a tasket, a green and yellow basket," repeating this absurd verse again and again.

As we made a circuit of the lawn I caught sight of Joan's face, expressing wondering horror.

I found I could direct our course by exerting pressure on the madman's arm. His hand in mine was slick with sweat. I pulled him toward the front steps of the house. We moved in that direction, bounding through a bed of zinnias and along the path of half-buried stones, still chanting our verse. His grasp was like that of a small child, his face entranced, joyous. We leaped up the veranda steps, skipped through the front door of the house.

It is not too much to say that our entrance created a prodigious sensation among the group of my relatives gathered in front of the living-room fire. They were actually struck stupid with wonder. Not one of them, even Dr Harvey, had sense enough to help me or to be frightened. Even the women weren't frightened. They just stared at us, eyes wide at this ineffable occurrence.

Still guided more by my subconscious mind than by an orderly process of reasoning, I led the madman past my relatives into the dining room, through the pantry, into the kitchen. I released his hand, pranced to the electric icebox and, chanting "A tisket, a tasket, nice food from the basket," brought out milk, part of a roast leg of lamb, potatoes and half a pie. I placed these on the metal table, drew up a chair and said, "Eat."

He fell upon the food like a starved animal. He drank the milk noisily, in great gulps; shoved whole potatoes in his mouth; chewed on the leg. Occasionally he would raise his eyes to mine like a grateful animal.

While I was watching him eat, still apprehensive, two men came in the pantry door. One of them was the sheriff. He looked frightened, and he halted in the doorway. The other was a thick-set, middle-aged man with level eyes and a firm jaw. "Well, Elmer," he said, smiling at the madman, "you certainly led us a merry chase."

The madman giggled proudly, continued to eat.

The thick-set man drew up a chair and seated himself beside the madman. He fastened a handcuff on his left wrist. "Go ahead and eat, Elmer," he said. "Plenty of time." He turned to me. "Thank you very much, Mr Coffin. You handled him just like a professional."

As I went into the living room, feeling now very frightened and sick, the radio spoke matter-of-factly:

"Attention, all cars. Madman Glunt recaptured. Return to your posts. All cars, return to your posts. . . ."

Chapter XX

I WENT UPSTAIRS to wash. I wanted to get the sticky feel of the madman off my hands. In the hall by my door I met Joan. Her face was as pale as a gardenia.

"Thanks for being so quick in summoning the sheriff and the captain of the asylum guards," I said. "Another minute in that kitchen would have done for me."

"It wasn't anything," she said.

"It saved me from a collapse. I was frightened enough as it was."

"I think you were marvelous."

"I was frightened."

"You were marvelous."

My heart began to beat faster at her insistence. The tone of her voice, too, was warm. I said, "You know, you never did answer the question I asked you by the lake."

"The question?"

"The question as to whether I deserve consideration as a suitor."

Her smile was half mocking, half tender. "Only the brave deserve the fair."

My heart sank. She had once called me a coward. "And you don't think I'm brave?" I suggested.

She moved slowly past me toward the stairs. "I'm

beginning to think," she called over her shoulder, "that you're the bravest man I ever met."

I watched her vanish down the stairs, a warm glow invading my veins. Could that mean she liked me? I went into my room and leaned on the bureau and peered into the mirror. Would my face attract a girl? I had never considered my appearance in this light before, and I was forced to confess, after a brief examination of my features, that Hollywood would never offer me a fabulous sum to appear in motion pictures. My skin was good, and my eyes were all right, but one of my eyebrows was arched more than the other, giving me an expression of waggishness, if not of insobriety. My jaw was fair, but my lips were crooked, and my nose was larger than it should have been. Definitely I was not handsome.

On the other hand, I was not altogether unattractive. Several co-eds at college had signified their interest in me, and there was Susan Briggs, the associate professor of biology, who had held my hand all during a symphony concert. Maybe Joan Leslie was the sort of . . .

"Peter!"

Startled, I drew back convulsively from the mirror, knocking off the silver vase I had taken from the mantel above the fireplace in my great-uncle's study.

"Sorry to disturb you," said Colonel Black from the doorway, "but I'd like to have you look at something."

"I'll be glad to look at it," I said. "Where is it?"

"In my room."

The colonel vanished, and I bent over to pick up the vase. As I lifted it from the floor a roll of paper fell out. The roll was composed of three sheets of fine bond paper, held together by a metal clip. The first sheet began, "I, Tobias Coffin, being in sound mind and body, do . . ."

Quickly I examined a paragraph on the second page. It began, "And to my nephew, Peter Nebuchadnezzar Coffin, I bequeath Graymere, my country estate at Crystal Lake, Michigan; including in said bequest all . . ."

It was the missing will. The new will! And it had been in my room all the time. I rushed to the colonel with it. "Look," I started to say as I reached his door, then halted in surprise.

There were trousers, at least twenty-five pairs, of all description strewn about the floor of his room. There were gray, brown, black, blue, green trousers. There were tweed trousers, cotton trousers, linen trousers, dress-suit trousers. The colonel stood ankle deep in trousers, and on his table, under a bright lamp, were a pair of Oxford-gray trousers. He was examining them through a magnifying glass.

"Colonel," I exclaimed, "I have found the missing will!"

"Excellent," he said without looking up from his microscope. His voice betrayed no surprise.

"But I've also found an important clue," I added.

He glanced up this time. "But I have found the murderer," he said calmly. "Or rather—his trousers."

The colonel leaned against the big table in the center of the living room, the trousers hanging over his arm. The sheriff had called a meeting, and everyone in the family and in the household, too, with the exception of Mrs Spotswood, was present. Both George and Burton Coffin, their wrists fastened by steel chains to burly deputies, were on hand, as was the asylum attendant who had taken charge of the madman. His name was Captain Marvin Anderson. He had sent Glunt on to the hospital in Traverse City.

"If Glunt had Mister Tobias' head," the sheriff was saying, "it's proof, ain't it, that he killed him?"

So the round object the madman dropped was my great-uncle's head!

"I think not," said Colonel Black. "He told Captain Anderson he found it, and I see no reason why he should have lied." He turned to the heavy-jawed captain. "I believe he led you to the place where the head had been hidden and showed you the other things concealed there?"

The captain prodded a wooden box with his toe. "Yeah, he did. And here's the junk we found."

Carefully the colonel laid the contents of the box on a newspaper. There was a bloodstained meat cleaver; a bottle marked "chloroform"; a revolver; a stained handkerchief with my great-uncle's initials, T. C., on it, and a piece of paper headed: "To Whom It May Concern."

The colonel picked up the paper between his thumb and forefinger and read:

" 'I have never let Fate master me, nor do I intend to start now. Yet Fate seems to be aiming at my mastery through my stomach.' "

"Ulcers," interrupted Dr Harvey. "Ulcers which stood a good chance of developing into cancer."

The colonel continued to read:

" 'I have five, perhaps ten, years to live, but they will not be pleasant years. Money, authority, possessions are of little value without health. I would rather leave these things to those who can enjoy them. I can think

of no better time to do so than when my family is
present.

"'And, too, in killing myself I shall defeat Fate. I
shall name the time and manner of my death instead of
having them named for me.

"'TOBIAS COFFIN.'"

The colonel paused, then said, "There's a postscript.
It reads:

"'This chloroform makes me sick. I'll name a revolver
instead. Fate be damned!'"

Mrs Coffin drew a gasping breath. She looked smaller
now, and much older. "But that fits Burton's story!"
she exclaimed. "You'll have to release him."

"Not until we find out who killed Bronson, ma'am,"
said the sheriff firmly.

"I killed him," said Burton, "just as I said."

George Coffin said, "No, he didn't. He doesn't know
how he crossed the court without tracks. I killed Bronson."

Mrs Coffin gasped. I was afraid she was going to
faint, and I moved nearer to her and took hold of her
arm.

"Where I come from," said the sheriff, giving them
both angry glances, "it's a crime to lie about a murder."

"Perhaps legally," said Colonel Black, "but you
know what Confucius said of the moral aspect of the
question, don't you, Sheriff Wilson?"

The sheriff stared at him blankly, and the colonel
said:

"Once the Duke of She spoke to Confucius, saying:
'We have an upright man in our country. His father
stole a sheep, and his son bore witness against him.'

" 'In our country,' Confucius replied, 'uprightness is something different from this. A father hides the guilt of his son, and a son hides the guilt of his father. It is in such conduct that true uprightness is to be found.' "

For the first time since he had been arrested I noted a glint of interest in George Coffin's eyes. He raised his face to the colonel in a long appraisal. There was a faint trace of color in his cheeks.

"I don't know about your dukes and so on," said the sheriff, "but I'm thinking that the evidence fits Burton's story to a T. I bet he did murder Bronson. He found his great-uncle dead by his own hand and wanted to save the insurance for his girl here." He jerked his thumb at Joan. "So he hid the suicide evidence. But when he knew Bronson had seen him hide it he killed him."

Colonel Black was fascinatedly testing the edge of the meat cleaver with his thumb. "The only fault with your theory, Sheriff," he said, "is that Tobias Coffin was murdered."

Like an echo in a deserted house the word "murdered" was repeated from all sides.

"Murdered!" exclaimed Burton Coffin.

"Murdered?" queried the sheriff.

"Murdered," whispered George Coffin as though he had known it already.

I looked at Joan. She was staring at Burton, fear in her eyes. Mrs Harvey had Mrs Coffin's other arm, so I released my arm and walked to Joan. She turned a white face to me.

"Could Burton have . . . ?" she asked.

"No."

She clasped my hand. "I'm so glad. I wouldn't want to be responsible for . . ."

She let her hand remain in mine.

The sheriff had recovered his composure. "How could it be murder?" he asked angrily. "You got powder marks on his collar, there's a bullet hole in his head, and there's the suicide note. Dr Harvey says it's in Mr Coffin's handwriting."

"It does resemble Tobias Coffin's handwriting," agreed the colonel, "and only an expert will be able to tell whether or not it is a forgery. But the note has little to do with the fact that Mr Coffin was murdered."

"I should think it 'd have everything to do with it."

"No. The chloroform's the thing. You remember the expert testified at the inquest that a large quantity of chloroform was present in Mr Coffin's lungs—enough to render him unconscious?"

The sheriff nodded.

"Well, how could an unconscious man shoot himself?"

The sheriff's mouth dropped open. Everyone was giving the colonel complete attention now.

"I might as well tell you the entire story," said the colonel. "I have it pretty well in my mind."

"And you know who killed Mr Coffin and who killed Bronson?" asked the sheriff.

"Yes. The same man killed them both. Shall I go on?"

"And you know how he crossed the court?"

"Yes. An amazing device."

"Who was it?"

"Wait. I'd like to outline the story of the murders first."

"All right." The sheriff sat down at one end of the davenport to the right of the fireplace. "Shoot." His tone sounded as though he was prepared to disbelieve everything the colonel had to say.

The colonel was still toying with the meat cleaver. "Our story opens the night Tobias Coffin was murdered," he began. "On that same night Elmer Glunt, who had cut off the heads of his wife and children, escaped from his guards while on the way to the state asylum.

"These two events are strangely connected.

"Mr Coffin had invited his family to come to Graymere to hear of the changes he had made in his will. I believe it was well known to everyone, with the exception of Peter Coffin, that he was going to leave the bulk of his property to the younger members of the family rather than to the older, as he had once intended."

The colonel glanced at George Coffin, who nodded interestedly. Everyone, indeed, was interested. I imagine the same thought was in all minds. Who could the murderer be? Was he, or she, in the room?

The colonel continued:

"This, then, is our setting. The murderer decides that the time is ripe to strike. He has something to gain by Tobias Coffin's immediate death."

I thought, "There is nothing pointing at anyone in particular here. Any one of us might have wanted to kill Tobias: some to destroy the new will, some to prevent its ever being changed." I wondered of the colonel had the same answer as I.

"So he went up to Mr Coffin's study after the household was asleep," the colonel went on, "and overpowered him with a chloroformed handkerchief. He had the suicide note already written, even the postscript, and after Tobias Coffin was completely unconscious he waited for a burst of thunder and shot him through the head. The noise of the thunder, of course, covered the sound of the revolver.

"Then the murderer arranged the body so that it would appear to be a suicide. He put the bottle of chloroform and the handkerchief on the desk, laid the note on the blotter and placed the revolver in Mr Coffin's right hand, bending the arm so that the muzzle was pointed directly back of the right ear, where the shot had entered."

Vividly I recalled the position of the body across the table. The arm had been bent in just that manner. From the expression on George Coffin's face I could see he recalled it too.

"But something happened to disarrange the murderer's plan," continued the colonel. "Burton Coffin, having seen the light in the study, came to investigate. When Burton's footstep sounded in the hall the murderer was examining the new will. Quickly he thrust it in a vase on the mantel, fearing that whoever was coming would catch him with it, and darted into Tobias Coffin's bedroom.

"Without the will he was fairly safe, for he could say, if caught, that he, too, had been awakened by a noise from the study and had come to investigate.

"But he wasn't caught. Burton entered the room an instant later and discovered his great-uncle. Naturally after reading the note and seeing the revolver and the chloroform he believed it to be suicide. As he says, the thought of the insurance, half of which he knew went to Miss Leslie, came to him. He knew that suicide would void the policy.

"He acted at once to conceal the suicide. He remembered Peter's account of his encounter with the madman and the scare the madman had given the household when he tried to break in. So he went downstairs and took Mrs Bundy's meat cleaver and with it cut off Tobias' head."

Joan's hand grasped mine convulsively.

"Then, followed by the murderer, he went out of the house with the head and all the evidence of suicide and buried them at the base of the tree in the pasture back of the barn." The colonel glanced at Burton. "He thought he was unobserved, but both the murderer and Bronson, from his window in the servants' house, saw him. Of course at the time Bronson had no idea what Burton was doing."

There was a click at the end of the living room, and Mrs Spotswood emerged from the elevator. I felt a thrill of horror at the sight of her wrinkled, inscrutable face with its deep-set, burning eyes. She glided noiselessly across the room, halting the wheel chair back of Mrs Bundy, who stood with her husband and Karl Norberg. Joan's hand, as she looked at the old woman, tightened on mine.

"Mrs Spotswood," the colonel said, "I have been explaining how Mr Coffin was murdered and how Burton cut off his head to make the death appear to have been the work of the madman."

Mrs Spotswood's voice was like the dry rustle of leaves. "I knew he was murdered," she said. "I have been looking for the will." There was no expression on her face.

"Well, to continue"—the colonel's voice sounded flat—"you found the body just as Burton, followed by the murderer, had returned to the house. Your scream aroused Peter and prevented the murderer from returning to the study and taking the will from the vase.

"Later, when everyone was in the room, the murderer looked for the vase, but Peter had taken it for a weapon. After everyone had gone to bed the murderer returned to the study to look for the vase. He thought possibly it was somewhere in the room. His light was seen by Norberg and the deputy left on guard duty, and with Peter they burst into the room. In leaving the room the murderer hit Peter with a poker.

"I don't know if this was a deliberate attempt to kill, but I think it was."

After gazing for several moments at the meat cleaver, which he still held in his hand, the colonel resumed his story.

"The searching of the various rooms thereafter, including the attack on Burton, was the work of the murderer. In the meantime Bronson let it be known that he knew something connected with the crime, perhaps even the identity of the culprit. He knew that Burton had buried the head and the suicide evidence, but the murderer was afraid that Bronson knew about him.

"So after dinner on the night of my arrival he crossed the court in the most remarkable manner imaginable (really, the trip was a stroke of genius), secured the cleaver from its hiding place and cut off poor Bronson's head."

Drawing a gasp of horror from the women, the colonel made a slicing movement of the cleaver in the air.

"Then, after he had hidden the head and the cleaver with the other head by the tree he returned to the house."

Sheriff Wilson's small eyes were alert. "Very good story," he said, "but you haven't told us how the murderer crossed the court yet."

The colonel eyed the people in the room. He glanced at me, at Mrs Spotswood, at Dr Harvey, George Coffin, Mr Bundy, Dan Harvey, Joan. For the first time he looked really dangerous. He looked like a cat ready to spring. A muscle in his jaw quivered.

"First," he said slowly, "I should like to name the murderer."

"Why, sure," said the sheriff. "Go ahead."

I noticed with a touch of amusement the expression on the face of Captain Anderson, the chief of the asylum guards. It was an expression of mingled amazement and incredulity. His heavy jaw had fallen down, and he stared at the colonel through bulging eyes.

"The man I'd like to name," the colonel said, "is Dr Thaddeus Harvey."

Despite the fact that this announcement did not come as a surprise to me I was unable to observe the reactions of everyone to the colonel's words. This was due partly to the relief I felt in having the name spoken at last and partly to the widely diverse nature of the reactions. Both George Coffin and his son were unmoved, their faces, if anything, apprehensive, as though they feared some trick. Mrs Harvey paled, and Joan left me to go to her side, but she didn't faint. The two younger Harveys gazed at their father in alarm.

"Dr Harvey," repeated the sheriff. "Dr Harvey?"

The doctor shook himself like a fox terrier. His eyes glowed angrily, his face flushed. "What sort of nonsense is this?" he cried.

"Then you don't care to admit you're guilty of both murders?" asked the colonel dangerously.

"Don't care to admit——" Dr Harvey was for the moment unable to speak.

The sheriff, his face worried, said, "Don't you think you ought to wait until . . ."

Colonel Black ignored him, spoke to the doctor. "Who beside you would have chloroform in the house?" he demanded.

"Why you mountebank! You cheap fourflusher!" Dr Harvey's voice was shrill with rage. "Trying to put this on me. Don't you know it's slander? I'll have you kept in jail for the rest of your life for this."

The colonel shrugged his shoulders. "As Juvenal said, 'Nihil est audacius illis deprensis; iram atque animos a crimine sumunt.' " He translated for the sheriff. "Nothing is bolder than they who are detected; they assume anger and spirit because they are detected."

If it was the colonel's object to enrage Dr Harvey he succeeded beyond all expectation. The doctor was struck dumb with anger; he was unable to do anything but shake his fist at the colonel.

The sheriff was still dubious. "But what proof have you, Colonel?" he asked.

"Plenty."

"Bah!" exclaimed Dr Harvey.

The colonel stared coldly at him. "Have you ever seen the new will drawn by Mr Coffin, Doctor?"

"No. Why should I have seen it?"

"You've never touched it?"

"No."

"Then why did you ask Peter Coffin what had become of the vase in Mr Coffin's study?"

I looked at the colonel with admiration. Dr Harvey's interest in the vase was what had given him away to me as soon as I had discovered the will. How clever of the colonel to see it too!

The doctor hesitated for an instant. Some of the crimson color faded from his face. "Did I ask him that?"

"Yes, you did," I said. "When you and George and I were in Uncle Tobias' room—just before the sheriff came."

"Perhaps I did if Peter says so. I presume I must have seen that it was gone from the mantel."

The colonel laid the cleaver on the table and took a paper from his pocket. "And you didn't know that the will was in the vase?"

"Of course not."

"Then how do your fingerprints happen to be on it?"

Dr Harvey was silent.

"Naturally you wanted to destroy the new will," said Colonel Black. "You wanted the money for yourself, not for your children. And the only way you could make sure of this was to kill Mr Coffin and then destroy the will. Too bad you hadn't time that night."

The doctor's teeth were bared in a sneer. "You have a fine imagination."

"You don't imagine fingerprints." The colonel's voice was soft. "Nor does Bronson's murder come under the heading of fancy."

"Well, how do you get me across that court without wings?" asked the doctor.

"I ride you across."

"Ride?" asked the sheriff.

"Yes. On Lady Cleo, the leader of Mr Coffin's Jersey herd."

"Oh, my gosh!" exclaimed the sheriff.

"It sounds almost impossible, but you remember Lady Cleo was accustomed to be ridden by Mr Bundy's boy. Dr Harvey, casting about for a method of reaching the servants' house to kill Bronson, hit on Lady Cleo. He went out to the rear of the house and caught her as she led the other cows toward the barn from the forest pasture."

"But the dog?" asked the sheriff.

"He was used to seeing Lady Cleo ridden. Dr Harvey rode the cow to the barn, killed Bronson, then rode the cow back across the court. As soon as he reached the heavy grass in back of this house, he slid off and allowed the cow to return to the barn. The result was that there was no mud on his feet and no tracks in the court."

Dr Harvey was pale now, and his eyes moved continually about the room.

"But why didn't Mr Bundy see him?" asked the sheriff.

"It was fairly dark, and Mr Bundy was in the barn."

"In the hayloft," said Mr Bundy, speaking for the first time. "But I wouldn't have seen him even if I had been down below."

Dr Harvey's voice was brittle. "That's a truly brilliant reconstruction," he said, "but you can't prove it."

"Oh, can't I?" The colonel spread the pair of Oxford-gray trousers on the table in such a manner that the seat was up. "These are yours, are they not, Dr Harvey?"

"I don't know. I have a pair like them."

"These, at least, have your name in them." The colonel handed the sheriff the magnifying glass and said, "Have a look at the seat."

The sheriff peered through the glass, one eye shut. "Hair," he said. "Silver hair."

"Lady Cleo's hair," supplemented the colonel.

The sheriff handed the magnifying glass to Colonel Black. "That's enough for me," he declared. He turned toward Dr Harvey. "I'll have to take——" He halted abruptly.

I turned toward the doctor to see what had happened. Dr Harvey's eyes were narrow slits through which the black pupils gleamed wickedly; his right hand held an automatic pistol. "Don't move," he commanded, moving the pistol in an arc before him. "Stay where you are."

While we watched in a stupor composed half of fear and half of terror, he backed out of the room, disappeared into the pantry on the other side of the dining room.

"I'll be doggoned!" exclaimed the sheriff, struggling to draw his revolver from its holster. "Come on, boys, let's git him." His face was angry.

Almost simultaneously the two deputies unfastened the handcuffs linking them to George and Burton Coffin. Joining the sheriff and Captain Anderson, who also carried a revolver, they cautiously made their way into the pantry.

I found myself standing in front of Joan. Unconsciously I must have moved there to shield her. I glanced at her oval face, but she was staring at Burton.

The colonel was moving toward the front door. I called to him, "Better take a gun, Colonel."

"Never used one in my life," he replied, passing

through the door. "I plan to confine myself to watching."

Burton looked up at Joan. "I'm all right," he said. For the first time, to me, he appeared boyish. His face had lost that sullen, arrogant expression which had made me dislike him. He smiled at Joan, his right hand fumbling at the steel bracelet on his left wrist. "I'd like to get rid of this, though."

She caught her breath, dropped down beside him on her knees and put both hands on his wrist. "Oh, Burton . . ." There was moisture in her gray eyes.

I felt a sudden constriction in the vicinity of my lungs.

"I was a fool to do it," said Burton, placing his hand on hers. "But I wanted to help you."

George Coffin had managed to remove his handcuff. He touched his son on the shoulder. "I'm sorry for everything I've said about you, Burton," he said. "You've got real courage. Not many sons would risk their lives by confessing something they believed their father had done."

"You did the same thing for me," said Burton.

I was dimly conscious that the other women, Mrs Bundy, Mrs Coffin, Mrs Spotswood and Dot Harvey, were trying to comfort Mrs Harvey, who had partially collapsed on the davenport, but my eyes were upon Joan and Burton.

"I've lived my life," George Coffin said, "and it isn't anything for me to die. My confession wasn't anything, but yours was, son." He looked down at Joan. "Especially when you've got someone to live for."

Burton's hand tightened on Joan's. "I don't know if I have," he said. "Have I, Joan?"

I didn't wait any longer. Joan's eyes turned toward me, in apology, regret or defiance, I did not know which; but I turned and fled from the room. How could she help loving Burton after what he had done for her? I had lost her. I had never had her. I felt as though the world had come tumbling about my head as, indeed, it had.

Chapter *XXI*

THE WIND was now from the east, and clouds made black patches among the stars in the sky. It was colder. My stomach felt very queer, almost as if I were faint from hunger, but I wasn't hungry. I leaned against the rail around the veranda, drew my coat closer about me for warmth and stared out at the lake. My life was going to be very lonely. It had always been lonely, but I had never known it before. I sighed. . . .

"Peter." It was the colonel's voice. "What's the matter?" His tone was kindly.

"I don't know."

"Come. Come. It must be something. People don't sigh like that for nothing. Is it Miss Leslie?"

I could make out his figure a few feet from me. He, too, was leaning against the rail. His face, his hands made faint gray smudges in the blackness.

"Yes," I said.

"You think perhaps she cares for Burton?"

I made no reply.

"Well, that *is* something to worry about, because she's a very nice girl."

"Yes, she is."

"What do you know about her?"

"Nothing . . . and everything."

He chuckled. "An excellent reply, Peter. But let me tell you something of her actual history. I had her looked up before I left New York."

"How about Dr Harvey? Aren't you going to look for him?"

"That's the sheriff's job. I'm a detective, not a bloodhound. Now about Miss Leslie . . ."

He told me what he had found out about her, and despite the fact that my heart ached painfully I listened with interest. She was, he said, an orphan. Up to her second year in Smith College she had been living with her aunt, but upon that woman's death she had been forced to leave school because of a lack of funds. Securities left her by her parents had ceased paying dividends, and her aunt's money went to a sister. She had refused a scholarship at Smith and had, for the past four years, earned a comfortable living drawing fashion illustrations for magazines and advertising agencies.

"She had courage and ability," concluded the colonel, "things many girls haven't."

"I knew that," I said gloomily, "but I'm afraid such a confirmation only adds to my sense of loss."

The wind blew from the lake, steady and chill. It was not terribly cold, but it carried a feeling of early fall. It was a damp wind. We stood for a while in silence.

In the rectangle of light by the doorway appeared Mrs Spotswood in her wheel chair, and George Coffin. The colonel called to them.

"Hello, there," said George Coffin. "Any signs of the doctor?"

"We aren't looking for signs," replied the colonel. "That's the sheriff's job."

Mrs Spotswood's voice sounded like two pieces of

sandpaper being rubbed together. "The doctor was a fool to run away," she observed. "He should have stayed."

"He knew he was caught," I said.

"Why?"

"Well, the fingerprints on the new will, for one thing."

"Those are hypothetical," said the colonel. "I merely guessed they would be there."

"You mean you lied?"

"To be frank, yes."

Mrs Spotswood laughed without mirth.

"But you had him cold on Bronson's murder?" asked George Coffin.

"Yes, I had him cold."

"George," I said, "you thought Burton had committed both crimes, didn't you?"

"Yes. Bronson told me he'd seen Burton with Tobias' head. So when Bronson was killed, what could I think?"

"And Burton thought just the other way. He thought you'd killed Bronson to protect him."

"That's it. Regular comedy of errors."

"Far from a comedy," said Mrs Spotswood.

The colonel spoke. "Just to clear the record, Mrs Spotswood, I'd like to ask you a couple of questions."

"All right."

"Why were you searching through Peter's clothes?"

"Looking for the new will. I thought it must be hidden somewhere in the house."

"And earlier this evening, what were you doing walking around the house?"

"Walking?" exclaimed George Coffin. "Mrs Spotswood walking?"

Mrs Spotswood's voice was dry. "I was walking around the house."

"But you never told us you could walk," I said.

"You never asked me."

"But why in the evening, Mrs Spotswood?" asked the colonel.

She hesitated before replying. "It's a somewhat painful subject, Colonel. You see, my method of locomotion is rather—grotesque. I'd prefer not being seen, as much for the sake of others as for myself. Yet I need the exercise. So I walk at night."

I broke the embarrassed pause which followed her words with a question. "How did the madman get Uncle Tobias' head and the suicide stage properties, Colonel?"

"As far as Captain Anderson was able to learn from Glunt, the madman had been hiding all the time in the vicinity of Graymere," replied the colonel. "On the night of Bronson's murder, perhaps, he saw the doctor place Bronson's head at the foot of the tree in the small pasture, with Mr Coffin's head, the revolver and the other deceptive paraphernalia. Naturally he was unable to resist the temptation to remove at least one of the heads to a hiding place of his own.

"Or else Dr Harvey, on the day following Bronson's murder, removed Mr Coffin's head and the other things himself, hid them in the woods where they were discovered by Glunt. This possibility seems more likely since Dr Harvey would just as soon have Bronson's head discovered; thus lending strength to the theory that the madman was the murderer of both Bronson and Mr Coffin."

"You were very clever to reconstruct the two crimes, especially the murder of Uncle Tobias, Colonel," I said, "but I'm afraid the insurance company won't thank you for proving that he was killed instead of being a suicide."

"They will certainly have to pay through the nose," agreed the colonel. He sounded as though the idea didn't disturb him.

There was a noise at the door, and Joan and Burton Coffin came out on the porch. My heart jumped violently at the sight of them.

"Where's Mother?" George Coffin asked his son.

"Upstairs with Aunt Mary," replied Burton.

Had they reached an understanding? I could tell nothing from his tone. His voice was utterly casual. I wished I could see their faces.

"I think I'll go up too," said George Coffin, walking toward the door.

A wild shouting arose in the woods to our right. "Halt!" commanded a voice. "Halt, or I'll shoot."

There was a sound of breaking brush, and then came the explosion of a shotgun. "This way," cried the sheriff's voice. "This way." Two shots followed this outburst, and we could hear the whine of bullets. Feet, pounding heavily on the sod, made a noise in the yard, and presently we caught, in the light from the living-room windows, a glimpse of a running figure.

"Dr Harvey!" breathed Joan.

"He's got his pistol too," added Burton Coffin.

I dropped over the veranda rail and started after the doctor. "Stop!" I commanded.

The doctor turned and fired at me without halting. The bullet clipped some leaves above me. "Stay back," he shouted, veering to the left toward the boathouse.

I followed somewhat more cautiously. I was filled with

anger at the doctor, especially because he'd killed harmless old Bronson, but I didn't want to let him shoot me.
Even though Joan Leslie didn't want me, and I didn't
care what happened, I desired to see Dr Harvey cap-
tured.

The fugitive ran into the boathouse, and I heard a
rattle of boards. He was going to take the canoe and
escape by way of the water. I reached the door of the
boathouse, but before I had even determined whether
or not to enter, another shot made me duck for cover.
Far in the rear I heard encouraging shouts from the
sheriff and his men. I dropped behind a tree and lay
face down on the cold earth. There was a heavy splash
in the boathouse and a groan of wood. He had dropped
the canoe in the water and had opened the door on the
lake side.

Quickly I drew off my shoes, trousers and coat,
scrambled to my feet and raced out onto the pier. If it
was cold I didn't notice it. The doctor caught sight of
me just as I saw him. He was only twenty yards from
the end of the pier, paddling furiously. He boated the
paddle and raised an arm at me. I dove a split second
before the flash of the pistol; something like a white-hot
iron seared my head, and I landed on the water in a
belly flop.

For an instant I was stunned, then fury overwhelmed
me. The only thing in the world I wanted to do was to
get my hands on him. My head cleared, and I struggled
to the surface, gasping for air, making a tremendous
turmoil on the water. My skull throbbed with pain. I
wondered if I was dying. I started to swim toward the
canoe. How many shots had he left. Three? Two?

A vertical black shadow on a longer horizontal one,

Dr Harvey waited quietly as I came toward him. I was only thirty feet away, yet he made no move to escape. Was he going to give himself up to me? Or was he going to wait until I was at the canoe's side, then kill me?

Twenty feet, and still he didn't move. The calm, the patience with which he awaited my approach was terrifying. He was sure he could kill me. I drew a long breath, thrust my head and shoulders into the dark water and took a powerful breast stroke, descending as quickly as I could. I heard a distinct "plop" and knew he had fired and missed me.

The water was pitch black; it was as though I was swimming with a blindfold over my eyes. I was safe from another shot, but how was I going to reach him? Instantly a plan formed in my mind. I guessed that once I disappeared under the surface he would paddle away as rapidly as he could. Moreover, he would go out into the lake, in the direction the canoe had been headed. Perhaps I could get to him before he was able to move at top speed.

I was going toward him anyway, and so I took five swift strokes, reaching a position approximately under that originally held by the canoe. But the doctor would be endeavoring to get under way. I took four more strokes and started toward the surface. Something solid grazed my shoulder. I reached up blindly and seized the doctor's paddle and gave it a terrific tug. With a splash the canoe overturned above me.

I came to the surface and listened. For a second there was silence, then, to the left, the doctor broke water. He was not more than five feet away, thrashing about wildly. Two crawl strokes brought me beside him. "Go away, or I'll hit you," he cried in a fury. I seized his shoulders, dodging a blow from his fist, and thrust him toward the bottom. I held him down with my feet for fully a minute and then let him up, stifling, I must confess, an impulse to drown him.

When his head emerged from the water he drew a great, gasping breath. "Are you ready to come ashore?" I asked. He clawed at my face, his nails cutting my skin. I pushed him under again.

This time when he came to the surface there was no fight in him. He had swallowed a great deal of water, and if I hadn't put an arm under his neck he would have sunk of his own accord. As I started for shore, abandoning the canoe, I heard shouting and saw lights on the pier. I headed in that direction.

During the pursuit of the doctor and in my brief combat with him I had been too excited to think of my wound. Now, pulling my captive over the water with one arm and swimming with the other, I found I was extremely tired. Faintness almost overcame me, and I felt a strong desire to let myself sink down in the dark water.

"Hello," called a voice from the pier. "Have you got him?"

A light shone in my eyes. I was hardly five yards from the wooden pilings. "Yes," I said, allowing myself to float for an instant.

A voice called anxiously, "Are you all right?" I recognized it as the colonel's.

I was too weary to reply. I wanted to stop swimming, but I forced myself on, saying, "Only six more strokes . . . only five more strokes . . . only four . . ."

After an eternity I reached the bathing ladder. "Take him," I gasped, hauling Dr Harvey part way out

of the water. In a second they had him on the pier. I
felt my strength leave me. I sank back into the water,
dimly hearing someone say, "Quick! Get him!" but not
connecting the words with myself.

Without opening my eyes I could tell it was daytime.
From the feel of sheets, of springs under me, I knew I
was in bed. My head didn't hurt very much, but I was
reluctant to open my eyes for fear it would. Someone
made a noise coming into the room, and Joan Leslie's
voice asked:

"Doctor, is he—all right?"

I was delighted to note a catch, an expression of concern in her voice.

The voice which replied had that tone of suave opti-
mism employed by doctors in replying to questions. "I
see no reason why the young man should not be all
right," it said cheerfully.

I wondered if the doctor meant to reassure Joan by
concealing the true state of my condition or whether
long practice at being confident had made him sound
insincere. I never believed doctors anyway.

Apparently Joan didn't either. She said, "Oh, Doctor, he's got to live."

"Oh, he will," said the doctor. "Good-by."

I opened my eyes a crack. It wasn't so bad. The ache
produced by the golden sunlight quickly subsided. Joan
was staring at the door with an expression of doubt. She
turned her lovely wide gray eyes toward me, and I
quickly closed mine.

Presently she was beside my bed. There was a faint
sweet odor of flowers about her. She touched my cheek

with a soft hand. "Oh, Peter," she whispered, "you must live."

I opened my eyes and said, "You can't kill me by way of my head. I've already demonstrated my skull is too solid."

She leaped away from the bed, her eyes startled. "You're conscious?"

"I think so," I said.

She was blushing. "You lie still," she said. "I'm going to get you some broth."

The soup, with crackers crumbled in it, was very good. I felt much better. "What happened to Dr Harvey?" I asked.

"He's locked up in Traverse City."

"And everybody else?"

"They've gone home—even the colonel."

"And you stayed behind to nurse me."

Her gray eyes crinkled at the corners. "I had two days left of my vacation."

"Oh! But Burton. Where's he?"

"Gone too."

"Gone!" I sat up in bed, causing my head to spin. "You mean he didn't wait for you?"

"No. Why should he?"

"You mean you're not—there's no understanding between you?"

"He understands me, at least."

"And he's gone?"

"Yes."

I sank back in bed. Did this mean she didn't love Burton? Would I be too bold to ask her? I felt confused, between hope and fear, so I changed the subject. "What's happened to the poor Harvey kids?" I asked.

"Oh, it's terrible. They're completely crushed. And Mrs Harvey had to be taken to the hospital. She had a breakdown."

"I don't wonder. What could have made that man commit those murders?"

"Colonel Black said the doctor had misappropriated some hospital funds and needed money to pay them back. The doctor told him this morning." She had been sitting on the side of my bed, and now she rose.

"Don't go," I said.

"I must. You need lots of rest." She leaned over me, her eyes suddenly solemn. "Peter, I wanted to tell you how sorry I am I ever called you a coward. That will haunt me the rest of my life. I think you did the bravest thing I ever heard of, going after Dr Harvey without a weapon."

"That wasn't bravery."

"Yes, it was."

"No. It was despair. I thought you cared for Burton Coffin," I said without looking at her, "and I loved you so terribly I didn't care what happened."

Her arms were about my neck. "Oh, my silly darling," she whispered, "my darling . . ."